Games
of God
and Men

Games

of God

and Men

Book Six of the Latter Annals of Lystra

Robin Hardy

Westford Press

Games of God and Men:
Book Six of the Latter Annals of Lystra
2nd edition
Christian fantasy/romance

ISBN: 978-1934776711
Copyright © 2008, 2014 Robin Hardy.

Portions of this book may be reproduced according to the fair use
doctrine as stated in § 107 of the U.S. Copyright Law; otherwise,
please contact the publisher for written permission.

Westford Press
mail@westfordpress.com

Cover image © Robyn Mackenzie Photography

Scripture quotations are from the RSV: Revised Standard Version of
the Bible, © 1946, 1952, © 1971, 1973 by the Division of Christian
Education of the National Council of the Churches of Christ in the
United States of America. The verses in Chapter 3 are Numbers
23:10 and Hebrews 10:38 (slightly paraphrased).

The riddles in Chapter 7 are mostly from the *Arts Forge Middle
English Book of Riddles*, translated by Tobin James Mueller on
http://www.artsforge.com/humor/riddles.html. A wonderful website
created by **Baron Modar Neznanich** describing games of the Middle
Ages is found at http://www.modaruniversity.org/Games.htm.

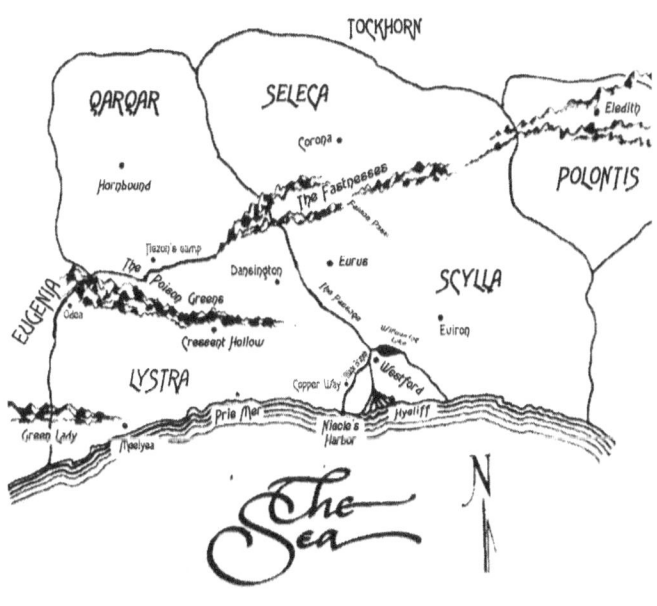

The Continent

TOCKHORN

QARQAR

SELECA

Corona

Eledith

POLONTIS

Hornbound

The Fastnesses

Tiezun's swamp

The Poison Greens

Eurus

SCYLLA

Danslington

EUGENIA

The Passage

Odaa

Wildrose Lye Lake

Eviron

Crescent Hollow

LYSTRA

Copper Way

Westford

Prie Mer

Nicole's Harbor

Hycliff

Green Lady

Npalyaa

The Sea

N

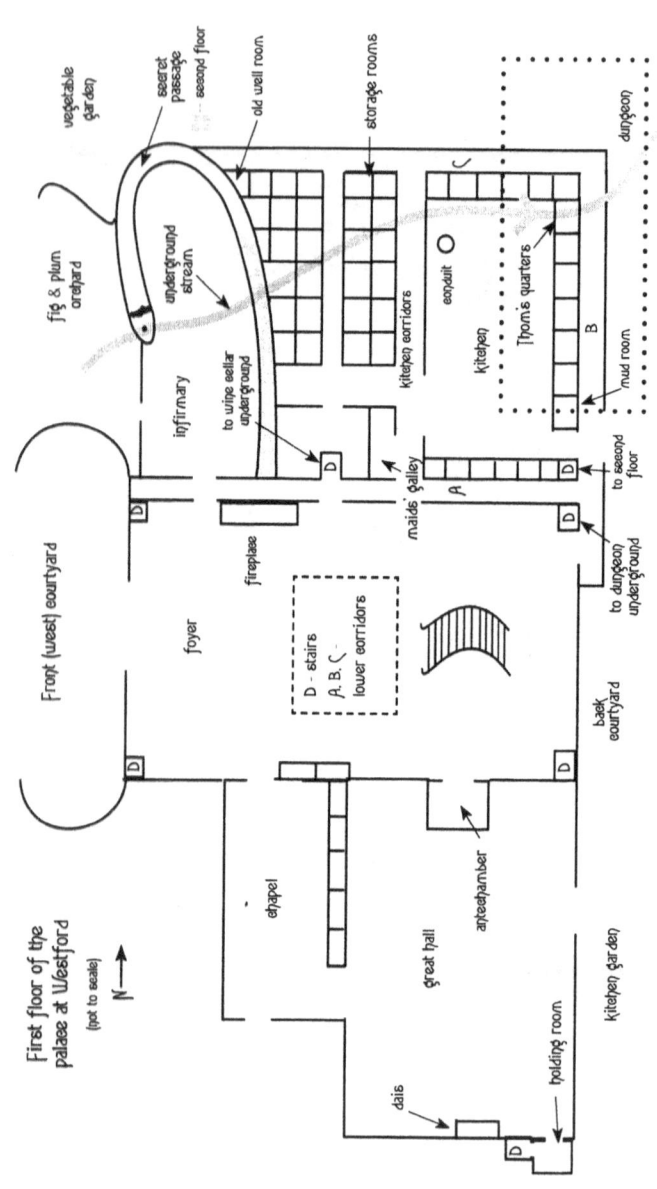

First floor of the palace at Westford
(not to scale)

N →

vegetable garden

secret passage

second floor

old well room

storage rooms

fig & plum orchard

underground stream

infirmary

to wine cellar underground

kitchen corridors

exit

kitchen

Thom's quarters

dungeon

mud room

B

Front (west) courtyard

foyer

fireplace

maid's gallery

A

to second floor

to dungeon underground

D - stairs
A, B, C - lower corridors

back courtyard

chapel

antechamber

great hall

kitchen garden

dais

holding room

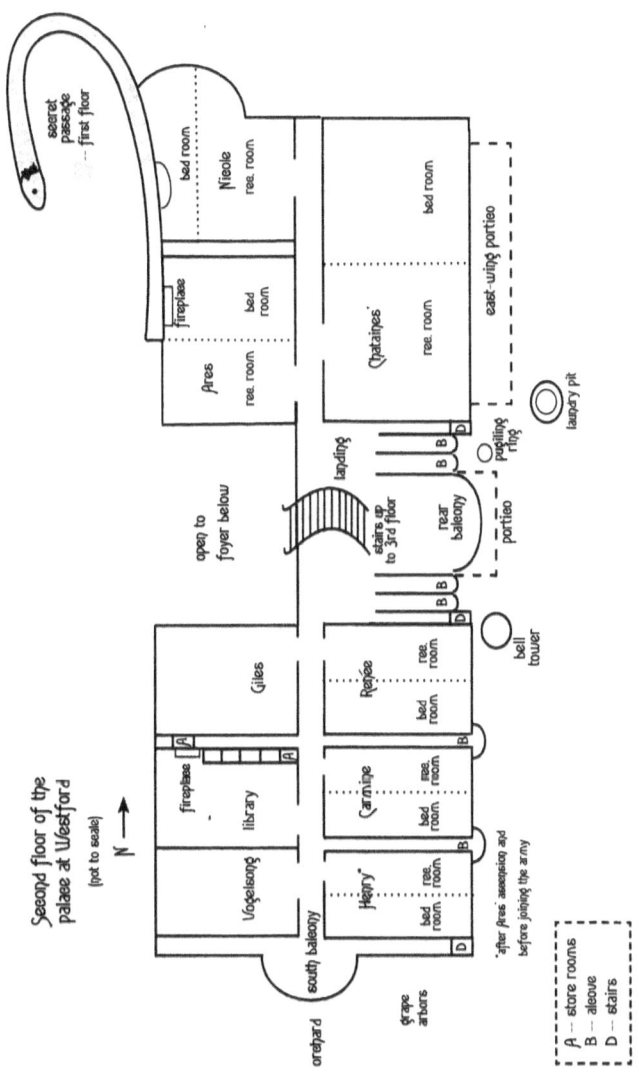

Second floor of the palace at Westford
(not to scale)

N →

Vogelsong

library

fireplace

Giles

A

A

Henny

bed room | rec. room

Carmine

bed room | rec. room

Repice

bed room | rec. room

south balcony

orchard

grape arbors

B

B

B

D

"after Ares ascension and before joining the army"

bell tower

open to foyer below

stairs up to 3rd floor

landing

rear balcony

B | B

B | B

D

D

portico

papilling ring

secret passage
--- first floor

bed room

Nicole

rec. room

fireplace

bed room

Ares

rec. room

Chataines

rec. room

bed room

east-wing portico

laundry pit

A — store rooms
B — alcove
D — stairs

We are in the world like men playing at tables; the chance is not in our power, but to play it is; and when it is fallen we must manage it as we can; and let nothing trouble us but when we do a base action, or speak like a fool, or think wickedly: these things God hath put into our powers; but concerning those things which are wholly in the choice of another, they cannot fall under our deliberation, and therefore neither are they fit for our passions.

My fear may make me miserable, but it cannot prevent what another hath in his power and purpose: and prosperities can only be enjoyed by them who fear not at all to lose them; since the amazement and passion concerning the future takes off all the pleasure of the present possession. Therefore if thou hast lost thy land, do not also lose thy constancy: and if thou must die a little sooner, yet do not die impatiently.

For no chance is evil to him that is content, and to a man nothing is miserable, unless it be unreasonable. No man can make another man to be his slave unless he hath first enslaved himself to life and death, to pleasure or pain, to hope or fear: command these passions, and you are freer than the Parthian kings.

Jeremy Taylor, *Holy Living,* 1650

Old Lystran Love Song

You have bound me with your eyes;
I am captive to your smiles;
Your tears rend my heart
You are such a part
Of me, my dove, my love.

If I loved you when we met,
I will love you ever yet,
For that love of mine
Was naught as it is
Now, my dove, my love.

What then shall I do
To win such a maid as you?
Is there hope for me
To ever touch your
Heart, my dove, my love?

—from Book One of the Annals of Lystra

I

Surchatain Ares sat in his receiving room with a small, soiled roll of parchment on the table in front of him. He took up the roll, deliberately breaking the wax seal on its edge, then unrolled the parchment and smoothed out the creases to read the hasty lettering on the inside.

While he was thus engaged, the door to the corridor opened to accommodate the rushed entrance of a nymph in a blue silk dress topped with a white rabbit surcoat. Being on the edge of young womanhood, she wore skirts that fell precisely midcalf—when they were not being blown about in tumultuous motion—and thick white hose over slender legs. She had long chestnut tresses, clean and curling, bound up in a ponytail by a single blue ribbon that threatened to give way from the stress at any moment.

"Papa!" the vision cried, rushing to the rear of the low-backed chair in order to throw her arms around his neck and kiss his cheek—the scarred one. That deep, ugly gash, and the man to whom it belonged, were so legendary in Lystra that admirers and imposters alike had begun mutilating their own faces in attempts to reproduce his likeness.

Eyes still on the letter, he did not look up as his daughter propounded, "Papa, today is the wolf hunt and you promised you would think about letting us go watch!" By "us," she was referring to herself and her twin sister. "Our guardians have the sleigh all ready and Bonnie is getting her cloak on now. I know that it snowed again last night, but we have plenty of furs, and Tobias says the snowfall didn't cover the stakes, so you can still see where the road runs. Please, Papa?" she pleaded with beguiling green eyes.

"No, Bonnie," he replied.

She let down in a disappointed pout before catching the discrepancy. Flustered, she began, "But, I'm Sophie—" Only then did her father look up with the barest twinkle in his grave brown eyes. She fell on him, consumed by embarrassed giggles. "Beast! How did you know?"

Smiling, he turned in his chair to lift her onto his lap despite the petticoats entangled around her long legs. "You are not your sister, dear one. The pretense is not convincing."

"Yes, it is! We can fool everyone but you and Mama!" she insisted, snuggling him, her forehead tucked under his smooth jaw. Ares expended the effort to shave daily around his scar mostly because his children preferred it. The last time he came home from an extended trip with a beard, Bonnie ran away from him in tears. He never understood how facial hair could be more frightening than the cleft in his face, but—

"Oh, Papa, please let us go watch the hunt. It's so boring not being able to go out at all. I hate the winter. I hate the cold," she fumed as someone who slept under downy quilts and never had to lift a finger to light a fire.

"Bonnie, how long has Tobias been your guardian?" he

asked. The question of the wolf hunt being a dead issue, he would not address it again.

"Um, I don't know. A few years, I think," she replied in disinterest, playing with the frill of his white shirt that peeked out from the black brocade coat. It amounted to meager adornment compared to the finery his daughter wore. "Papa, why do you always wear black? It's so tiresome. Wouldn't you like to wear something colorful for a change?"

He shifted to look at his daughter, soon to be twelve. Now forty-seven himself, Ares had already exceeded the life expectancy of men in this century. But visitors to the court at Westford were awed by his vigor. They whispered that he must have found some magic potion, else what could account for his still-muscular build, his clarity of sight, hearing, and mind, his full brown hair?—only slightly greying at the temples. And he still had all his own teeth! He was imposing enough to rule with little distraction, for the most part. In the last three years, he had been challenged only once for the throne.

That challenger, a young man from Dansington named Sulander, discovered the hard way that the old man was not to be trifled with. As the challenged party, Ares was entitled to choose weapons. He chose the estoc, which the unfortunate Sulander had never seen before. Given no time to practice with the newfangled sword before Commander Thom shouted, "Begin!" the young contender attempted a cut, which did indeed nick the Surchatain's arm as he deflected the blow. But he answered with a straight thrust which, much to Sulander's surprise, pierced his jerkin clear through to his heart.

Following, Ares had sent ten units—a hundred men from the Red Regiment—to seek out all of Sulander's family and friends. Anyone who might have known of his ambition, and supported him in it, were collected with all their possessions and driven out of Lystra into southern Qarqar. Ever since then, whenever any young man began boasting over his ale how he could whip the old Surchatain and take over the throne, he was inevitably beaten senseless by his own companions first.

In response to his daughter's question about his attire, Ares replied, "What could I wear that would grace me better than two beautiful daughters? Would I be more attractive in motley, like Twomey?"

Bonnie laughed, clinging to his neck. "Only if you told stories like Twomey! He is so wonderfully amusing!" Her father nodded slightly, narrowing his eyes, and she quickly turned serious. "Oh, Papa, I know you don't like jesters— or don't like Twomey—but please don't send him away. He makes me laugh myself silly. It would be unbearable over the winter without him," she pleaded.

He regarded her. "Would it mean that much to you to keep this fool around a while longer?"

"Oh, yes, Papa, so much! Be a dear and let him stay. He doesn't eat much and Uncle Giles says he doesn't drink nearly as much as Carmine," Bonnie urged.

Ares allowed not so much as a flicker of pain to cross his face at the mention of his old friend, and only said, "Then, for you, he may stay."

"Thank you, Papa," Bonnie sighed, hugging his neck.

"Now, about Tobias, your guardian," Ares broached. When Bonnie had nothing immediate to offer on the guardian's behalf, her father went on, "He must be rotated out of service soon, you know. All guardians are rotated."

"I know," she said. He listened hard for any particular inflection in the words, but found none.

"So," he posed, "would you like a say in selecting your new guardian?"

She sat up in his lap. "Can I?" she asked with gleaming eyes.

"Yes. After I have the Commander nominate candidates, I will narrow them down to the top three or four, then let you make the final choice."

"Oh, Papa, really?" she breathed.

"Yes. It's important for you to feel comfortable with your guardian, and I think you are mature enough to base your selection on something other than how he wears his hair or whether he has nice eyes," he said dryly.

"Certainly, Papa," she said with that touch of haughtiness that children mistake for maturity.

"Well then, Chataine, let me get the Commander up here to start on it," he said, nudging her from his lap.

She stood, shaking out her petticoats from habit. "How long will it take to get them ready for me to choose from?"

He considered the question as he rose from behind the table to stretch his legs. Although the room had been plastered to seal cracks in the stone, and a fire burned heartily in the large fireplace, it was still cold enough that he had to move around frequently to shake off the stiffness. His old battle injuries haunted him daily during the winter. "Give us at least a fortnight, Chataine." She exhaled impatiently, and he nodded. "Call the sentry in."

She went to the door and opened it, gesturing to the sentry in the corridor. He stepped into the room, saluting. Ares told him, "Go tell the Second Oswald that I give permission for the twins to be taken sleigh riding out to Willowring Lake and back. Not on the wolf hunt."

"Papa!" Bonnie cried in joy, jumping up and down.

Ares looked down on her. "Uncle Oswald will take you

himself. And see if your mother wishes to go." Neither Oswald nor Giles was related to the royal family. The gentle, massive Oswald had earned their love through his unflagging loyalty, and Giles, the palace Steward, had adopted the twins with a vengeance when it became apparent that, because of the numerous gifts they constantly received, they cared little for spending anything themselves.

"Papa, you're wonderful!" Bonnie cried, catapulting herself amid a flurry of skirts into his arms.

"If my daughter thinks so, then my life is complete," he murmured. In a flash she was out the door into the corridor, the sentry trailing her. "And don't run," he said long after the blue lightning had vanished. When a second sentry approached to take the place of the first, Ares instructed him, "Summon Tobias."

As that sentry departed, a third came to take his place. And so they would continually replace themselves, which is what they had been trained to do. Everything went so much better when they did what they were supposed to do. Ares sighed and shut the door.

Returning to the table, he dropped heavily into the chair and took up the small scroll once again. It read, "My darling. We will leave today on the wolf hunt but I have made arrangements not to come back. It will be well. I am yours forever."

This message had been intercepted from the hand of a maid who confirmed that she had been instructed to deliver it to Bonnie. The informer who brought it to Ares told him that its author was Tobias. But Ares did not know this for a fact.

At the knock on the door, Ares placed the scroll in the pocket of his jacket and stood. "Enter."

The sentry opened the door to announce, "Tobias, as you summoned, Surchatain."

"Very good," Ares said genially. "You stay as well," he told the sentry.

The man stood aside respectfully as Bonnie's guardian entered. He was young—probably no more than twenty-three—and pretty, as little girls liked. "Tobias." Ares greeted him with outstretched hand. "You have served so faithfully that I fear I have abused you. How long have you been Bonnie's guardian now?"

"I believe—about two years, Surchatain," Tobias replied, visibly sweating.

Ares winced. "Too long to be saddled with babysitting. Forgive my negligence in not rotating you out sooner."

"It has been an honor to serve her—you, Surchatain," Tobias replied.

"Yes, yes, I know," Ares said dismissively, ignoring his slip of the tongue. "And you have performed honorably, for which I commend you." Practiced negotiator that Ares was, he still had to turn away as he said this, to hide the telltale clenching of his jaw. Tobias' manner did not lend credence to his innocence.

But Ares had seen enough innocent men put to death to make him cautious in issuing judgments; therefore, he would not hold Tobias guilty unless it was certain. With the honor of his daughter at stake, however, he had to act. "Now go gather your gear, for you will be released to genuine soldiering today."

Tobias paused. "I thank you, Surchatain. But might it not wait until after the wolf hunt? I have been conscripted to help."

Ares smiled on him in apparent approval, but any longtime associate who saw him smile like that would have been shaking in his boots. "Faithful to the end, eh, Tobias? But have no fear; I will not hold you to petty obligations when your release has already been granted. Go get your gear and report to the Second Rhode."

Turning back to the table, Ares could feel the young man's hesitation. "Oh—one more matter," Ares said, facing him again, and Tobias straightened. "I would like your recommendations as to who should take your place. Sit and write out at least ten names for me." He gestured to a pile of blank parchment and a quill in ink on the table.

"As you wish, Surchatain." Tobias sat distractedly in the Surchatain's chair, then took up the quill, wiped the nib on the lip of the inkwell and began to scrawl out names. Ares watched him steadfastly.

When he had achieved a short column of names, he looked up, but Ares prompted, "A few more."

Dipping the quill and biting his lip, Tobias added three names to the list. Ares said, "Excellent." He gestured to the sentry, instructing, "You will assist Tobias in collecting his gear and taking it to the officers' quarters. He is to wait there until he receives his orders from the Second."

As the sentry saluted, Tobias asked tightly, "Where am I to be stationed, Surchatain?"

Ares glanced at him in mild surprise. "That is your superior's decision. I'm sure he will place you wherever you are most needed. You are dismissed."

Grimacing, Tobias saluted and turned out with the sentry down the corridor. When the next sentry approached, Ares told him, "Summon the Commander." That sentry saluted, sprinting away, and Ares shut the door. He sat at the table and removed the crumpled roll from his pocket. Opening it, he laid it beside Tobias' list to compare the lettering point by point.

He was still poring over the two documents when a knock signaled Thom's arrival. Ares sat back as he entered, and the two eyed each other for a moment. Thom still sported a short, stiff beard, along with new, deepening lines in his face and an extra ten pounds. "Congratulations, Thom. Another son, I hear." This was the second; Thom's firstborn Ryal was eight years old.

The Commander glanced down. "Thank you, Surchatain."

"What is his name?"

"Tor, Surchatain."

Ares smiled slightly. "I hear that he required the large tub for his first bath."

"He's—adequate, Surchatain. Deirdre had a time of it, but Doctor Savary says she'll be fine. She is highly dissatisfied with the nursery mistress," he added thoughtfully.

Ares leaned forward. "Then the Surchataine Nicole will find an appropriate gift with which to placate her." Diverting to other matters, he extended the scroll to the Commander. "This was to be delivered to Bonnie this morning."

Thom read the message, his lips tightening. "From Tobias?"

"Twomey says so," Ares replied.

Thom paused. "If this is true, it means death for the guardian. Have you any way of verifying this?"

"I asked Tobias to write out recommendations for his replacement. Judge for yourself." Ares handed him the list.

Thom compared the two writings for several minutes while Ares waited without comment. The Commander then decided, "They are the same hand."

"I felt so, yes," Ares said softly.

19

Handing both back to him, Thom said, "Then he must suffer the consequences."

Ares stood with a troubled sigh. "An execution? No, I cannot see that. Not a hint, not a breath of scandal must touch Bonnie from this. I do not believe she even understands the young man's feelings—when I told her he must be rotated out of service, she accepted it without a murmur. She was far more fearful of losing Twomey!"

Thom allowed himself a thin smile. "Distancing yourself from the jester publicly seems to have served you well. But, you are saying that you cannot punish Tobias without also casting suspicion on the Chataine."

"Exactly. So I wish you to write out a commendation, and then instruct Rhode to send him to Nicole's Harbor. The moment the snows abate, he is to be dispatched to Odea."

This was an outpost on the far western border of Lystra, a rough station in inhospitable country at the foot of the Poison Greens, four days' travel on horseback in good weather from Westford. Its existence was due to Eugenian merchants, escorted by mercenaries, constantly trying to break the border without paying tariffs. Also, slave traders rebuffed from entering Lystra through southern Qarqar routinely attempted to gain entry around the western edge of the Poison Greens instead.

The spartan outpost, originally built to house five hundred men, now accommodated a thousand, so the soldiers stationed there spent most of their off-duty hours building additions. It was not a popular place of deployment, to say the least.

Thom stiffened. "Yes, Surchatain, but—I strongly protest commending this traitor in writing. That cheapens the commendation for those who deserve it."

Ares eyed him sideways. "Your rebuke is noted, Commander. I have commended him verbally before one witness. That will have to suffice."

Relaxing, Thom acknowledged, "Thank you, Surchatain. And how long shall Tobias be stationed in Odea?" His lip curled knowingly.

Ares nodded at the Commander's assumption. "Forever. If he returns to Westford of his own accord, I will certainly put him to death."

"Done, Surchatain," Thom said. To warn the renegade guardian of his peril did not cross the mind of either man. All guardians pledged their lives to protecting the lives and honor of their charges; Tobias' egregious disregard of that vow merited no special favors. If he obeyed orders from here on out, well and good. If not. . . .

Almost lightheartedly, Ares tossed both parchments into the flames. "Ah. That reminds me. You're to nominate ten men to be potential guardians. After I have interviewed them, I promised Bonnie the final choice."

Thom's bristly jaw dropped. "You're going to allow the Chataine to choose her own guardian?"

Ares smiled back at him. "So we had better make sure that any we present to her are worthy, eh?"

"The burdens you place on me," Thom muttered, and Ares chuckled.

Then he sobered, adding, "The Second Oswald is about to take the Chataines out in the sleigh. He might need to be informed that he is responsible for warding Bonnie, and why."

"Surchatain." Thom saluted on his way out.

At that moment, having been summoned for the sleigh ride, Sophie's guardian, Seane, was meeting up with the Chataines in the foyer. This stone hall, sixty feet long from the foot of the wide, curving stairway to the tall, iron-banded double doors, was almost large enough to be a banquet room itself. Still, it was adequately warmed by the mammoth fireplace to the right of the stairway, across from the chapel doors. It helped that the hall was crowded as usual with merchants and tradesmen who conducted business on a daily basis with the palace. The thought that a mere snowfall should interfere with such business was ludicrous.

Seane's charge Sophie and her sister had just descended the stairway, giggling and whispering, while Seane anxiously looked from one to the other. He was relieved, firstly, that they were not dressed exactly alike—one wore white furs while the other wore brown. That enabled him tell them apart, once he ascertained which was which. Those first few minutes were perilous: if he guessed and was wrong, they laughed at him. Occasionally, they tricked him, pretending to be each other.

Recalling the time that he had spent the whole day ignorantly warding Bonnie still made Seane break into a sweat. The Surchatain had glimpsed him escorting his charge back from town and paused to query where Sophie was. In heart-stopping panic, Seane had deposited Bonnie in the foyer and ridden back like a madman to the confectioner's shop where Tobias and Sophie had been lingering.

Taking possession of her, Seane had informed Tobias of the girls' deception. Tobias was wroth, Seane remembered. He still wondered at it.

There was every reason to be afraid of these pranks, because if something happened to one of the girls when she was supposed to be in her guardian's care, the Surchatain would not countenance the explanation, *"They tricked us."*

But Tobias had been exceedingly angry about it.

In the foyer now, Seane ventured, "Chataine Sophie?" and they both turned toward him.

"I'm Sophie, Seane," the one in brown said.

"No, *I'm* Sophie," said the one in white, a wicked glint in her eye.

The first turned back to the second. "We agreed not to fool our guardians any more, Bonnie. They could get in very bad trouble with Papa." While her sister considered this with a disappointed pout, the foyer doors opened amid a blast of icy air. The Second Oswald, in his regular uniform with a threadbare army cloak tossed over his shoulders, gestured. "Your sleigh waits, Chataines."

Hoisting the hood of his cloak, Seane took each girl's arm to escort them down the slippery stone steps into the courtyard. Due to the traffic in and out, the cobbled courtyard was a mess of trampled snowdrifts, dirty slush and icy patches.

At the foot of the steps, Oswald reached down to lift each girl on a trunklike arm. He carried them that way through the crowded, treacherous courtyard, secure in his footing. Seane slipped and slid behind him until they had exited the palace gates to the sleigh waiting on the snowy road.

Here, Oswald deposited the girls directly into their seat. Seane scampered up behind them, glancing at the mounted bodyguard that stood nearby. But when Oswald climbed into the driver's seat and clucked to the pair of horses harnessed to the sleigh, Seane leaned over the rail. "Wait! Where's Tobias?"

The Second glanced over his shoulder. Even with three passengers in back, his large frame on the driver's seat caused the front of the runners to dig down into the snow.

"He's been rotated out of service. Chataine Bonnie's got me today."

Seane's mouth hung open. "Rotated out? In winter? Why—?"

Oswald slapped the reins on the horses' backs, causing the sleigh to lurch forward so that Seane landed at the Chataines' feet in a heap. While they laughed at him, he scrambled back onto the seat across from them. Right now he almost envied Tobias, because guarding these girls had to be the most painful, humiliating duty imaginable.

In the Surchatain's suite on the second floor, Ares steeled himself against the cold to open the leaded-glass windows and look out over the pristine white countryside beyond the front courtyard. Few tracks marred its smooth skin, as few men or beasts roamed in this weather.

True, the Village Branch to the southwest of the palace and the paved roads on either side were thronged year-round with travelers from Westford to Nicole's Harbor or back again. The wolves were always a plague in winter, however, which was why the hunt had been organized to begin with. At a bounty of two royals a pelt, a good bowman could earn the equivalent of three months' standard wages in one day.

Movement beyond the gates caught Ares' eye, and he looked down on the Chataines' sleigh heading out toward the lake. He could discern both girls wrapped up thoroughly on one seat and Sophie's guardian in the seat across from them. Nicole was not with them. Oswald himself was driving the sleigh while four soldiers rode alongside—a precaution that must have originated with the Second.

Ares inhaled the cold, stinging air in gratitude. Had he known nothing of Tobias' plans, and allowed the girls to go watch the hunt with their guardians *and Oswald*, Tobias would have had no more chance to abscond with Bonnie than he could walk out of the treasury with an armful of gold, and live.

He heard the Commander reenter the receiving room behind him. "What of Seane, Thom?" Ares asked, eyes below. "How is he performing?"

Approaching to glance down through the window, Thom raised his brows. "I hear that he is overvigilant to the point of nervousness, Surchatain."

"He has only been on duty for—what? A few months?"

"Five weeks, Surchatain," Thom replied.

Ares nodded. "Good." After closing the window, he was mildly surprised to see the Commander's face settle into a troubled, indecisive expression. "Thom?"

He exhaled. "Captain Crager recommends, again, that Henry be promoted to the Blue." Of the four regiments in the army—the Green, Gold, Red, and Blue—the Blue was the highest, comprising men who had exhibited uncommon valor on the field.

Ares lifted his chin. "And you don't agree."

Thom, known for his logic and fair-mindedness, took his time to phrase his objections and still stumbled over the words. "It just seems—obscene, in a way. His grandfather Talus killed your grandfather to usurp the throne, and his father Cedric almost succeeded in having you beheaded."

"Which Henry prevented," Ares pointed out.

"Which the Law prevented," Thom countered. "True, Henry has served bravely, but . . . for those of us who remember his lineage—" Thom broke off, glancing at the old banner on the wall, that of Ares' great-great-grandfather, Roman. Those faded, frayed patches of fabric depicting a lion and a cross had come to be practically revered by those who lived by Roman's Law. "It is a hard thing to swallow."

"So . . . Talus was more equitable than we," Ares said.

"What?" Thom said, shocked.

"Talus promoted me to lieutenant, though I was the one who most threatened his line," Ares observed.

Thom's color rose. "Talus would have sent you to the block but for his brother Reynard, who stood in as your guardian. I resent that you equate us, Surchatain."

Ares smiled, glancing down. "Well said. Let me ask you this, though: If it had been anyone but Henry who spotted the brigands swimming up the Passage in the dead of night, and disabled the five of them virtually unaided when the watchman refused to open the gate, would he have been promoted by now?"

Thom's jaw tightened. "Yes."

A few seconds of silence passed, then Ares said, "If you are waiting for me to order you to promote him, I won't do that. I am no longer his guardian, but you are his Commander. Your decisions stand."

Thom passed a hand over his face in resignation. "Barring specific knowledge to the contrary, I must accept the recommendations of my officers. Henry will be promoted." He felt compelled to add, "But, being already certified in the Law, that makes him eligible for promotion in rank."

"So it does," Ares observed. "You are dismissed, Commander."

Saluting, Thom withdrew, and Ares sat reluctantly to attend the ever-pressing correspondence on the table. He perked up at the sound of the bell tolling, but sank back down when it struck only one. Afternoon drills with the Greens would not be for another two hours yet, and Ares was restless for the exercise they afforded. Sometimes he desired to go back to simple soldiering and leave all the administration to others. In that area, Carmine always excelled—

At this point, Ares blocked out thoughts of anything but the next letter atop the pile. It was yet another overture from Surchatain Fanchon of Seleca to reopen trade between the two provinces. Ares was wary of the idea, given Seleca's history of slave trade, but Fanchon maintained that he had purged his province of it as much as possible, and there was some evidence that the slavers had mostly relocated to southern Qarqar.

Given the horrendous suffering that the slavers inflicted on whole populations, Ares wanted to do more than make them move; he wanted to eradicate them. A few notorious slavers had large bounties on their heads, but anyone caught participating in the slave trade was subject to death upon discovery. The only people who had nothing to fear from the slavers were the lepers.

In the last few years, a virulent form of leprosy had sprung up all over the Continent, everywhere at once, it seemed. The disease was so feared that its sufferers were branded on their right hands as identification and warning. They were shunned wherever they went, given no lodging nor even food, and slavers would not touch them, lest they infect their whole stock.

Lepers were not branded in Westford, as Ares considered it unreasonably cruel when Doctor Savary insisted that the disease could be cured. But neither were they welcome here. In an attempt to alleviate their plight, Ares had set aside funds for a leprosarium to be built not far from the abbey south of Westford. It was slow going up because no laborers could be found who would do the work other than the lepers themselves. But now it was almost completed.

All that aside, Ares studied the seal on Fanchon's letter, which depicted a gryphon—a beast with the body and hind legs of a lion and the wings and head of an eagle. Because the gryphon was reputed to feast on the flesh of men, Fanchon's choice of emblem was not particularly reassuring to Ares.

He simply couldn't know whether it would be prudent or disastrous to resume trade relations with Seleca, as an earlier venture into that province in cooperation with Lord Lieterstad had produced middling returns. And since any Selecan traders would of necessity pass through Scylla to reach Westford, Ares would need the cooperation of the Scyllan Surchatain, irascible Magnus.

Yet, on the outside chance that it would prove profitable—Ares pushed back from the table and headed for the door, intending to summon the Counselor for his opinion on the matter.

Opening the door, he had an instant to brace himself before Henry, who had his hand on the outer latch preparatory to rushing inside, smacked into him with such force that they both were knocked down.

2

The flabbergasted sentry stood over the Surchatain as he struggled up to a sit, fingering the cheekbone which had met with Henry's forehead. Henry, likewise, was pushing himself up onto his knees, groaning, with a hand on his head. "How many times have I asked you not to run through the corridor?" Ares asked calmly. The sentry snapped out of his shock to offer the Surchatain a hand up, which Ares accepted.

"I was just opening the door," Henry grunted.

"Which the sentry is supposed to do," Ares said, hoisting the young man up by his uniform jacket. With a nod, Ares dismissed the sentry to his post in the corridor, and he carefully closed the door on his way out. Then Ares returned his attention to the newest member of the Blue Regiment, who was still squinting in pain.

Henry, 20, was as tall as Ares now—a little leaner, but still well-muscled. He seemed to have shot up in stature so recently that Ares kept having to readjust to looking at him straight on instead of down.

But as of late, every time Ares looked at him, the bile rose in his stomach, for Henry had grown into the physical likeness of his father, Cedric, who had tried to take Ares' wife and his life . . . the man who had risen to the throne by his father's murderous hand. From the curling, reddish blond hair to the delineated jaw and straight nose, Henry's face evoked bitter memories of Cedric in Ares' mind—and evidently in Thom's, as well.

It was most unsettling, especially as Ares felt that Henry had nothing of Cedric's black spirit. Henry certainly never spoke of him, but the boy had been only seven at the time of Cedric's murder. Ares did not know how much he remembered of his father.

"Captain Crager just now told me," Henry said, and Ares refocused his attention from the bright red spot above Henry's left eyebrow to his eyes. "Did you talk to the Commander about promoting me?"

"He confirmed to me the decision that had already been made," Ares said. "Surely you know that I would never instruct him to promote anyone. Least of all you."

Henry grinned. "You made me wait forever to sit for certification. But I got the best of it—I even answered Giles' questions right!" The Steward was notorious for tripping up examinants with obscure financial questions technically unrelated to the Law.

"Not all of them," Ares noted, feeling his right cheek. The blow to his scar had caused it to start bleeding. Opening the door again, he told the sentry, "Bring me something to wipe my face." The sentry knew exactly where to go upon this command: a storage room nearby was kept stocked with cloths for just these emergencies, as the Surchatain would demand one on a moment's notice while refusing to keep any on hand.

Turning back, Ares saw the pensiveness in Henry's grey eyes. "Which one did I miss?" Having looked at Ares' scar all of his life, Henry acted as though it were non-existent. That it bled under certain circumstances was no more consequential than a nosebleed.

"The tax rate for a Prie Mer shipper during the winter months," Ares replied.

"That's twelve percent of gross," Henry said, affronted.

"Fifteen percent," Ares corrected.

Henry gawked at the news. "The ledger I was studying from said twelve percent!" he protested, outraged. "Giles gave me an outdated ledger!"

Receiving the clean, soft diaper from the hastily approaching sentry, Ares said, "So what does that teach you about using someone else's information without ascertaining that it is trustworthy?" He blotted his scar with the cloth, closing the door.

Henry absorbed this, blinking, then howled, "Giles is the Steward! He's supposed to be trustworthy!"

Ares' brow arched and he lowered the cloth. "To me, yes. But to you? Who are you but an unranked soldier? Why should he go out of his way to make sure that you have the most recent information? That is your responsibility."

Henry stared at him, then broke into an affable grin. "You made the Commander promote me to the Blue."

"You are wrong," Ares assured him, daubing at the scar and checking the cloth.

"You lie, foul dog," Henry uttered. Ares stopped dead, leveling on him the gaze that made cold-blooded mercenaries quake, but Henry suddenly threw his arms around Ares' shoulders in a childlike embrace. "Thank you."

Ares started, remembering when he himself, at Henry's age, had thrown his arms around Reynard in a fit of gratitude for something long forgotten. Reynard, good man though he was, could not abide that, so had pushed him away laughingly. Ares still remembered the embarrassed hurt.

So he patted Henry once or twice on the back, waiting the few seconds necessary for Henry himself to disengage. When he did, Henry said, "You have been the best father ever to me. You taught me everything I know."

Ares was shocked. Then he wondered why he was shocked. He knew that, as a child, Henry had transformed his guardian into a father figure. In the back of his mind, Ares had supposed he would outgrow that fantasy eventually. But then he saw himself spending hour after hour with the boy, attempting to inculcate upon him the attitudes he would require to rule justly—when it was thought that Henry would attain the throne at his maturity.

Even after Ares had assumed rulership, Henry seemed to be always at his elbow, especially after Ares had brought him back from slavery in Hornbound. Ares had tried to be patient with him when he made a pest of himself in his demands for attention. Only now, after years of endlessly listening to Henry's childish prattle, did Ares begin to realize just how deep Henry's learning went.

"I want permission to court Sophie," Henry said, snapping Ares out of his contemplation.

The Surchatain strained to evenly modulate his voice. "No, Henry. She is too young."

"When will she be old enough?" Henry asked with a shade of petulance.

"I will let you know," Ares replied.

Henry regarded him eye to eye, and smiled faintly. "Then I will wait. Again."

"You are dismissed," Ares said. Unoffended, Henry saluted and withdrew.

After a moment's thought, Ares went to the door to instruct the sentry, "Whenever the Chataines return from their sleigh ride, summon Chataine Sophie to me. But . . . I want you to do it out of her sister's hearing. I don't want Chataine Bonnie to know that I have summoned her."

The sentry hesitated, a look of terror crossing his face. "Sophie is wearing the brown rabbit today," Ares clarified.

In immediate relief, the sentry replied, "I understand, Surchatain," with the requisite salute.

Closing the door after him, Ares sighed, "Who knew that those tiny things would grow up to be so troublesome?" He paused, reflecting on the day he had held the newborn Henry in his arms and recited the oath of guardianship: to protect the life and honor of his charge, and to pay for failure with his life. He had often wondered why Cedric would entrust his heir to the last surviving descendant of Roman—now, twenty years later, he believed that Cedric did so looking for an excuse to send him to the block. But Ares had taken the oath too seriously.

He understood, as far as any man could understand, that he was making that vow before God—but how dimly he perceived the far-reaching effects of that vow! His face changed slightly at a related thought: Much as he admired his ancestor Roman's charisma in gaining the love of the Chataine he warded, Ares was not about to let that happen with one of his daughters.

Resting both hands on the stone hearth, he leaned over the fire and closed his eyes. Henry wanted to court Sophie! Upon reflection, that, too, seemed inevitable, as Henry had been drawn to her from earliest childhood.

Significantly, Henry had no difficulty telling the twins apart. The last time they had attempted to fool him, he played along with their game, confiding to "Sophie" (who

33

was really Bonnie) how vain and childish he thought Bonnie was until she, in a fit of rage, exposed her identity by endeavoring to thrash him. Henry had made the incident famous with so many retellings that the next time the girls opted to switch roles, they were careful to exclude him from the group of intended patsies.

Exhaling, Ares looked up at the large portrait over the fireplace which depicted the twins on either side of their mother. He did not consider it a particularly good likeness: the artist had taken liberties with his subjects' faces and necks, elongating them according to the current fashion. The reproduction of their eyes also fell short—there was a luster, a fire in Nicole's eyes that the artist had failed to capture. Still, despite the portrait's many shortcomings, Ares liked to look at it.

When this was commissioned two years ago, Nicole had begged him to be included, but he refused to immortalize his scar for future generations. He wanted to preserve only that which was beautiful. And that beauty was already drawing attention from around the Continent. Stuffed into a corner niche was a thick wad of marriage proposals to his daughters from Chatains and nobles as far away as Eugenia and Tockhorn. These he refused to entertain for at least another two years.

But Henry. . . . When Ares had accepted the throne, he decreed that Henry would retain his title of Chatain, just as his half-sister, Renée, retained her title of Chataine. But when Henry joined the army as a Green recruit, he discarded the meaningless title. He now had no more standing than any other member of the Blue Regiment. And Ares could not see wasting the great political advantage of an astute marriage alliance by allowing Sophie to marry a mere soldier . . . unless her heart was set on it.

With a soft groan, he returned to the table to make a half-hearted effort at answering correspondence, but the letter from Fanchon must be considered first, and he wouldn't summon the Counselor to ask him about it until he had spoken with Sophie. So Ares occupied himself with relative trifles until the sentry opened the door to inform him of his daughter's arrival.

Ares watched as she came in. While Bonnie's entrance was as the cataract of the northern Passage where it descends from the Fastnesses, Sophie's was like the stream whose tranquil surface belies the depth and strength of the current beneath. She came to him where he sat, bending to kiss whichever cheek was closest. "Good afternoon, Papa."

"Sophie." He nodded to the chair across from the table, and she gathered her skirts properly to sit. She wore a red silk dress (of identical cut to Bonnie's blue one) topped with a brown rabbit surcoat. Like Bonnie, her long chestnut hair was gathered back in a high ponytail. But observant admirers might notice that her hair was a few inches shorter than her sister's, as Sophie made frequent, clandestine efforts to cut it. "How was your ride?" her father asked.

"It was fun," she admitted. "Bonnie made poor Seane stand up to get off the furs just before we hit a little hill and he fell out of the sleigh. Then he had to run to catch up with us because Uncle Oswald didn't know he was gone and he wouldn't call out. You should have seen him jumping over the snow! The other soldiers were about to fall off their horses laughing. But he made it back in. And when we got out to the lake, we saw snow foxes and deer. Papa, the deer looked so hungry—they were standing on their hind legs trying to reach the last of the green willow branches. Can't we put fodder out for them?"

"We will, after the wolf hunt. We don't want them to

35

starve over the winter, either," he assured her. She glanced down, knowing that they were being kept alive for the Surchatain's table. But she comforted herself with the knowledge that the hunters' thinning the herd was kinder than letting the lot of them die of starvation.

Ares leaned forward, drumming his fingers indecisively on the table, and Sophie read his face. "Is this about Tobias?" she asked in a small voice.

He cleared his throat. "Has he molested your sister?"

Her eyes widened in horror. "No!"

"You're sure," he said, relaxing a little.

"Oh, yes, Papa," she said firmly. "Bonnie would have told me. But I don't think she would have let him—when Mama started telling us about how babies are made, Bonnie thought it was the most disgusting thing she ever heard and wouldn't listen. I had to go back and ask Mama about it later. But, Papa, I still don't understand something. When men—when a man—"

"Ask your mother," Ares interrupted. "She knows more about it than I do." Sophie giggled and Ares smiled momentarily. But as his face settled into its usual gravity, she grew still. "If Tobias has not wronged your sister, how did you know that I wanted to talk to you about him?"

"He didn't go with us today," she said. "And . . . Seane thought it strange that he would be rotated out in winter. He can't go anywhere."

Ares regarded her. "What Seane thinks wouldn't mean anything to you unless you had put it together with something else. Sophie, I know that you don't like to tattle, but you really must tell me what you know about Tobias."

She glanced aside, sighing. "He . . . took her too seriously. Bonnie plays with them, you know. She doesn't mean anything by it, and she never does anything wrong.

She just flirts, like Renée. He started acting like—treacle, all gooey and sweet, but to Bonnie it was all a game."

"Something else I have to thank Renée for," he muttered. Bonnie's role model Renée was Henry's half-sister, also a child of Cedric's. Twelve years older than her brother, blonde and blue-eyed, she was renowned for her heartless playing of suitors. After Lord Lieterstad died, passing his considerable fortune to his nephew Nicklos, Renée had married him and gone to live in Crescent Hollow. But then Nicklos had died in a drunken fall from a horse, and Renée had returned to Westford—

"Papa, what have you done with Tobias?" Sophie asked in alarm.

He smiled hazily. "He will be stationed in Odea once the weather clears."

"That's all?" she asked suspiciously.

"He must never come back to Westford," he said, and it was unnecessary for her to ask what would happen if he did. "Why do you care? Did you like him?"

She made a small face. "Not really, Papa. I just don't see that it was wrong for him to care about Bonnie, especially when she led him to."

Ares made the deliberate decision not to burden her with the knowledge of Tobias' plans. "Well," he exhaled, passing a hand over his face. "Henry has asked my permission to court you."

Sophie quickly looked up, but, having studied her father's manner in delicate council meetings, mimicked his inscrutable expression. "What did you tell him?"

"No, for now, because you are too young."

"Of course I am," she murmured.

"Do you like Henry?" Ares asked. She hedged and he said, "Sophie, I need to know how you feel about him."

"I don't know!" she said, vexed. "I know that he is brave, but he is also annoying. He is a very annoying boy."

Ares sat back, laughing. Sophie looked simultaneously irritated and pleased; she did not see anything funny in the statement, but she loved to hear him laugh. It happened rarely enough.

Wiping his eyes, he said, "Dear one, I must agree with you there: he is very annoying. But . . . we care for him anyway."

Sophie squinted dubiously at his use of the plural pronoun. Then she said, "Why is your cheek red?"

A knock at the door elicited a testy "What?" from him, as interruptions in the precious little time he had with his family chafed him.

When the door opened, he stood and came around the table. Sophie also bounded up from her chair; being swifter and closer to the door, she reached her mother first. "You've been crying," she murmured, closing her arms around her mother's waist.

Nicole smoothed her tousled ponytail. "No, dear; it's only the smoke from the fireplaces that irritates my eyes. But your sister has been looking for you, and if she discovers that you've had your father's ear in private, she will demand an hour of his time in return."

"I'll go," Sophie said, looking to her father, who nodded. When the door closed behind her, she glanced back in concern—her mother's story about dry eyes did not fool her—then progressed down the Surchatain's corridor toward the landing.

Henry met her at the head of the stairs. "I . . . saw you come back in the sleigh," he opened.

"Yes," she said, pausing out of courtesy, not to give him any encouragement.

"The lake is nice, but you should see the fountain in the market square. It has these great icicles hanging down that Breckett the confectioner carved into wonderful shapes—fish and birds and even dragons. Then he carved one in the shape of his wife's face, so people are bringing him chunks of ice to carve into little statues. I . . . would like to see him do one of you," Henry said, swallowing.

"Then it would look just like me, and I'd be doing this!" Bonnie, behind him on the stairs, stuck out her tongue at him.

"Yes, that's how you usually look, Bonnie," Henry said levelly.

She blew a vigorous raspberry at him, then grabbed her sister's hand. "Where have you been? Wait till you hear what I heard—" She began dragging her down the Surchatain's wing toward their quarters. Sophie glanced back at Henry, still standing by the stair. She really did rather want to see the fountain, but said nothing to Bonnie about it.

After Ares' receiving-room door had closed upon Sophie's exit, he came up to his wife to take her hand and kiss her palm. She was the original, the pattern for the twins' looks that turned so many heads. Thirteen years after first setting eyes on her, he still got weak-kneed upon seeing her after any length of absence.

To his eyes, she looked unchanged from the seventeen-year-old who stepped into his path in the foyer. He never confessed to anyone, not even her, that after clutching her to avoid falling down with her, and feeling her soft firmness under the linen bodice, he knew he was going to lie with her, and soon. For honor's sake, he just had to contrive a way to marry her first.

Only today, she looked rather pale. That, he noticed.

Lifting heavy eyes, she told him, "Doctor Savary said it was a miscarriage." He did not respond other than to press his lips harder into her palm. Despite evident attempts to contain herself, her eyes filled with tears again. "All I wanted was to give you a son," she whispered. "That's all I ever wanted—"

"Which would be superfluous," he interrupted, lowering her hand, and she looked at him in wounded wonder. "I already have been given one, whether I would have him or not, and a second would simply create more problems than I care to deal with now."

As she stared at him, he noted that the tears had stopped. She floundered, "What . . . ?" But she knew what, or rather whom, he was talking about.

The bell tolled two, and Ares turned away from her to the door. Opening it, he spoke in a low, deliberate voice to the sentry: "I do not wish to be interrupted for the next hour. No one is to be granted entrance unless an army shows up at the palace gates. Do you understand?"

That voice, used solely to pronounce judgments of life and death, produced the quick, "Yes, Surchatain."

Satisfied, Ares closed the door and returned to his wife. "When was the last time," he murmured, "that I was *not* deprived?—when I could have you at leisure without worrying that I would get my head chopped off because of it?" So saying, he reached under her velvet surcoat to begin unlacing her bodice with rough, sinewy fingers.

Her lips parted in a slight, flushed smile, which he took as permission to proceed more aggressively. So he opened the full front of her dress to look at her. "It's cold, my lord," she protested coyly, while making no move to cover herself.

"You shall be well warmed soon," he said. In pursuit of

this promise, he yanked the remaining velvet and linen from her shoulders to drop them in a great heap on the floor, then pressed his face into her skin.

She closed her eyes, embracing his head, and shortly he picked her up to carry her into the bedchamber adjoining the receiving room. A fire was kept burning here as well, so while Ares laid her on the fur-covered bed and closed the door behind him, the fragrance of apple wood being consumed in heat wafted through the room.

Sinking back into the furs, she watched him remove his black coat and white shirt with measured haste. "It really doesn't matter that I bear you a son . . . ?" she murmured.

"All that matters is your pleasuring me," he said, dropping his pants to climb onto the furs. She waited as he paused to unbind her rich chestnut tresses, scattering them across the downy pillow before laying his weight fully atop her. Smiling, she arched into him, and his intense reaction confirmed that pleasuring him was something she knew how to do quite well.

At three of the bells, Ares was down in the rear quadrangle, knee-deep in snow, wearing only a light cotton shirt and deerskin pants. Under dark grey clouds, the young Green recruits gathered before him in shifting, uneven rows, and he began putting them through their paces so vigorously that heavy outer clothes were quickly thrown off around the yard.

Windows facing the quadrangle were cracked open for spectators to watch the Greens run in place, jump, shout, and fall into the snow on command. The frozen field quickly became a pit of muddy slush as hundreds of boots trod on the same space over and over. Ares grew hoarse shouting at the boys, chastising them for their laziness and inattention as he demonstrated moves that most of those past the first few rows could not see (their number having swelled in recent months).

Then, for some reason, they became a little more orderly, executing the commands a little more ably. Pausing, his breath issuing in puffs of stream, Ares discerned the reason for their sudden acuity: Henry was in the midst of them, carrying out Ares' commands without having to see him. Those who could not see Ares at the front could watch Henry to see what to do.

All at once, because a member of the Blue (identified by the insigne on his collar) was out drilling with the Greens, members of the Red or Gold began appearing in various places among the rows, even far in back, to translate Ares' orders for the benefit of the lowly recruits. Ares stopped berating them, saving his voice for one- or two-word instructions which were then reliably translated and executed.

The hour passed in profitable drills and much-needed exercise. When Ares dismissed the sodden, panting recruits to return to their regular chores, he watched Henry melt away in unconcern as to whether Ares knew he was there or not. Pensive, Ares stripped off his shirt to wipe his face.

As new snow began drifting down from overstuffed clouds, he reentered the palace by the mudroom at the rear of the kitchen. He removed his boots for cleaning, then hastened to the nearby stairwell. Whenever he had to go up or down from his receiving room, he most often took the back stairs to avoid appearing in the foyer, where he was likely to be detained by any merchant or noble wishing to air a complaint personally to the Surchatain without the inconvenience of going through the Counselor or, infinitely worse, the Steward.

Today, Ares was successful in reaching the Surchatain's suite without mishap; in the sleeping chamber, he stood in the sunken tub under the gentle waterfall. (Water was piped in from the cistern above, replenished by the continual snowfall which melted upon reaching the heated conduits).

He bathed quietly so as not to waken Nicole, still curled up in the fur bedcoverings. She was very tired. Smiling privately, he pulled out a fresh set of dress blacks and attired himself for the afternoon. When he came out to the receiving room and noticed Nicole's clothes still heaped on the floor, he resisted the impulse to leave them there as a monument to himself, and carried them back into the bedchamber.

With fresh enthusiasm and four hours until he was required to appear at dinner, Ares summoned the Counselor for his opinion on the prospects for successful trading with Seleca. While waiting for him, Ares left Fanchon's letter on the table and turned to the honeycombed shelving on the wall behind him which housed all his maps. He selected the map of routes into Seleca, spreading it open on the table in front of him.

He was standing over this map when the Counselor arrived with a knock on the door. Ares looked up as Vogelsong entered, appearing young and slight as ever, though perhaps more lavishly dressed. "How may I serve you, Surchatain?" he asked, bowing, and Ares allowed himself to be momentarily chafed. He didn't like people bowing to him in private. Carmine never irritated him with shows of humility.

"Counselor, some weeks ago I received a letter from Fanchon of Seleca proposing to renew trade. I am just now getting around to considering it," Ares said, extending the parchment to him. Vogelsong took it in hand to read, and Ares knew not to clutter the air with more words while the young Counselor was digesting the proposal.

Finally, Vogelsong handed the letter back to him. "I see, Surchatain. What do you think?"

Ares drooped slightly. "That is what I wish to hear from you: what do you think? Fanchon says that he has expelled the slavers to allow for safer travel. What have you heard?"

"What have I heard?" Vogelsong repeated, and Ares suppressed the urge to shake him. The Counselor went on, "Nothing from Seleca. What is there to hear, given this abominable weather? When did you receive this communication, Surchatain?"

"About three weeks ago, before this last storm hit," Ares said, looking at the letter again. It was dated January 15—a little over a month ago. "Fanchon's messenger said that the Surchatain was anxious to get the formalities out of the way early so that trading could commence in the spring."

The Counselor looked appropriately thoughtful. "If I knew anyone in Eurus who traveled frequently—or who was mad enough to brave this weather—I might be able to tell you whether the slavers still haunt Falcon Pass or not. But . . . my small circle of acquaintances does not include any such souls. Carmine would know."

Ares turned away with an audible groan and Vogelsong winced. "I know he was your great friend, Surchatain, and believe me when I say I wish he had not died."

B

Ares stared at the translucent lozengy windowpanes which revealed nothing beyond except the shadow of snowdrifts packed on the sill outside. "I do not resent that Carmine was taken from my service, Counselor, only . . . that he chose to go, whether by accident or design," he said, his voice gravelly.

Fourteen years ago, Carmine and Renée had been lovers. When her father, Cedric, discovered the affair, he chose to keep the brilliant young counselor in service, but had him castrated. Something of the flame remained between the lovers, however, for about the time that Ares ascended the throne a year later, the two were married.

Finding that the self-sacrifice required for a happy marriage was beyond two such strong personalities, Ares allowed them to divorce to prevent Carmine's drowning in wine. But the divorce did nothing to sever the bonds between them; Carmine lived and died daily by the attentions Renée bestowed on him or other men. Still, she remained at Westford, where he could daily drink in her beauty—but not satisfy himself with it—where he could daily hear her voice, usually in the form of taunts.

Then she married Nicklos and moved to Crescent Hollow, two days away by fast carriage. And despite Ares' best efforts to prevent it, Carmine turned to his closest, dearest friend for comfort. By all reports, Carmine was deeply besotted his last night among the living. Some time in the early morning hours, unseen by anyone, he mounted the back stairs to the parapet of the sparsely watched eastern wall, past the practice fields, armory, and barracks. And there, some time before sunrise, he either fell or leaped to his death.

That had been about six months ago, in late summer. No one sent word to Renée. But then Nicklos died, and she had returned to Westford in September, before the snows set in. Discovering that her longtime patsy was no more had affected her deeply, in ways that were just now coming to light.

Ares turned from the window. "So I am now dependent on you, Counselor, to give your best advice: how should we proceed with this proposal?"

"Well, Surchatain." Vogelsong's voice cracked and he cleared his throat. Whenever he was nervous, he had a habit of shaking out his embroidered sleeves in imitation of Carmine's practiced gesture. This he did now. "It would seem prudent to send a unit of soldiers to scout the Pass and bring us direct word of slaving activity."

To his considerable relief, Ares agreed. "The slavers keep camps year-round in caves hidden in the Fastnesses. It's maddening—we know the names of the most notorious slavers; we even have good descriptions of them: Ticzon has but four fingers on his right hand; Dorn has a large scar traversing his forehead; Morguloff is very tall and very fat —but they melt away like fog whenever we send a regiment after them. Any information that the scouts could glean about them would be helpful. But it would be most dangerous, this time of year. So instruct the Second Rhode to call for volunteers to make up a unit. We'll see how the weather looks in a fortnight, then send them out."

"Very good, Surchatain. I will attend to this immediately." Vogelsong bowed again on his way out, and Ares placed Fanchon's letter on his pile of pending actions. He picked up the next letter, but stared over the top of it for several long minutes. Then he went to the door again.

Any time he could simply call the sentry, but he disliked raising his voice, especially if Nicole was in the next room. Opening the door himself also afforded interesting surprises, such as the time he found Renée's maid Eleanor listening at the door pursuant to her mistress' instructions. That was when he was hosting a Polonti emissary who had brought a marriage proposal to Renée from his master. Shortly thereafter, she had married Nicklos.

Ares told the sentry, "Summon the priest." Then Ares returned to the table to wait, but shoved aside the stack of unanswered mail. Instead, he reached over to finger his little book, in which he copied down quotations or verses that he wished to meditate on. He opened the book to the latest entry, which read, "Let me die the death of the righteous, and let my end be like his!" Inhaling, he fixed a troubled gaze on the scrawl.

Father Birondo, a learned and gentle man, entered the receiving room with a benedictory gesture toward the Surchatain. Ares nodded at the chair across from him, inviting, "Have a seat, Father."

"Thank you, Surchatain." He sat easily, waiting in attentive silence for the Surchatain to speak his mind. The priest had little trepidation over an unexpected summons. Early in his career at the palace, he had gained Ares' approval with his piety and simple dress (a coarse brown robe with rope belt); later, having secured Ares' trust with his closed lips, the priest sometimes found himself called upon to act as a sounding board—particularly if it involved a matter that the Surchatain did not wish to tell his wife.

"Father, what is your knowledge of dreams?" Ares asked with a glance toward the closed bedchamber door.

The priest paused to adjust his spectacles over eyes weakened by incessant reading in poor light. "There are different classes of dreams, Surchatain: there are fanciful dreams that mean nothing and are quickly forgotten; there are troubling dreams brought on by spoiled meat, fever, or fears; there are nightmares that are visitations of Satan; then there are messages from God."

Ares nodded pensively. "How do you tell," he asked, "whether a dream might be of Satan or God?"

"Tell me your dream, Surchatain," the priest urged.

Ares unconsciously fingered the little book again. "It is the same one over and over. I am out riding to battle. I come across a knight in white armor, from his coroneted basinet to his sabatons."

"You mean, I take it, that he is in plain, polished armor with no coverings?" the priest asked.

"Yes. But I do not have on armor; I am in dress blacks as I always wear." Ares gestured at the soft, brocade short coat. "He calls out a challenge to me, so I dismount. He is on foot. I advance to meet him, drawing my sword.

"As we meet, I cut off his head, straight through his camail. The head falls to the ground, but there is no blood. And then . . . he grows a new head! As I watch, a new head sprouts from his shoulders, wearing the same coroneted basinet! He raises his sword and pierces me through. I fall, and as I lie dying, he places his foot on my chest and says,

'The righteous shall die by his faith.' And then I wake."

"Allow me to correct your nighttime adversary on one point, Surchatain: the quotation is, 'The righteous shall *live* by his faith.' Not 'die,'" Father Birondo said firmly.

"Yes, I know; I have read it. But the white knight clearly says, 'The righteous shall die by his faith,' and his words never change. What do you make of it?" Ares asked, peering at him.

The priest was silent for some minutes. "It is clearly a dream of import, Surchatain, and the fact that it is given you repeatedly reinforces that. But as to what it may mean, I have no immediate answer. I ask that you give me time to think and pray on it, and that you pray on it as well."

"I have been, Father, but the author of the dream has not seen it fit to enlighten me," he muttered. "Can you tell me, though, whether it would be from Satan or God?"

"For a Christian, there is but one First Cause," the priest said. "Were the dream crafted by the master devil himself, the fact that it comes to a child of God can only be because the Father allows it."

"I see," Ares acknowledged, leaning back.

"Meanwhile, I shall pray and meditate on the matter," Birondo assured him.

Yet another knock came at the door, so Ares said, "Do so. You are dismissed."

Rising with the same gesture of benediction, Birondo turned as Counselor Vogelsong came in. The Counselor stopped short in embarrassment. "Forgive me, Surchatain; I entered too hastily."

He started to back out again, but Ares said, "Come in, Counselor; the Father was just leaving."

The two nodded to each other as Birondo passed by, then Vogelsong shut the door and advanced to the table, extending a scrap of parchment. "The Second Rhode found more volunteers than are needed for our mission, Surchatain—here is the list for you to pare to ten. The men seem to have had enough of looking at walls."

"They might feel differently after sleeping under snowfall," Ares muttered, reaching for the list. Scanning the twenty-odd names, he went on: "They're so used to fighting with swords and spears, they don't stop to think how dangerous a little frozen water might—"

He stopped midsentence, for his eye had landed on Henry's name. What if the dream referred not to himself, but to someone close to him? What if the white knight represented snow and ice?

Ares looked up with glazed eyes. When should he stop being Henry's guardian? Vogelsong waited in mild concern —the Surchatain could hardly pick ten volunteers if he wasn't looking at the names.

Ares deliberately returned his attention to the list, then noted, "Most of these are members of the Blue: Buford. Quince. Stauch. And I am wondering why I should put the cream of my men in grave peril to meet Fanchon's timetable for reestablishing trade."

Vogelsong stared at him in confusion. "I thought that our aim was to gather information on the slavers' activity in the Fastnesses, Surchatain."

"Which we can do just as well when the snows melt. Fanchon can wait," Ares said, thrusting the list into the fire. "You are dismissed, Counselor."

Vogelsong collected himself to bow, feeling that he had miscalculated something dreadfully.

Dinner at Westford was a nightly extravaganza of the best foods, the liveliest conversation, the brightest table shimmering with the reflected light from scores of candelabra and chandeliers. Sixty guests graced the Surchatain's banquet hall nightly, with three times that number on a waiting list to attain a coveted seat.

Midwinter dinners were particularly festive as Georges, the dinner master, strove with all his considerable experience and ingenuity to relieve the residents' boredom of confinement as well as the tedium of winter fare.

Fish and meat were available year-round (praise God) but the spoiled Westfordians had to settle for dried fruits and compotes in place of fresh produce. Tonight they feasted on green turtle soup, broiled bloaters, and fricatelli (pork chopped with seasonings, eggs, and onions, then fried), with wheat pudding for dessert.

All children at table (usually just Bonnie and Sophie) were now given kumyss—fermented milk—to drink instead of diluted wine, as had been the custom. And while Ares was not stinting with refreshment at dinner, guests who were foolish enough to get themselves noticeably drunk found their prized seats given to someone else in short order.

At the head of the table, in tall-backed wooden chairs, sat Ares with Nicole at his right. Around the corner of the table on Ares' left sat Sophie, Thom, his wife Deirdre, the Second Rhode and his wife Soucie, and Doctor Savary. On Nicole's right around the corner of the table sat Bonnie, Counselor Vogelsong, Steward Giles and his wife Genevieve, the Second Oswald and his new bride, Evangeline, who was such a modest, shy, sweet girl that she found instant favor with everyone who loved Oswald. The rest of the seats were occupied by shifting ranks of lesser palace administrators, courtiers, captains and nobles of Westford.

The question of where to place Renée at the table when she returned to Westford almost spun into a state crisis. Since she had moved back into her old suite on the second floor, she expected to reclaim her old seat next to Bonnie.

Vogelsong was more than willing to move down to accommodate her, but Giles, after having seen the young Counselor leapfrog over him, dug in his heels about giving up chairs three and four on the Surchataine's side of the table.

Ares, in turn, refused to displace Thom or his Seconds, as the Surchatain sometimes quietly conferred with his Commander over dinner. (Sophie, in between them, absorbed everything that was murmured over her head.) And everyone agreed that the doctor had earned his place.

Finally, Ares offered Renée seat number seven on the Surchatain's side of the table, next to Doctor Savary and across from Father Birondo. This she rejected out of hand until a few days' exclusion from the table convinced her that it was the best she could hope for.

So she accepted it, appearing at table in dramatic, low-cut widow's weeds specially designed for her by Lord Preus, the once-premier dressmaker of Westford. She was graciously received and liberally condoled, but . . . it was not the same. Conversations did not immediately cease just because she started to speak.

Her status changed in other ways, as well. After years of ruling the dance floor, she discovered that a few months' absence usurped her, and the dancing altered completely. The more elaborate, anxiety-producing dances were dropped in favor of line dances and simple couples' dances that almost anyone could learn in minutes. Bereaved of her longtime dance partner, Carmine, she found no one else sufficiently skilled at the old dances to partner her—except

Ares. And he gently refused; he danced with no one but his wife and daughters.

Being removed seven places from the head of the table served to blunt Renée's acerbity, as well. The one time she forgot her place and directed a comment to Rhode's wife, Soucie, about her dress (created by Tailor Gathing) it elicited a snapped, "She dresses to please me" from Rhode and silence from the rest of the table.

Whereupon Renée looked at sweet little Evangeline, one seat up and across the table from her, and all movement at the table ceased while Renée contemplated *her* dress, which the fashionable widow considered even more ridiculous than Soucie's. But seeing the faces of her dinner companions, and reading them accurately, Renée held her tongue.

At that moment the *coup de grâce* of the evening was innocently delivered by Bonnie, who leaned over to her mother to whisper a little too loudly, "Mama, why is Aunt Renée wearing such an old-fashioned dress?"

Nicole quietly rebuked her for calling attention to the deficiencies of anyone's clothes. And over the next few weeks, Renée began to notice that all the women of the court, led by Nicole, were now wearing soft, modest dresses created by this Tailor Gathing.

But Renée's new life had its consolations, as well. Since she brought Nicklos' fortune with her when she returned to Westford, she was not dependent on the palace treasury for the finery or frivolities that she desired. And since it was *her* money she was spending now, she became somewhat more conservative in her purchases.

Giles became a new person, as well, without having to balance the books around her spending binges. In the amazed sight of everyone, he and she struck up a warm, flirtatious friendship, much to the annoyance of his wife.

Tonight, as large platters of fricatelli were passed around the table, several animated conversations were generally interweaving each other. First, there was the immediate alarm provoked by the sight of the bruised swelling around the Surchatain's scar. This he dispelled with the one-word explanation: "Henry."

Thom looked to Rhode for a more thorough accounting. The Second snorted, "My newest Blue was called to account for his black eye—he said the Surchatain hit him, and he hit back."

The upper half of the table looked in astonishment at Ares, who sighed, "Partially true. In spite of all mishaps over the years, Henry has not ceased to run through doorways."

Bonnie (who ran down corridors) chortled, "Silly boy," but Sophie had to study her father's face to assure herself that no further permanent damage had been done. It had not been that swollen when she saw him earlier in the day.

At this time, Giles offered the foremost thought on his mind: "You will be pleased to hear, Surchatain, that I was forced to pay out a total of seventy-four royals to wolf hunters today." He had long ago taken to concealing his bald pate with the finest headwear that Lord Preus produced, but the wild fringe of hair that ringed it had turned (overnight, it seemed) from a dull brown to a distinguished silver-grey. That, combined with the fact that Westford's finances were healthier than ever, served to make the Steward glow with ruddy cheer.

"The hunt took thirty-seven wolves? Excellent!" Ares said. He was most pleased with Giles for changing the subject from the condition of his face.

The Steward smiled brilliantly on all within sight to

make sure they noted Ares' praise, for Giles had been the organizer of that event. Then he added, "As soon as the pelts are cleaned and tanned, they will be taken to the abbey, Surchatain. They should fetch a silver piece or two for the orphans' care."

Genevieve patted her husband's hand lovingly. Their performance was staged, of course, as everyone passing their chambers at night heard the screaming fights. But everyone also knew how important the sustenance of the abbey was to Ares. He had lived there as a child himself.

Ares glanced at Nicole for the third time in as many minutes, though she had not spoken, and she smiled back at him. Her pallor had given way to a warm blush, and she looked lovely in her contentment. Preferring to think himself responsible for that, Ares lifted her hand to kiss it.

Bonnie leaned toward them with an impatient sigh. "Papa, I've been waiting all day for a list of guardians. When will you have them ready for me to choose from?"

Ares raised a brow at Thom, who averted his eyes as though he had no knowledge nor responsibility in the matter. So Ares replied, "Bonnie, I told you that it would take us a fortnight to make preliminary selections. It's too important a matter to rush."

"I get to choose my new guardian," Bonnie announced to the upper table.

When no one responded immediately, Vogelsong jumped into the gap lest the matter appear to be trivial. "That's wonderful, Chataine. Tell me—what shall you look for in a new guardian?"

She screwed up her pretty face to concentrate on the question. "Well . . . Papa said that I can't go by his eyes or his hair. . . ." She looked dubiously across to her sister, who smiled in amusement but offered no help.

When it became apparent that Bonnie had no idea what she should be looking for, the Counselor determinedly rescued her again. "Perhaps the Surchatain would enlighten us as to what he expects in the Chataine's new guardian?"

"Certainly," Ares said, waving away the wine steward from refilling his goblet. "I expect that he will be heartless, ruthless, unsympathetic, unfeeling, and uglier than me. Those are our primary criteria," he informed Thom, who nodded assent.

Bonnie stared at her father in dismay. Lest she burst into tears on the spot, Vogelsong hastened to tell her, "I am sure that your father is jesting with you, Chataine."

"Oh, yes, Papa!" She wheeled to him. "Summon Twomey! Please summon the jester now!"

The rest of the table voiced their approval of this idea despite Ares' slight sneer. "I had hoped to eat dessert in peace, at least," he grumbled. Turning to his wife, he inquired, "What does the lady desire?"

"Whatever is my lord's pleasure," she murmured, and he regarded her in anticipation.

"Well—" He glanced at Sophie, who nodded excitedly in favor of the jester. "Summon Twomey," he said in resignation to the sentry. At this, the hall resonated with the sounds of wood scraping stone as the guests on the Surchataine's side of the table turned their chairs to face outward, where the jester would soon appear.

Only moments later the very Twomey entered to enthusiastic applause and bowed to the head of the table. Even disregarding the red-and-green motley, or the fool's cap split into two tails with bells on each end, he was a funny little man. He had huge ears, high cheeks, a long nose, bulging eyes, and almost no eyebrows or eyelashes to speak of. Moreover, he had the silliest grin ever seen, with his wide mouth curving up and his pointy chin sticking out. Just by walking in and bowing, he sent Bonnie into fits of suppressed giggles.

"Flog your sentry, Surchatain Ares; he told the meanest lie to poor Twomey just now. He said you sent for me. Is that not folly? You did not send for silly Twomey, did you, Surchatain Ares?" he demanded in a high, piercing voice that had Thom wincing.

Ares inhaled tiredly. "I sent for you, Twomey."

"You did?" Twomey made a show of clasping his hands in fond hope over his heart. "Why did you send for foolish Twomey, Surchatain Ares?"

"With the foolish idea that you might entertain us," Ares said dryly. Most of the guests were now tittering. Vogelsong watched in morbid wonder, as he could not imagine baiting the Surchatain the way this fool did. Renée eyed the jester in bored disgust, then turned away in her chair, slouching.

"Ooooohhh!" Twomey's exclamation of delight sounded like the baying of a hound, and Thom took a long swig of wine. "Then what shall poor Twomey do to entertain good Surchatain Ares? Dance? Dance! Twomey will dance! Musicians!" he cried with a grand gesture. Stone-faced, the courtly musicians appeared just behind him with their vielle, tabor, flute and bells ready. Upon his exaggerated signal, they began to play, and Twomey began to dance.

At the opening strains of "Wasserleben," Renée sat up suspiciously. This was one of her favorite dances, complex and challenging. Most of the guests knew it well enough to recognize it, but not perform it. So they quieted down to watch Twomey's solo interpretation.

He was unnaturally agile, and would have been a

lovely dancer but for the exaggerated motions and deliberate missteps. Nonetheless, the guests watched in amazement as he sailed through difficult movements without a partner, adding a flash or two to make them even more difficult. Then he would fall flat, or pretend to slip, or turn himself in dizzying circles—and then miraculously pick up the correct step at the next beat.

He knew the breathtaking dance so well that he turned it inside out, creating an even more breathtaking parody. Moreover, his mincing carried an underlying statement about the absurdity of pretensions: when he paused in the middle of the dance to fart (to howls of laughter) it was a reminder that people who performed such wonderful feats still had to relieve themselves like any beast.

At his concluding bow, the guests broke into boisterous applause. After a moment, even Ares grudgingly brought his hands together. Someone near Renée gasped, "I'll never be able to watch anyone dance the Wasserleben again without laughing!" Renée was incensed—it amounted to sacrilege.

Upon seeing the Surchatain's straight-faced applause, Twomey squealed and ran toward the head of the table. Before anyone could move, he launched himself as out of a trebuchet to land squarely in Ares' lap.

Half the table stood—the officers in alarm, the rest to see better. With bony arms around Ares' neck and skinny legs draped over the right chair arm, Twomey planted a firm, luscious kiss on the Surchatain's unscarred cheek.

The table waited in suspense as Ares turned cold eyes to Twomey while he toyed with his white frilled collar coquettishly. Then Ares uttered, "I've had better."

Nicole laughed outright; Thom dropped his head, and the twins fell upon the table in laughing fits. As the

Surchatain's utterance was passed down the table for those who had not heard it, the laughter shook the chandeliers. Only one spectator was clearly unamused: Renée.

Still sitting, Ares lifted Twomey off his lap and dropped him over the side of the chair, where the jester landed flat on his bottom with a wail. Then he began rolling away in somersaults which the twins stood up to watch.

But neither Ares nor Thom was watching the jester at this point, for a sentry had quietly entered to bend at Thom's ear, whispering. Thom nodded, waving him away. While Twomey launched into song, holding the table spellbound, Thom leaned over to Ares to whisper, "Tobias has deserted his unit en route to Nicole's Harbor, and disappeared."

4

res blinked, whispering to Thom, "Tobias intends to come back for Bonnie."

"Yes," Thom returned in a whisper.

The two glanced up at a fresh burst of laughter from the table over Twomey's antics. No one was looking at the Surchatain and Commander. Ares resumed whispering, "Then we must assign Bonnie another guardian straightway. I need names on the morrow." Thom assented, settling back into his seat.

Ares leaned back as well, placing two fingers over his lips in contemplation. At this point the jester was standing on his head near the end of the table, his bony legs in wrinkled green hose flailing the air. "See what Twomey knows!" he cried, which meant that he had seen Ares' signal.

"Fine. You are dismissed," Ares said, gesturing. He had to give Twomey time to circulate before their meeting tonight, which had been arranged just now. When the guests murmured in disappointment, Ares offered as consolation, "You may dance." He waved at the musicians to bring their instruments forward. A score of dancers rushed the floor then, all clamoring to try the Wasserleben.

As Ares turned, he was met by his wife eyeing him in expectation, a delicate hand at the silk lacing of her bodice. "Why has my lord dismissed everyone so early tonight?" she murmured.

He raised his chin. This was an offer he would not refuse; they had time before he was to meet with Twomey. "Come upstairs and I will show you," he directed. Lifting her soft, flowing skirts, she turned promptly to the doorway.

Following her, Ares was detained by a firm hand on his arm. Reluctantly, he turned to meet Renée's imperious blue eyes. Nicole was already out the door. "Ares, they're butchering the Wasserleben. You must help me show them how it's properly danced!"

He demurred, "Chataine, after watching Twomey tonight, I'm fortunate to remember how to place one foot in front of the other. Excuse me." He pulled loose from her grip to follow his wife.

Ares was the only one who still called Renée "Chataine," either by force of habit or because of his promise that the title would never be taken from her. But even she was beginning to realize that with two genuine Chataines at Westford who were younger and far more marriageable, her own claim to the title appeared rather pale. That, too, had changed.

Bonnie and Sophie watched the courtiers make fools of themselves at the Wasserleben for a little while, but since they were not nearly as good at it as Twomey, the girls grew bored with that and began to head upstairs.

On the way, Bonnie spotted a new sentry, a young one. Contrary to protocol, he glanced at the girls when they passed, so she tossed her head every so slightly, with a provocative glimpse in his direction. As usual, his heart almost stopped in his chest. While he watched, the twins began to ascend the dark stairway, lit only by globed candles at each end of every other step.

When the girls were out of his sight on the stairs, Sophie turned on her sister. "You have to stop that!"

"What?" Bonnie blinked at her.

Aggrieved, Sophie explained, "Bonnie, you have to stop playing with them like that. They think you're in love with them. It gets them in trouble!"

Bonnie pooh-poohed her. "What do you know? You're just jealous that they don't react that way to you."

"I'm not jealous. I get enough attention. A member of the Blue came to Papa today and asked permission to court me," Sophie said in her own defense.

"Really? Who?" Bonnie asked, all agog.

Sophie paused. "Henry," she admitted.

"Henry!" Bonnie screeched in laughter. At her sister's unamused expression, she turned serious. "Sophie, do you like him?"

"No," Sophie insisted, choosing not to examine the question.

"Well, I can't stand him, either. I wouldn't want him to court me. All I want to do is get back at him for telling everyone that I'm *vain* and *immature*," Bonnie vented. Sophie was quiet. "Let's sneak down to the wine vault and snatch a bottle!" Bonnie suggested in a whisper.

Sophie turned on her violently. "No! That would kill Papa and I won't do it!"

"All right, how about a bottle of kumyss?" Bonnie offered.

"Okay," Sophie agreed, so they began a clandestine descent.

While the girls were downstairs raiding the kitchen storerooms, their parents were upstairs satisfying their thirst for each other. Ares was gratified by Nicole's demands— he had seldom known her to be so lustful. By the time the final bells of that day rang (at ten), he was just in the process of disentangling himself from her, flushed, sweating, and lazily satisfied. "Where are you going?" she murmured, reaching up to his wet chest.

Still winded from his exertions, he took a moment to catch his breath. Desirous of preserving her peace of mind, he was judicious in what he told her; for instance, she knew Twomey only as a jester. But there were some things Ares was forced to tell her.

Lowering himself to her arms again, he said, "My love . . . we had a problem with Bonnie's guardian, Tobias, today. It seems that he had made plans to run off with her."

"What?" Nicole bolted upright in bed. "And Bonnie agreed to this?"

"No, no," he said soothingly. "It was all in his own mind—Bonnie knew nothing of it. But I relieved him of duty and sent him to Nicole's Harbor. Tonight, I received word that he disappeared. So, I must go make arrangements to secure Bonnie until she receives a new guardian tomorrow. I will only be gone a little while."

"All right," she said hesitantly, sinking back to the bed.

"Do not worry over this, Nicole," he ordered. "I will not be deprived because you are busy entertaining needless worries."

"Of course not." She smiled sleepily, and had drifted off before he even finished dressing.

Ares trotted downstairs to the chapel off the foyer. Any witnesses would see nothing unusual in such late visitations because Ares' regard for Father Birondo, who slept in a small side room off the chapel, was widely known.

Entering, Ares closed the chapel doors behind him and scanned the small hall. Past the rows of rough wooden benches, worn smooth by centuries of use, he saw the robed figure sitting quietly underneath the large cross on the far wall, ancient even in Roman's time. The figure was sitting on the dais facing the door to the foyer. Ares advanced to the dais, then turned to sit beside the man, who lowered his cowl. It was not Father Birondo. It was Twomey.

The funny little man had appeared one day last August at the palace kitchen begging for a bite. Ares had a protocol for beggars: they were given kitchen refuse at a designated place away from the palace, not at the kitchen door. But the man was in such a sorry state—parched, palsied, covered with sores—that the kitchen mistress made an exception, feeding him then and there.

In gratitude, he had delivered a spontaneous recital from the new hit *Piers Plowman* that so delighted the kitchen staff they kept him around for further performances, feeding him from worktables and allowing him to sleep by one of the great kitchen fireplaces at night. They even drafted one of Doctor Savary's assistants to treat his painful sores, which soon healed.

Word of Twomey's various talents spread until Giles interviewed him for possible dinner entertainment. After seeing him audition in rags, Giles ordered him dressed in motley provided by Tailor Gathing. Twomey performed after dinner the very next evening.

Ares was not particularly impressed, but everyone else was so taken with the jester that he was summoned to perform practically every night thereafter. He was always doing something different—he could dance; he could sing; he could recite long passages from the classics (with immodest alterations), and his wit carried the sting of truth.

A few days before Carmine's untimely death, Twomey had stopped Ares in the corridor with a cringing bow to murmur, "Pardon, Surchatain. Please pardon. Poor Twomey fears the wine will kill the Counselor." Ares had stared him down and gone his way, but the disregarded warning came back to haunt him soon enough.

Thereafter, Ares had tested Twomey on various matters around the palace, questioning him about this or that. If Twomey did not know, he asked for time to find out. Sometimes he was able to uncover information, sometimes not; but whatever he chose to pass along to Ares proved to be accurate every time. So Ares worked out a system by which he could glean from Twomey's field of knowledge in secret. Only Thom and Father Birondo knew of the relationship.

Several people—Thom and Ares included—asked Twomey about his background, as his antics indicated a knowledge of not only the Holy Canon but other classical forms, such as the Wasserleben. But the jester would tell no one anything of his past, not even the Surchatain. Father Birondo confided to Ares that, because of certain expressions Twomey used, the father was sure that Twomey had been either a monk of some order or a priest in some royal court. The man himself steadfastly refused to say.

About a week ago, Twomey had expressed to Ares vague concerns about Tobias. Then there was the incident this morning in which Twomey was caught stealing a cream pastry from the kitchen. He appealed to the Surchatain, who arrived downstairs to interview the accused in private, receiving from him a small scroll and a few words. Twomey was whipped for the theft, but allowed to stay on as palace jester. He also ate the pastry.

Ares, his back against the wall underneath the cross, eyed Twomey as he gingerly adjusted the rough wool away from his neck. Twomey had sensitive skin, and suffered rashes from the wool which gave him great discomfort, but he was never heard to complain. He also said nothing to Ares about the welts that covered his back from this morning's punishment—but neither was he leaning against the wall. Uncovered, his head sported sparse grey hairs shaved short, almost identical to the bristly grey hairs on his face. And when he was not performing, as he was not performing now, his pinched face settled into lines of vague sadness.

Ares said, "I was told at dinner that Tobias never arrived at Nicole's Harbor. What have you heard?"

Twomey replied, "I hear that he debarked the barge headed for Nicole's Harbor at Copper Way"—so named because a barge trip from the small station either way to Westford or Nicole's Harbor cost a copper pence. "That was early this afternoon, so he had plenty of time to make it back to Westford before nightfall." Without the cringing tone, his voice was cultured and precise, though hoarse.

"Has anyone seen him?" Ares asked.

"No, Surchatain. Not a soul that I've talked to suspects that he might come back here. The feeling is that he got so weary with the babysitting, he set out to have himself a good drunk before showing up for duty in Nicole's Harbor. Even Captain Derrick expects to see him there in the morning." Derrick was the officer in charge of the outpost at the harbor.

Ares chewed his lip in thought. "Will Tobias try to take her tonight?"

Twomey narrowed his eyes at the closed doors across

the room. "I cannot see how, Surchatain." He squirmed in the uncomfortable wool. "But I believe he is hiding somewhere around the palace tonight—the stables, the servants' quarters, maybe even the washhouse. Tomorrow, if he can lure her with a message to his hiding place, then all he has to do is put her on a horse and ride out."

"His message of this morning said that he had arranged not to come back from the wolf hunt. Did he have an accomplice?" Ares asked.

"Perhaps," Twomey said hesitantly.

"Someone in or close to the palace, who would still be around to help him now?" Ares asked.

"One would think so," Twomey replied.

"I need to know who, Twomey," Ares said mildly.

The jester regarded him with watering eyes, again pulling at the cowl neck. "We are seeking a shadow, Surchatain. I need more time." Ares nodded at this, and Twomey added, "All will hang on the guardian that you assign her."

Ares looked up quickly. "Then I should ward her myself."

"But you cannot, any more than you can dictate Sophie's choice of suitors," Twomey pointed out, and Ares was taken aback by his prescience. "More important than being strong or smart or brave, the Chataine's new guardian must be loyal. Any one of the soldiers could be Tobias' accomplice, and any number of them might be sympathetic to his cause," Twomey lectured in a barely audible rasp.

Ares straightened, groaning, "I see."

"Meantime, Twomey listens," he said in a whisper. "And there is someone listening at the door now."

Ares quickly looked at the chapel doors. Sure enough, he could see the shadow of feet under the doors just outside. While there was no way that an eavesdropper could hear what was whispered on the dais, Ares signaled to Twomey that the interview was ended.

While the jester pulled the hood back over his head and rose to leave by the back door, Ares stealthily crossed the chapel in hopes of catching their eavesdropper. But the feet disappeared, and by the time Ares opened the doors, there was nothing in the dark, echoing foyer but the red glow from the log slowly burning to ashes in the great fireplace. So he went on up to bed and Nicole.

Deep into the night, Ares started awake. Once again, he had severed the head of his adversary only to watch it grow back. And once again he had felt the sear of metal through his chest, driving him dying to the ground. As his blood drained onto the earth, the white knight planted an armored foot on Ares' pierced chest to utter, "*The righteous shall die by his faith.*" It took a long time for Ares to get back to sleep after that.

He woke early the following morning, long before the first bells rang at seven, and climbed out of bed to put another log on the fire, for the room was icy. Nicole was burrowed somewhere down in the furs. Standing by the hearth, he reached for the soft woolen undergarments he wore when it was this cold, and paused.

A queer feeling rose up in him. He remembered for the first time that this action of putting on woolen under-garments was part of his recurring dream. Did he meet the white knight in wintertime? Deliberately, instinctively, he changed that action, reaching for the cotton undergarment instead. He would just be a little colder today.

By the time Ares had finished his morning prayers and meditation, when the first weak light of day appeared through the window, Thom was in his receiving room with a list of eighteen prospective guardians for Bonnie. Most were from the Red or Blue Regiments, though a few were from the Gold. There were two lieutenants on the list, but Thom was reluctant to pull a captain from regular duty to be considered for the position of guardian.

It was not that guardianship was beneath a ranking officer, he explained to Ares, it was simply that by the time any man reached the rank of captain, he had been so thoroughly indoctrinated with the specific demands of his position that replacing him for a temporary assignment would be greatly disruptive to the regiment as a whole. It was far better to tap an up-and-comer who was free of such encumbrances. Since Ares already knew this, he agreed.

Mindful of Twomey's advice, Ares spent all morning interviewing the proposed candidates. While he was thus engaged, his Commander was taking care of a few matters in town. First he stopped by the swordmaker's shop to confirm his appointment at the palace in a few hours. Thom reminded him, again, to bring his daughter.

Then the Commander stopped by the shop of Aron the jeweler, just to look in. He received a bristly, perfunctory welcome from the jeweler, for the two men did not like each other. Thom never bought anything, and Lord Aron felt as though he was merely spying.

Outside his shop, Thom paused to watch a minor fracas in the street. Gowin, the flower merchant, was forcefully shoving away a child when a young woman got between them to argue on the child's behalf. Seeing Thom, Gowin shouted, "Banish these street urchins, Commander! I do not want their weeds or their services!"

With a couple of soldiers at his side, Thom came over to mediate. "What is the problem?" he asked mildly.

The two combatants spoke at the same time, both standing over the frightened child, but the young woman prevailed by sheer passion. She was Polonti, Thom noted. He listened to her explain, "These children are not street urchins! They are in my care. They do not beg or steal, but sell what they can to earn a piece or two honorably." Thom glanced aside at four other children waiting in the shadows of a nearby house.

"What is your name?" he asked.

"Mayra, Lord Commander," she said cautiously.

Gowin attempted to interrupt but Thom motioned him silent. "And who are you to these children?"

"I . . . found them alone. They have no one else to care for them," she said, chin out.

The Commander squinted at the children again. They looked to range from about three to eight years old. They were mostly clean, skinny but not starving. Appraising the young woman, he found her in a like state, although there was obviously no one taking care of her. Thom said, "The Surchatain does not permit street vendors—"

"I told you!" Gowin vented.

"Would you have them banished to slavery?" she exclaimed.

Thom told one soldier at his side, "Have all the children taken to the abbey."

As the soldier bent to pick up the nearest child, Mayra cried, "Where? Where are you taking them?"

"Come see," Thom said. "I have a place for you, too."

"At this abbey?" she asked doubtfully, gesturing the rest of the children to her. They came running.

"No," Thom said.

Meanwhile, Ares was completing his preliminary selection of candidates to be Bonnie's new guardian. A few who were clearly disdainful of the opportunity he eliminated at once. Fulfilling the obligations of the position would be difficult enough without a bad attitude. A few who were rather repulsive in their appearance or manner Ares also crossed off the list; Bonnie would simply refuse to be attended by such a one.

In interviewing the candidates, Ares was careful not to imply that there was anything urgent about filling the position, nor did he mention Tobias. The guardian whom they selected would be fully apprised of the threat, but not a whisper of it would be aired prematurely.

By the time the bell chimed one, Ares had his list narrowed down to three candidates for Bonnie to interview: Garren, Wordie, and Van Laeke. Coincidentally, they were respectively members of the Blue, Red, and Gold Regiments.

They were all young, earnest, intelligent, and (for Bonnie's benefit) better-looking than the average soldier. But Ares already had in mind the precautions he would take to see that the new guardian did not fall into the trap that had virtually assured Tobias' death.

When Ares summoned Bonnie to his receiving room, she arrived almost immediately, tired and crabby. Because the cold permeated every room of the palace, she was bundled up head to foot in blue fox. "Papa, we've been stuck in the library for hours! *Why* did we have to stay in lessons all morning long? That's just mean! I've never been so bored in all my life!"

"Think how hard it was for your tutor," Ares rejoined.

"Why?" she said blankly.

He went directly to the matter at hand. "Bonnie, I have narrowed our list of guardians to three, and I'm about to summon them one at a time for you to examine. I want you to think about what you want to ask them," Ares instructed, sitting behind the table.

She bit her lip, wavering, then climbed onto his lap. "You examine them, Papa. I don't know what to ask."

"Well, let's talk about that. I don't think that what you ask is as important as how they answer. You will be listening for how they talk to you—are they nice to you? Are they respectful? Do they listen to you? And so on," Ares said.

"I still don't know what to ask," she said.

At that point they were interrupted by a knock on the door. The sentry leaned in to say, "Pardon, Surchatain. The swordmaker is here, and the Commander wished you to watch his daughter demonstrate his new blades. The Commander was highly impressed."

"I will have to see him later," Ares said a little brusquely, so the sentry saluted and withdrew.

To the daughter on his lap, Ares said, "All right, Bonnie; let's make a list." He reached around her for a stack of scrap parchment. "We'll make a list of questions for you to ask all three." Dipping the quill in the inkwell and putting it to the parchment, he suggested, "We'll start with, 'Why do you want to be my guardian?'"

"That's a good question!" Bonnie said, sitting up. "And ask, 'How *long* do you want to be my guardian?'"

Ares hesitated. "That's a good question, too, but it won't be up to them how long to serve. Your new guardian will be rotated out of service no later than August. So why don't we ask instead, 'How long would you be willing to serve if it were up to you?'"

"They'd better answer that right," Bonnie said ominously, and her father agreed.

So the two of them worked up a list of five questions

which Bonnie clutched as Ares summoned the first candidate, Garren, of the Blue Regiment. He entered with a salute and stood at attention as Ares sat behind his table and Bonnie in a chair to his right.

This candidate was tall and blond with a clean-shaven, square jaw. He wore the standard uniform of deerskin jacket and pants with a woolen dress cape over his shoulders. "Bonnie, this is Garren. Garren, this is the Chataine whom you will be warding if you are selected," Ares began. The young man bowed nicely to her while studying her intently. Apparently, he had heard something of the difficulties in telling the twins apart.

"Hello, Garren." Bonnie smiled politely, but in her father's presence there was no hint of flirtation. Businesslike, she held up the list to read the first question: "'Why do you want to be my guardian?'"

"Chataine, what I want is of no import. I will do whatever I am commanded," Garren replied respectfully.

It was an absolutely commendable answer, but Bonnie turned to her father, wailing, "Papa!"

He tried to soothe her wounded feelings. "Bonnie, all he is saying is that he'll do whatever we want, and not what he wants."

She raised the list once more, eyeing the young man. "'How long would you be willing to serve if it were up to you?'" she asked suspiciously.

Garren caught the gist of his error. "I would serve forever, Chataine, if I could."

Appearing slightly mollified, she progressed to question number three: "'What do you think would be the best part about being my guardian?'"

Garren paused to assess the subtext of the question, and very fine beads of sweat appeared on his forehead. "I believe the best part would be simply to be around you all the time—" He broke off to glance at her father, suddenly aware that this point should not be stressed. "It would be a great honor to me to be in your presence, and to know that I had a hand in keeping you whole and safe."

"All right," Bonnie said. Referring to her list once more, she asked, "'What would you *not* like about being my guardian?'"

A look of mild consternation crossed the young man's face, and the sweat became prominent on his brow. "I cannot imagine any drawback, Chataine, unless I were to die. Not that I would mind dying," he quickly amended. "It would be an honor to die in your service, were that required," he said desperately.

"Dying is the worst thing you can imagine? Worse than if I got snatched?" she asked crossly.

Open-mouthed, Garren feebly replied, "Then I would die."

"Hmmph." Unimpressed, Bonnie looked to her list for the last question. "'Finally, what would you like for me to say about you when you have completed your service?'"

"I would like for you to say that I did my job well," he said sincerely.

"Next!" Bonnie said, waving him away. Gulping, Garren bowed to her, saluted Ares, and staggered out into the corridor where the other two candidates were waiting.

Before the next man was called in, Ares sat tapping his fingers on the table a moment. At this rate, Bonnie would quickly disqualify the entire Blue Regiment from consideration. He leaned toward her to suggest, "Let's revise the questions a little, Bonnie. The men don't understand what we are asking."

So once the next candidate, Wordie, of the Red Regiment, was called in and introductions made, Bonnie began her list of questions with, "'What do you think is the most important quality my guardian should have?'"

"Faithfulness, Chataine," he replied. He was shorter than Garren, with wavy brown hair and a gentle face. Ares began to entertain high hopes for him.

Noncommittally, Bonnie looked to her second question. "'Why would you make a good guardian?'"

"Because I would do whatever your father instructed me without question, Chataine," Wordie replied.

"What about what I instructed?" Bonnie asked, deviating from the list.

"That would not be regarded, Chataine," Wordie answered correctly and honestly.

"Next!" Bonnie shouted. Ares slumped at the table.

There was a short father/daughter conference before the final candidate was called in. Van Laeke, a member of the Gold, stepped into the room to crisply salute the Surchatain. But when he turned to the Chataine, he went down on both knees before her and bowed his head. "Your humble servant Van Laeke at your summons, Chataine."

Enormously pleased, Bonnie held out her hand. "You may rise, Van Laeke." According to form, he took her hand and lightly kissed her fingers before standing and stepping back.

He was definitely the most handsome of the three, with black curls hanging over his brow, a delicate nose, and white, healthy teeth. He looked at Bonnie, not Ares, and she lifted her list of questions. "'What do you hope to accomplish as my guardian?'" she began.

"I hope to earn your favor so that you think of me fondly enough to invite me to your wedding, Chataine," he said in dead earnest. Bonnie looked gravely pleased and

Ares tightly repressed a smile. This candidate had been doing quick research in the corridor.

"'What would you consider the greatest personal benefit of serving as my guardian?'" she asked.

"To preserve the life and honor of the most celebrated beauty on the Continent," he replied.

Bonnie began wiggling happily in her chair and Ares had to cover his smiling mouth. Then she asked, "'If you are allowed to take me on an outing into town, where would you want to go first?'"

"Lord Preus' dress shop, Chataine," he answered, smiling.

Bonnie's happy face vanished. "Lord Preus' shop? Why Lord Preus?"

Van Laeke looked concerned, and Ares held his breath. "Well—isn't he the Chataine's dressmaker—?"

"No!" screamed Bonnie. "Not mine! He does old ladies' dresses! Why do you think I would be interested in going there?" Confounded, poor Van Laeke began stammering, and Bonnie shouted, "Oh, you're hopeless! Get out!" He bowed and fled.

Fuming, Bonnie sat with arms tightly crossed and Ares sat contemplating how she had required only minutes to vanquish three of the most promising soldiers in the whole Lystran army. He was vaguely wondering if it was possible to mass an army of spoiled girls to bring against invaders when Bonnie demanded, "Who's next?"

He sighed, eyeing her. "Bonnie, that's all. Those three are the very best we could find. You're going to have to pick one of them."

She flopped back into the chair, chin thrust down in her folded arms. This wasn't going to be any fun at all! She couldn't see any way to—

Suddenly the light dawned, and she slowly sat up. All at once she saw a way to get some measure of control, not to mention entertainment, out of this whole proposition. So she straightened and said, "Very well, Papa. I've made my selection."

Surprised, he dropped a hand onto the table before him. "Excellent! Which one do you choose?"

"I don't choose any of them. I want Henry to be my guardian," she said.

5

Ares eyed his daughter. "Henry is not on the list of candidates for guardian."

"So?" Bonnie said. "He's qualified, isn't he? Wasn't he just promoted to the Blue? Or was he lying to everybody about it?"

"No—yes, he was promoted," Ares said reflexively. "But—"

"Well then, why are those three more qualified than him? Is there anyone more loyal to you?" she demanded.

At that, Twomey's words came back to him. "No, there's not," Ares murmured. But then he turned his scar toward his daughter, and her eyes flicked down. "Why do you want Henry?"

"Because . . . he would do a good job. He's very conspicuous," she said aloofly.

"Conscientious?" Ares asked.

"That, too," she said.

Studying her innocent face, he perceived quite well that she wanted Henry as her guardian in order to torture him. And Ares had little doubt that she would accomplish her objective exceedingly. But these three interviews had enlightened him to the fact that she would accomplish this with whoever was finally chosen. Moreover, she was correct in that Henry was as qualified as anyone. But most important, Henry was loyal. Unable to tolerate her father's scrutiny during his deliberation, Bonnie looked away.

Ares shifted and she looked back at him hopefully. "If you choose Henry, you are stuck with him until August. You cannot unchoose him when you get tired of him," he warned her.

She weighed that. "What if he quits?"

"He can't quit," Ares said.

Now her smile was pure evil. "Then I choose Henry."

"Then Henry it will be," he stated. Gloating, she picked up her list of questions to inflict them on the newest candidate, but Ares stopped her. "Since you have made your selection, there is no reason to interview him. Go call in the three who are waiting outside."

Sulkily, she went to the door, opened it, and said, "Papa wants to see all of you." They entered, saluting, and stood straight-backed in a line before him.

Ares told them, "Thank you for your time, gentlemen. The Chataine has chosen a guardian who was not on our list. Garren, you're to take the Chataine downstairs to the audience hall and stay with her there until I come down. Wordie, you're to tell the Counselor to announce an open audience right away. Send word of the audience to the Commander and the Surchataine, and bring Chataine Sophie down to the hall. Van Laeke, you are to fetch Henry to me here. You are dismissed."

The three saluted again; Van Laeke and Wordie left at once while Garren bowed to Bonnie. "Chataine?"

She turned to her father. "Papa, I want to be here when you tell Henry."

"Oh, no," he said. "You don't get to start in on him until I have a word with him, first. Go down with Garren *now*."

As his tone indicated that compliance was advisable, she curtsied submissively and departed with her guardian of the hour. On the way out, Garren glanced back at the Surchatain in relieved gratitude, and Ares smiled grimly. Henry would not be so pleased. Teeth chattering slightly with the cold, Ares stood over the fire to wait for him.

Scant minutes later, Henry was announced by the sentry, and entered. While Henry looked at the bruised knot on Ares' cheek, Ares studied his black eye. "Surchatain?" Henry saluted.

"Henry," Ares sighed, "Bonnie has selected you to be her new guardian."

Henry stared at him open-mouthed as the separate words connected into a coherent sentence in his mind. Then his eyes widened, his hackles rose, and he choked out, "Bonnie's guardian?—no. No!"

When Ares got really angry, his whole being changed into that of an iron god and his voice dropped to a metallic whisper. It was thus as he said, "I did not offer you the choice. I am your Surchatain, and as such I expect complete, immediate obedience. If you are unwilling to give it, I will see that you are out of Westford within the hour."

Henry gazed at Ares as his scar throbbed with the blood rushing so close to the tender, exposed skin. The young man's brows drew down and he said, "I owe you my life many times over. How could I do anything but obey?"

Ares turned human again, knowing that Henry's first response was blurted in honest shock, while his second was the truth. "Here is the matter, Henry: Tobias apparently sent a message to Bonnie this morning that he had arranged for them to elope during the wolf hunt. Bonnie never received this message; I did. But I did not confront him or punish him"—and Ares now looked regretful of that decision. "I relieved him of service and sent him to Nicole's Harbor as if he was being routinely rotated out. But he deserted, and I have reason to believe that he will attempt to kidnap her."

Ares began pacing the receiving room while Henry watched his every move. "I know that Bonnie has chosen you as her guardian in order to torment you, which will not make your job any easier. But you are also the only one I can trust with this knowledge, for Bonnie's sake. Until the matter with Tobias is resolved, you will have to stay close by her every moment, because I believe he will try to reach her with another message. If he does summon her to him, you must be close enough to follow."

"How will I know if she receives anything from him?" Henry asked. "I can't demand to see everything in her hands."

Ares nodded. "I will solicit her sister's help. Sophie will tell you. But if it happens this way, you will have only minutes to intervene. Needless to say, both girls must stay in the palace for the time being."

Henry hesitated, then voiced his question. "Does Bonnie want to go with him?"

"She knows nothing of it. If he is successful in luring her away, she is bound to think it all a game," Ares said heavily.

"I see," Henry said, suddenly looking older. "And . . . if I find Tobias, what am I to do with him?"

"You are to kill him," Ares said.

Henry's chin came up slightly. "I understand, Surchatain."

"Come then," Ares said, extending an arm toward him. "We have an audience to attend."

Together, they crossed the second floor to descend the south stairwell which led directly to the holding room off the dais of the great hall. When the sentry saw them enter, he hastened to tell Georges. Then the dinner master (who had a larger, more sonorous voice than Counselor Vogelsong) announced to the crowd gathered in the audience hall, "Surchatain Ares of Lystra."

Ares entered the hall, mounted the dais, and sat on the scrolled wooden throne. Following him, Henry stood between the dais and the crowd, and Thom took his position at the right hand of the throne.

First, Ares checked to make sure that Garren, Bonnie, Nicole and Sophie were all in attendance near the front, then he looked to see that the amanuensis was ready with quill and ink at his small table near the dais. Open audiences were always recorded for the history books.

When the noise of several hundred people's bowing had abated, Ares lifted his head and said loudly, "This audience is to announce the appointment of a new guardian for Chataine Bonnie. Bonnie, step forward. Henry, on your knees."

As required, Henry dropped to his knees before the throne while Bonnie came forward to stand beside him. Ares said, "Henry, here is your charge. And here is your vow: Do you, Henry, swear before God to guard the life and honor of Chataine Bonnie with your life, whether inside or outside the palace, until such time as you are relieved of your duty?"

"Yes, Surchatain," Henry said.

"Do you understand that failure to protect her life or her honor will mean your death?" Ares asked.

"Yes, Surchatain."

"Then rise; you are appointed the Chataine's guardian," Ares told him. As Henry stood, Ares addressed Bonnie. "Chataine, you have chosen Henry to be your guardian, so I am honoring your choice. But I want you to understand that this is no light matter. If you test him, or tease him, or thwart his efforts to protect you, and anything happens to you as a result, he will die for it, and his blood will be on your hands. Do you understand that, Bonnie?"

Thoroughly frightened, she murmured, "Yes, Papa."

"Then this audience is concluded. You are dismissed." He gestured to the crowd. While they went down on their knees again, he descended the dais to tell Bonnie, "Wait here with Henry. I have to tell your mother and sister how this came about." They were already at his side, Sophie staring between him, Henry, and Bonnie in disbelief.

"Yes, Papa," Bonnie said meekly.

Ares directed a glance at Thom, who was also watching with raised brows. So the four of them entered the small holding room, and Ares shut the door. "Papa, how could you make Henry her guardian?" Sophie cried. "Do you know what she will do to him?" Thom eyed Ares with a similarly dubious expression. Nicole looked on silently.

Ares drew up a chair and sat, taking both Sophie's hands in his. "Dear one, do you trust me?"

"Yes, Papa," she said, downcast.

"Well, I trust Henry. I think he may be the only one I can trust with Bonnie. But here is the problem, Sophie: Tobias did not go to Nicole's Harbor yesterday as he was ordered. No one knows where he is. But I think he may try to come back for Bonnie," Ares said. Sophie looked at him in alarm.

He continued, "I need your help, dear one. If Tobias

tries to send a message to Bonnie to meet him, you must try to prevent her going. If you can't prevent her, then you must find out what the message says and tell Henry. He may be our only hope of preserving your sister's honor. Do you understand, Sophie?"

"Yes, Papa," she said grimly.

Ares looked up at Thom, who nodded, and Nicole, who smiled. "Well done, my lord. Henry will not fail you," she quietly observed.

Thom eyed her in mild surprise. "I wish I knew what gives you such confidence, Surchataine."

She turned her deep hazel eyes on him with a slight smile. "Henry loves him." Her eyes misted as she remembered something from years ago. "Henry taught me to love him when I did not know my own heart."

In the midst of the dispersing crowd, Bonnie studied Henry, her apprehension displaced by calculation. Before departing the hall, Garren paused to salute him in a friendly manner. "Congratulations, my friend. And good luck."

Henry acknowledged the good wishes, but his eyes swept those who remained nearby. Bonnie shifted as a precursor to speaking, and he looked down on her. "So, do you still think that I'm *vain* and *immature*?" she asked.

"I daresay you're maturing by the moment, Chataine. And why shouldn't you be vain? You're beautiful," Henry said with a whiff of boredom.

She glanced at him sharply, then her face smoothed. "So is Sophie. You must think so, anyway, since you asked permission to court her."

Henry might have winced before nonchalantly replying, "I only did that to make her feel better, since you get all the attention." Still scanning the crowd, he watched the jester eye him before turning away.

One of Bonnie's friends, the daughter of a courtier, came up to whisper in her ear. They both looked at Henry, then turned away from him in a barrage of laughter.

Seane, Sophie's guardian, came to his side to mutter, "Welcome to my little corner of hell."

Henry grinned at him. "Is it so bad?"

Gesturing helplessly, Seane said, "What do you think, when I can't even tell them apart?"

"You can't?" Henry glanced at Bonnie, still occupied with her friend, then assured Seane, "Sure, you can." He leaned over to whisper in Seane's ear. At once glimpsing the movement, Bonnie watched suspiciously.

Eyes fixed on her, Seane listened to Henry's short exposition, then said, "I never noticed that."

"Noticed what?" Bonnie asked.

At that moment Sophie joined her sister, and the two guardians looked back and forth between them. "See?" Henry said. Sophie wore red fox furs of a similar design to her sister's blue, but the young men were not regarding the girls' clothes.

"You're right!" Seane exclaimed. Then he threw back his head and laughed as one of the redeemed.

"What is the difference?" Bonnie demanded.

"What are you talking about?" Sophie asked.

Bonnie wheeled on her. "Henry found some way to tell us apart!"

Sophie frowned at her. "Bonnie, we've known that ever since he told you that you're vain and immature—"

"Oh!" In a fit of pique, Bonnie ran off through the thinning crowd. Henry was after her like a shot.

Ares, Nicole and Thom stood watching them from a distance. In capitulation, Thom admitted, "You may be right, Surchataine."

"I usually am," she said, lifting her skirts to move away with a sidelong glance at her husband.

There followed the longest hours of Henry's existence to date, worse even than his enslavement in Hornbound. Once Bonnie understood that he had to be in the same room with her all the time (an unhappy fact confirmed by the Surchatain) she set about punishing him in every conceivable manner.

She made him hold her furs for her while she went to the garderobe; upon reclaiming them, she brought out a half-filled ewer of water from behind her back to throw on him. Then she gave it to the maid to refill. Unable to leave her to go change, Henry spent the rest of that cold, interminable day in wet clothes.

She and Sophie sat in their receiving room (which years ago used to be his) to stitch on a large tapestry that was their own special project, depicting their mother and father in one of the palace gardens. To help ease the tedium for Henry, he was allowed to request a book from the library to read while sitting with the girls.

So he sprawled out with his book on the rug (which absorbed some of the moisture from his front) while they sat nearby with their canvas. The greenish panes in the leaded glass window over them allowed sufficient light to work and read by, as it was one of those maddeningly bright winter days—the sun invited you out while the cold air drove you back in.

Bonnie stitched carelessly, pausing often to evaluate Henry with dark glances; Sophie worked intently on her section of the canvas. She glanced at Bonnie's work, then exclaimed, "Bonnie, those are daisies! They're supposed to be white, not blue!"

"It looks fine to me," Bonnie said indifferently. "Why doesn't Seane have to be up here with us, too?"

Sophie lowered the stitchwork. "Bonnie . . . Papa thinks Tobias might try to come back."

"Really?" Bonnie said, her face lighting up. "To see me?" Eyes on his book, Henry blinked just once.

"To snatch you! Papa is afraid he's going to try to snatch you away!" Sophie said.

Bonnie laughed, "That's silly! Tobias was my guardian! He wouldn't do that." But she began playing with the idea of his coming back to pledge his undying love for her. How crushed he would be when she kissed him goodbye! She hoped he wouldn't hurt himself. But she began humming to herself as she sorted through the colored threads. She looked up just in time to see her sister exchange exasperated glances with Henry.

Tossing her curled ponytail, Bonnie said defiantly, "I would love to see Tobias again. Papa sent him off before I could even give him his guardian's gift! And he was a *much* better guardian than Henry. He was bigger, and stronger, and all my friends said he had such a manly face. They all think that Henry looks like a *girl*," she sneered.

"With a black eye?" Sophie murmured.

Declining Bonnie's bait, Henry returned to his book. That seemed to pique her further: "Besides, everybody knows that *your* father tried to put Papa to death."

Sophie looked up in dismay but Henry said, "Ares is my father."

Throwing down the threads, Bonnie hooted, "Who do you think you are? I don't hear anybody calling you 'Chatain' Henry! You're just—"

"Stop it, Bonnie! That's just mean! Everybody knows that Henry saved Papa's life when he was just a little boy!"

Sophie cried. Shrugging, Bonnie picked up the needlework again, but Henry looked at Sophie. When she glanced at him, he quickly looked back to his book.

There was a short silence, then Henry said, "Ares made me his son a long time ago."

"We know that, Henry," Sophie said hastily. "Bonnie's just tired of being stuck inside all the time. Don't pay any mind to her." Bonnie stuck out her tongue at her sister, who rolled her eyes.

The hours crept by like graveyard duty. Tiring of the needlework and too chatty to read, both girls desired to go out to the back quadrangle to play in the snow. Henry sent a query to Ares. Permission was granted, as long as Henry went with them.

So while the twins donned long waterproof coats, Henry dispatched the sentry to bring him a standard army cloak which he put over his wet clothes. Then he stood near them in the quadrangle, jumping up and down to keep warm while they rolled snowballs and threw them at each other. A large percentage wound up hitting Henry, whose cloak became encrusted with ice.

When he was blue-lipped, the twins finally decided to go back inside. Shedding the sodden cloak, he stood over the fire in their receiving room while waiting for them to change out of wet clothes in the bedchamber.

A maid entered with a sealed message for Bonnie that Henry snatched out of her hand. He broke the seal and read it before the maid could even knock on the bedchamber door. Finding it to be an innocuous message from one of Bonnie's girlfriends, he handed it to its intended recipient as she emerged into the receiving room.

Bonnie took one look at the broken seal and demanded, "What do you think you're doing, reading my letters?"

"I am following the Surchatain's orders," Henry said tiredly.

"Papa would *not* tell you to read my messages," Bonnie corrected him.

"Enough!" Sophie shouted, sounding much like Ares. "I'm sick to death of this! Do I have to go tell Papa how you're needling him?"

"Tattler," Bonnie muttered, but she quieted down.

Two of the girls' friends, Artavia and Roux, came to join them in the receiving room, so they pulled out the board to play shatranj. Grabbing the box with the black pieces, Bonnie said, "Roux, you partner me. We'll play the black!" So Sophie and Artavia set up the white pieces on the other side of the board.

Shatranj was a difficult game of strategy which Ares had encouraged the girls to learn. Bonnie had only a passing acquaintance with it, whereas Sophie had a solid understanding of the rules but little imagination in applying them. Of the four girls, Giles' niece Roux, two years older than the twins, was the most experienced player. When Bonnie simply moved the pieces where Roux told her to, they two usually won. Henry watched the first game, then picked up his book again.

After losing three straight games, Sophie's partner, Artavia, lost interest and wandered over to play with Bonnie's dolls. As Bonnie (who liked winning) was setting up the pieces again, Sophie complained, "Two against one isn't fair."

"Papa says you learn more from losing than winning," Bonnie offered, lining up the pawns on a row.

Sophie looked over to Henry, who raised his eyes. "Come help me, Henry," she pleaded. He dropped the book and scooted over to her side. Roux accepted the new challenge, pushing Bonnie out of the way just a little bit. So with Bonnie moving the pieces at Roux's command and Sophie moving the pieces for Henry, they began to play.

Henry required only four moves to defeat Roux. At his "Checkmate," Roux stared glumly at the board and Bonnie got up to join Artavia with the dolls. Roux demanded a rematch, so Sophie moved aside to let Henry play unhindered.

After each of the next four games, all of which Henry won, he explained his strategy to Sophie while showing Roux her mistakes. He was so matter-of-fact about it that even thin-skinned Roux took little offense at his tutoring.

By that time, evening had fallen and the girls were required to dress for dinner, so Henry was shown into the corridor to wait. Then, as the bell tolled eight, he escorted his charge and her sister down to the great hall.

Here, another surprise awaited the girls: Henry was given Vogelsong's seat next to Bonnie for the evening. The Counselor, the Steward, the Second Oswald, and everyone on that side of the table were moved down one seat.

As Ares and Nicole were seated, and he waved for the wine steward, Bonnie whined, "Papa, why is Henry at table? He's not dressed nice and I'm tired of looking at him!" Henry still wore his uniform, still slightly damp, of brown deerskin.

Ares glanced between them with a grave smile. "I want him here."

"Then where's Seane?" Bonnie pressed. Sophie's guardian was not at table.

"Seane has eaten with us on other occasions. Tonight is Henry's turn," Ares replied. To make matters worse, the wine steward set a goblet of kumyss before Bonnie, but poured wine for Henry.

"Congratulations on your appointment, Henry," Renée smirked, a tinge of sarcasm in her voice. That her younger half-brother should be given a seat five places above her was almost too much to bear.

He looked down the table toward her to utter the most devastating comeback possible: "Thank you."

Bonnie, detecting the undertones in Renée's voice, was given to understand that her mentor, her role model, was implying that it was no great honor for Henry to be selected as her guardian. But then Bonnie shook it off and craned her neck to see what was being served tonight. The counter-intimation that Renée was not a person worthy of rejoinder was as effective as any spoken retort.

Baked whitefish with egg sauce was followed by quail pie and snipe stuffed with mushrooms. Eating, drinking, and talking warmed everyone to good cheer, though every time Henry looked up, he saw Ares' gaze resting on him. Henry lowered his head, feeling the weight of the responsibility.

By the time the savarin and hot hippocras were coming around for dessert, the guests (led by Bonnie and Sophie) were calling for Twomey. But Ares announced, "I regret to tell you that I have given our overworked jester the night off. You may dance instead." He nodded to the musicians, who appeared only too happy to play for genuine dancing and not comedy.

"Finally," Renée uttered in relief, standing. She approached her little brother (who was now taller than she) with extended hand. "Come, Henry; make yourself useful." Having danced since early childhood, Henry was probably the best dancer in the hall right now. Probably better than Ares.

He bowed to her. "Excuse me, Sister." While Bonnie

was safely in the midst of a line dance, Henry went to Ares and asked permission to visit the common latrine outside. This favor was granted.

It was almost a relief to trudge through the snowy quadrangle to the row of holes surrounded by a three-sided shed with a roof. It stood in the shadows, feebly lit by a torch at each end. Bales of hay sat at random intervals around the holes.

Standing over one hole and dropping his pants, Henry closed his eyes, breathing a weary sigh. In his preoccupation, he hardly felt the cold air biting into his flesh. He must not disappoint Ares; the assignment must be completed before it killed him with boredom.

Gazing at the dilapidated backside of the latrine, Henry wondered what made Ares think that Tobias would be insane enough to come back for Bonnie. Who in the world would want her that badly? Listening to her whine for a half hour would douse any smoldering love.

He hitched up his pants and plucked a few handfuls of hay to drop into the hole. Then he trudged back toward the back door of the palace, lighted beyond. Pausing at the large laundry basin to wash his hands in the icy water, he detected the slight crunching sound of feet on snow behind him. He turned, hands dripping in the cold night air, to scan the quadrangle.

He saw nothing. With a slight frown, he wiped his hands on his pants and trotted up the steps to the back door. When he reached it, he glimpsed the jester move silently as a shadow down the lower corridor.

Reentering the hall, Henry picked out Bonnie quickly in a circle dance. Renée approached him again to dance, but he replied, "I am on duty, Sister." She made a face at him and turned in a huff.

Bonnie caught sight of him and halted the dance midmeasure. "Come here, Henry!" she called, as if he were a dog. Shoulders slumped, he obeyed the summons. Bonnie then instructed the musicians, "Play the Wasserleben."

As the opening strains sounded, the floor cleared. Everyone at court knew who could dance and who couldn't, who was willing to be a fool and who wasn't. Bonnie could dance, and she wasn't willing to be a fool.

Beaming, she followed as Henry led her in a perfect performance. The one gratification he got from it was seeing Renée on the edge of the floor, seething. The only other male in the room who could execute those steps was relaxing in his great chair with his wife's head on his shoulder, and would not be budged.

Following the Wasserleben, Bonnie imperiously called for one after another of Renée's favorite dances until the elder Chataine finally roped a noble into dancing with her. But Henry could dance with no one but his charge; knowing this, Bonnie was free to monopolize his talents all evening long.

At length, Ares called an end to the entertainment and bid the girls goodnight. Henry saluted him and bowed to Nicole, then trod heavily up the stairs after his ward. He would sleep outside her door tonight.

When the twins were safely within their receiving room, Henry dropped to the corridor floor in exhaustion, for boredom drained him as nothing else. A servant brought him a long, hooded cloak to sleep in—guardians were not to get too comfortable on duty, even while sleeping. Bunching the hood under his head, Henry wrapped the rest of the great cloak around him and lay down in front of the door. He dropped off into a dead sleep.

Some time later, movement woke him. He sat up

weaving, and for a few moments he did not know where he was. Someone was shaking him.

He blearily looked up into Sophie's anxious face, illumined by candlelight. "Henry!" she hissed, shaking him. "Henry!"

He came awake then. "Sophie! What—?"

She handed him a charred piece of parchment. "A maid gave this to Bonnie when I was bathing. She looked at it, got into her furs, and threw it in the fire. She ran out before I could stop her."

Heart hammering, Henry looked at the scrap, which read, "My love. Meet me at t—" and the rest was burned away.

6

Henry lurched to his feet. First he looked at the door, which opened away from him into the receiving room. A horde could have gone in and out over him, were they quiet. Then he stared down the dark, deserted corridor. Sophie said, "She went toward the stair! Hurry!"

He flung himself around the corner to the obscure stair. It also was dark, and he almost tumbled down it in his blind haste. Bursting out of the stairwell onto the ground floor next to the east-wing portico, he stopped, scanning the grounds. The pugiling ring was to his right, the laundry pit to his left.

All was dark and quiet. The snow on the grounds was trampled and dirty under multiple, crisscrossed paths. Frozen edges and small patches of unblemished snow glittered under the full moon.

Holding his breath as he gazed sickly into the night, he heard a voice at his side rasp, "She went to the stables." Without looking to see who was speaking, Henry leaped off the walkway like a hound on the scent and bounded through the snow toward the stables. Approaching, he saw flickers of faint torchlight through the cracks in the planking. He gained a side door, heaved it open, and rushed inside.

Immediately he saw two figures beside a saddled horse, both of whom started at his sudden appearance. "Oh. It's just Henry," Bonnie breathed. She was bundled up in her blue fox, her luxuriant chestnut hair spilling loose over the fur. Henry looked from her to the tall, broad-shouldered man beside her.

"Hello, Henry." Tobias grinned at him. "You won't give us away, will you? That's a good lad."

"Bonnie, go back inside," Henry said, slowly advancing. He had no weapon. He could not see whether Tobias was carrying one under his cloak, but he probably was.

She coaxed, "Oh, Henry, don't spoil our fun. We're going to pull the greatest prank on everyone! But I promise to be back in the morning."

He addressed her by her rank to remind her who she was. "Chataine, your father will not think it very funny. Think how he will feel to find you gone in the middle of the night." Henry came closer by degrees, watching Tobias all the while.

Bonnie looked down, pouting. "Oh, you're probably right."

As she began to turn away, Tobias said lightly, "Bonnie—dearest—if you go back in now, you'll be punished anyway. You'll be confined for the rest of the winter. We might as well have a lark while we can!"

The torch he held sputtered under drips of melted snow falling from cracks in the roof. Glancing up, Henry saw hanging down from the roof a broken board with a protruding nail. It was almost within his reach, hanging by only a corner.

She paused again, and Henry said, "Bonnie, did you

cry when your mother was taken from her bed? Why do you want to make her cry like that?"

"Oh, I don't," Bonnie breathed. Then she said firmly, "I'm sorry, Tobias; he's right. I can't make Mama cry over a prank. I'll see you when you get back from Nicole's Harbor."

She reached up to kiss him on his cheek, then skipped out, having gotten what she wanted out of the evening. Besides, it was cold out here. Tobias made a perfunctory grab at her, but realizing the futility of attempting to take her by force, let her go.

Expelling a frosty breath, he directed a brief glare at Henry. "Well, thanks for spoiling everything, friend . . . for now," he said, turning to mount.

In the moment that he was fitting his boot to the stirrup, Henry leaped up to grab the loose board and yank it down. While Tobias was turning in surprise, Henry swung the board at his head, nail out.

The board made contact with a sickening crack. Tobias jerked up and then fell with a thud onto his back, dropping the torch to the frozen mud. There it continued to burn with halved brightness.

With a choked cry of pain, Tobias reached up to grope for the nail embedded in his skull. But as he was doing this, Henry opened his cloak to find the sheathed knife on his belt.

Extracting it from the sheath, Henry raised it with both hands and plunged it directly into Tobias' chest. He stared at Henry in fixed surprise, then fell back onto the hard ground with a last gurgling breath.

The horses stalled nearby began stamping and whinnying with the smell of blood and smoldering straw. Plucking up the torch, Henry snuffed out the smoking bits of straw, then held the torch over Tobias to make sure he was dead.

About this time he heard the alarm sounding in the quadrangle. A sentry rushed in, coming to a dead halt at the sight of Henry standing over Tobias' body. Then the sentry backed out again in slow, respectful fear, turning to run only when he was out of Henry's sight.

Moments later guards who had been standing else-where on the grounds—everywhere but where they were needed—rushed into the stables. Shortly, they were followed by other hastily armed men roused from the barracks.

They came in staring, dumbfounded, at one of their own on the ground with the hilt of a hunting knife sticking up obscenely from his chest. Then there was Henry standing over him with a dying torch and blood splattered across his front.

The sentry that had been on duty in the quadrangle refused to approach further, so one man, still hazy from sleep, brought a torch forward to study the scene. Raising the torch to Henry's face, he uttered, "This is Tobias. You killed the Chataine's guardian."

The others then pushed forward. One said, "He just came to say goodbye to her. The Surchatain never even gave him the chance to tell her goodbye." Henry turned his perspiring face away from the hot, smoking torch.

"You killed him, you stinking murderer!" one shouted, and suddenly they had surrounded him, wrenching the sputtering torch from his unresisting hand.

One pinned Henry's arms behind his back while two others stood at his sides, hemming him in. A fourth bent to extract the bloody knife from Tobias' chest. He straightened with the dripping blade. "Son of a murderer."

Henry glimpsed Paramore, Captain of the Blue Regiment, enter the stables. Only then did the disgraced Blue speak. "I appeal to the Surchatain."

"Stand down!" Paramore barked, and the men fell away, releasing Henry. The one who held Tobias' knife dropped it.

While Paramore assessed the situation at a glance, the first man on the scene said, "This is Tobias, Captain— Chataine Bonnie's guardian. The Surchatain took him off duty all of a sudden and he only came back to tell her goodbye. This—murderer's whelp killed him."

Henry repeated, "I appeal to the Surchatain." According-ing to the Law of Roman, anyone accused of a crime had the right to appeal his case to the Surchatain. Meting out punishment before the appeal could be heard was strictly forbidden, and failure to honor an appeal before execution was murder.

Eyeing him, Paramore said, "Come with me." With Henry at his side, the Captain paused to address a servant. "Wrap the body, weight it well, and roll it into the Passage." The ground would remain far too hard-frozen to dig a grave for months yet.

One of the men behind them protested, "He was a Blue! He deserves a burial with honor, Captain!"

Paramore turned. "He defied orders and deserted duty in order to meet an underage Chataine in secret and alone. If I were the Surchatain, I would have killed him myself for this." Paramore resumed escorting Henry toward the palace, but both of them heard the grumbling behind them.

When they reached the back door, Henry said, "Allow me to see that she returned to her rooms safely, Captain."

Paramore looked momentarily shaken. He whispered, "Do you mean that she had made it out there to him?"

"Yes," Henry replied. "She was with him when I got there. He was about to put her on his horse."

Paramore straightened in comprehension. Then he tightened his lips and gestured to the stairway. Henry led up the stairs to the door of the girls' receiving room. Guards had filled the corridor, now lit with sconced candelabra from end to end. Glancing around distractedly, Henry knocked at the door.

It was opened by a maid. He cleared his throat to say, "Urhmph . . . is . . . ?" Seeing him, Sophie came to the door in her night robe. Her large hazel eyes took in the blood on his hands and chest, and she looked up, too stricken to speak.

"Did Bonnie come back all right?" he asked.

"Yes," she said, blinking. "She's in bed. I ran to Papa's room after you left, and he sent out the guards. But he was too angry to speak to her tonight."

"Very well," he said formally. "Good night."

She mouthed *good night* reflexively, and the Captain bowed to her. Then they two turned up the corridor to the Surchatain's chambers, and Henry wondered if this was all a dream.

He wasn't sure whether he knocked at the door or the sentry opened it as he and Captain Paramore approached. Entering the receiving room, Henry saw Commander Thom, Surchataine Nicole, and Surchatain Ares awaiting him. The sentry stepped back out and closed the door.

Immediately Nicole was upon him with worry in her face. "Henry, are you hurt?"

"No." He looked down at her, trying to see her through the mists that seemed to descend around them. She had on a heavy velvet night robe, with her hair pulled back hastily but decorously.

"Henry." That was Ares speaking, so Henry looked at him. "What happened?"

He blinked, coming to. "I . . . went to sleep at the doorway. A maid got over me to give a note to Bonnie while Sophie was in her bath. Bonnie ran out over me, and Sophie woke me to give me the note, partly burned. He just said he was going to meet her—somewhere. That part was burned off."

"Yes, I saw it," Ares said, his voice gravelly.

Henry continued, "I ran down to the quadrangle, and someone told me she'd gone to the stables. I found her there with him. He had a horse saddled, ready to leave. She did not know what he was doing," he said with sudden passion. "She thought they were playing a joke on everyone. She did not understand."

"We know, Henry," Nicole said, reaching up to brush his damp hair back from his forehead. She had tears in her eyes.

"When I told her how it would hurt you, she relented and went back inside," he said to Nicole. Then he looked back at Ares, and his voice became detached. "Tobias said he'd come again. He was going to come back for her later. So I knocked him on the head with a board, took his knife, and stabbed him."

Ares turned his eyes to the Captain, who confirmed, "Tobias was dead when I got there. I instructed that his body be rolled into the river. But . . . he was popular among the men, Surchatain. They all believe he came back just to tell her goodbye. When I got to the stables, I found a mob about to avenge his death with Henry's blood. He appealed to you."

Closing his eyes, Ares turned to lean upon the hearth until he could control himself. Then he straightened to face the four of them. "I erred greatly, and Henry will pay the price for it. I should have confronted Tobias at once and put him to public trial."

Henry glanced at Nicole as her breathing deepened. Then he contradicted the Surchatain. "No. Bonnie would have been ruined. I will survive, but Bonnie never would have lived down the shame. Look at my sister."

Years ago, Magnus made public the fact that Renée was not a virgin when she married him. And somehow, afterwards, she never married another Chatain. While Bonnie had not been physically violated, just the suspicion that she might have been would have done as much damage —at least for a Chataine.

Gasping, "Henry," Nicole put her arms around him, and he placed a bloody hand lightly on her shoulder. Thom studied the floor.

Paramore cleared his throat. "Commendable, soldier. But . . . the man who camps next to you may not see it that way, and slit your throat in your sleep for something he misunderstands." Addressing Ares, he added, "At the least, his presence is a catalyst for anyone wishing to act violently on a complaint."

Ares nodded heavily. "Wake the riverman. He's to transport Henry to Nicole's Harbor tonight. When the snows clear, you're to be stationed at Odea," he told Henry.

Stepping away from Nicole, Henry saluted. "You are dismissed," Ares sighed. Nicole ran weeping to the bedchamber.

As the banished soldier turned to leave with his former Captain, Ares said, "Henry!" The young man looked back.

Ares came forward to take hold of his shoulders and embrace him. Closing his eyes tightly, Henry laid his head on his father's shoulder.

"I will not forget this, Henry. I will send for you again when it's safe."

With great effort, Henry released him. Saluting again, he formally replied, "As you wish, Surchatain." He saluted the Commander, who returned it. Then he left.

In the quietness of the receiving room, Thom stared at the log breaking upon the grate in a shower of fleeting sparks. Then he looked at Ares and shrugged. "So I was wrong about him."

Captain Paramore himself accompanied Henry to the landing on the Village Branch. He was not allowed to go back to the barracks for anything, so left with nothing but the bloodied clothes on his back. Waiting for the riverman, Henry crunched fistfuls of snow, watching the sticky brown stains infect the glittering whiteness.

The riverman appeared; the Captain bid Henry farewell with a pat on his shoulder. As Henry sat alone on the barge, huddled in the cloak, the riverman poled and muttered to himself about the ridiculousness of being wakened in the middle of a frosty night to transport one single passenger all the way to Nicole's Harbor. He vented bitterly over the injustice of life, and Henry watched the pole dipping and rising from the dark water, shedding great drops on the railing of the barge. Then he buried his face in the cloak and wept silently.

Bonnie was wakened the following morning by her maid, Ninian, who persistently whispered, "Chataine. Chataine. You must get up. Chataine, your father summons."

That roused her, and she pushed herself up groggily. By habit, she looked over to the other side of the bed. "Where's Sophie?"

Assisting her out of the deep feather mattress, Ninian replied, "She was summoned a while ago, Chataine. She has dressed and gone already. Come, have a quick bite. Quickly, Chataine."

For once, Bonnie did not balk or fight. She had rather a bad feeling about last night—a lot of people were coming and going in the corridor long after she got back. Now, she was really glad she had listened to Henry and didn't try to pull a foolish prank on her parents. She resolved to be nicer to him from now on.

She had toast with butter and strawberry jam along with a nice cup of cool, sweet milk for breakfast. After using the garderobe (flushed out by water from the rooftop cistern) she let Ninian wash her face and hands and put up her hair. But when the maid brought out a plain woolen dress as if to put it on her, Bonnie rebelled. "What is that thing? I'm not wearing that!"

"This is what the Surchataine sent for you to wear, Chataine. You must be doing something special today," Ninian said, trying to sound encouraging.

"Is Sophie doing something special with me?" Bonnie asked apprehensively.

"I do not know, Chataine."

"Well—did she have to wear a bag like this?" Bonnie asked, raising her arms for the maid to slip the dress on over her head.

"I don't know what Chataine Sophie is wearing today," Ninian replied.

While the maid fastened the buttons on the back of the dress, Bonnie distrustfully eyed her reflection in the looking glass. She looked like a servant! But the wool was nicer than what the servants wore—it was very soft, and much warmer than her silks.

She sat to let Ninian slip sturdy leather shoes over her stockinged feet and lace them up. That must mean she was going out!—because she wore silk slippers indoors. Looking toward the open wardrobe, Bonnie decided, "I'll wear the silver fox today. Sophie didn't get it first, did she?"

"Chataine, you won't need a fur over this. Come now." The maid held out her hand, smiling, and Bonnie took it glumly. She was forever piqued that Ninian was older and plainer than Sophie's maid, Menchal, and a lot harder to intimidate. Papa had picked her.

Ninian escorted her charge down the corridor to the Surchatain's suite. Seeing them approach, the sentry rapped on the door and opened it straightway. Ninian then gave Bonnie a little push to propel her into the room and shut the door after her.

Ares was sitting behind his table as usual. He looked up to say, "Good morning, Bonnie."

"Good morning, Papa," she said diffidently, as she did when she was expecting punishment. He paused to weigh his words, but she could not know how much he had been deliberating what to say to her this morning. She preempted him by asking, "Where's Sophie?"

"She and your mother have gone on an outing," Ares replied.

"Without me?" Bonnie said indignantly.

Again Ares paused. "Bonnie, since you are becoming a young woman, I am going to treat you like a young woman, and not like a baby. So I believe you should know what happened last night."

"All right," she said, fidgeting.

"I trust you to listen to me carefully and accept what I tell you in a mature manner," he stressed.

"Of course, Papa."

He evaluated her. "Tobias came to snatch you last night, Bonnie. Henry killed him to prevent it."

She stared at him dumbly for several seconds, then tossed her head in denial. "No, Papa—it was just a joke. It was just. . . ." Ares was regarding her fixedly, the way she saw him look at others who were about to receive the shock of their lives at open audience. "He . . . wasn't going to bring me back in the morning?"

"No, Bonnie."

"But—I came in! Henry didn't have to kill him!" she cried.

"When Tobias couldn't take you last night, he was going to try again later, Bonnie. He was going to keep trying until he was able to take you away from your home, and your family, and everyone who could protect you."

"But . . . Tobias swore to protect me," she whimpered.

"He betrayed us, Bonnie," Ares whispered. "Stop and think: was it right for your guardian to lure you out at night alone? It was not to tell you goodbye. He did not even ask me to let him tell you goodbye when I discharged him."

She looked down at the brightly woven rug on the floor, trying to understand the incomprehensible—and could not. "Well, I hope you're going to punish Henry for killing him!" she said indignantly.

Ares bit his lip. "Henry has been sent away for his own safety."

"Then I get a new guardian?" she asked hopefully. "I know better now, Papa. I can pick a good one this time."

"You won't need another guardian for a while," he said.

"Oh," she said. He couldn't tell whether she looked relieved or disappointed. "Well, why am I wearing this old bag today?" She lifted the skirt of the lambswool dress.

Ares tapped his fingers on the table contemplatively, and she wondered why he was having to think so hard about everything this morning. "Bonnie," he said as if reaching a decision, "your mother and I believe you have many talents that are not being put to good use. You're bored because you don't have anything interesting to do. So I think we have found something interesting and profitable for you to do."

"What?" she said warily.

"Bring in the sentry," he instructed. When she did, Ares told him, "Summon Mayra."

When the sentry saluted and departed, Bonnie turned curiously to her father. "Who's Mayra?"

"She's your new . . . friend," he said carefully. "You are going to be helping her."

"Will Sophie be helping my new 'friend,' too?" she asked, eyebrow elevated.

"Maybe," he parried. "But this is not about Sophie; this is about you. Sophie didn't get so bored that she left her room and went outside to meet a man last night."

"Oh." Bonnie asked no more questions.

Shortly, a young woman came to the receiving room and curtsied to Ares. "Good morning, Surchatain," she said to him, then looked at his daughter.

"Bonnie, this is Mayra," Ares said.

The Chataine eyed the young woman, a Polonti. But what seized Bonnie's attention was her dress, a replica of the one Bonnie herself was wearing, with the additional attribute of vaguely disagreeable odors wafting about it.

As Bonnie's lip was beginning to curl, Mayra said, "Well, Chataine, we are so privileged to have your help. I know that everyone will have just a grand time."

Bonnie's attention snapped from Mayra's soft woolen dress to her face. Superficially, her tone was bright and friendly, but there was a knowing undertone to it. More than that, there was . . . fearlessness. She spoke as a superior to a subordinate.

Bonnie narrowed her eyes, then glanced at her father. His impassive face signaled his full support of this person. Guardedly, Bonnie asked, "Doing what?"

"Come see, Chataine," she said cheerily, ushering her out the door. "Again, thank you, Surchatain."

"A pleasure," he replied, saluting her in respect.

Mayra took her new helper upstairs to the third floor. All Bonnie knew of this floor was that the council chambers and guest quarters were here. Intensely curious, she strained to see down the corridor. She and Sophie were never allowed up here unescorted, because the treasury was on the floor above. There were guards at every stairwell and more guards patrolling the corridor.

By the time Mayra and Bonnie got to the end of the corridor, strange wailing sounds came to Bonnie's ears. She was growing alarmed when Mayra stopped at a half-door and looked in.

It was the nursery. Bonnie gazed into a large room containing a score of babies and toddlers lying on blankets, crawling on the floor, chewing on soft rag toys, crying, nursing, spitting up, or sleeping. A handful of maids attended them.

Mayra unlatched the half-door and opened it. "You are so kind to volunteer to help us, Chataine. The little ones do keep us busy! Go on in and I'll be back directly. I've got to run to the kitchen for fresh milk. There's a dear." She nudged the stunned girl into the room and latched the half-door behind her.

With a groan and a start, Henry came to. His head hurt; he was cold; he was hungry. Sitting up on the pallet, he looked around the spartan barracks. A few other men, now off-duty, were huddled by the center firepit, trying to stay warm.

Henry crept on hands and knees toward the meager fire. He opened and closed his numb fingers, sticky with dried blood. Pulling himself close to the ring of rocks surrounding the embers, he reached stiff hands over the heat.

One of the fellows glanced at his hands, then at his face. "Nice eye. Hope you got the best of the brawl."

"I killed him," Henry muttered.

"Ah. That's why you're off to Odea. Congratulations," he snorted, and the others chuckled.

"Henry!" He started, burning his hand. "Present yourself!" The other men glanced over with mild curiosity at Captain Derrick in the barracks doorway. Henry scrambled up on shaky legs. He had trouble controlling limbs he couldn't feel, so smacked himself in the head trying to give a proper salute.

Derrick shook his head in pity. "You've got visitors, Henry." Jerking his head for Henry to follow, the Captain walked out of the barracks into a bright, icy morning. He went down the path, which had been shoveled clean of snow, and headed toward the only decent building in the outpost, that of the main hall.

Henry stumbled after him, turning his head at the crisp sounds of men and beasts at work. Wagons rolled past on narrow roads while chains of men unloaded supplies from one set of arms to another.

Arriving at the hall, the Captain pushed open the door and stepped back. Henry felt the warmth first, then smelled the aroma of ham and lentils on the fire. Finally, he caught sight of two of the most beautiful creatures he had ever seen on God's earth.

"Nicole!" he murmured, then, "Sophie."

7

Henry demanded, "What are you doing here?"—as if the Surchataine and her daughter owed him an explanation for their movements.

"We're here to see you, silly," Sophie said, studying him.

Nicole turned to the officer. "Captain, may we have wash water? I must smell like fish after the barge trip down."

He laughed, "Not hardly, Surchataine; but we'll get you water all the same." He motioned to a soldier, who shortly brought a basin and ewer, with clean cloths, to set on a side table.

"Come here, Henry," Nicole said, standing over the basin. Obediently, he stood before her, shucking off the cloak. She took his hands and began washing off the caked blood and dirt while he watched stupidly.

Meanwhile, Sophie commandeered an empty table in a corner, where she began unpacking treasures from a basket: smelts, wheat buns, cheese, dried venison, and peach compote, along with a few bottles of sweet Valley wine.

The large shank of ham that had been cut up and put on

the fire with the lentils was also from the palace store, intended to supplement the morning porridge of all new arrivals at the outpost—not just Henry. Nicole had given a second basket of treats to the captain when asking for Henry, just so Derrick would know that the young man was special to the royal family.

When Henry had been cleaned up to Nicole's satisfaction, the three of them sat at the table to eat. The Surchataine's armed escort, two Lystran soldiers, sat near the door to share in the victuals but not the conversation.

Sophie poured a cupful of wine for Henry, which he downed in one gulp. She refilled it, then poured cups for her mother and herself. Henry paused. "You don't get wine."

"Mama said I could have a little today because I was so brave last night," Sophie said, then lowered her voice. "I'm sorry I couldn't stop her, Henry. She was out the door before I could climb out of the tub."

Henry stared at the distorted reflection of his black eye in the green glass bottle. "It doesn't matter. If she hadn't gone out to him then, it would have been another time when I may not have been able to follow. I keep wondering who told me that she had gone to the stables," he muttered.

"Eat, Henry," Nicole urged, but he looked offended at the suggestion. Sighing, Nicole broke off a corner of the cheese to begin eating first. When Sophie picked up a roll to dip it in the compote and eat it a piece at a time, Henry helped himself to the box of smelts.

One of the soldiers brought over a trencher of hot ham and lentils, which the three of them shared. Sophie was quietly astonished at how much Henry ate. But he knew that he wouldn't get fare like this again for a long time.

When he finally began to slow down, Nicole opened

the purse at her side and withdrew a sealed letter which she handed to him. It was addressed to Captain Yonge, the officer in charge of the outpost at Odea. Henry recognized the handwriting as Ares'.

Nicole said quietly, "You're to deliver this to the Captain when you arrive, Henry. It tells him that you performed a great service for the Surchatain, and that the Captain is to treat you accordingly. I myself watched Ares write it and seal it." Henry took the letter and carefully stashed it in an inner pocket of his coat.

"I have something for you, too," Sophie said self-consciously. While he watched, she lifted a silver locket on a chain from around her neck and handed it across to him. Opening it, he found a short lock of chestnut hair bound by a tiny pink ribbon. He looked up at her, and she explained, "We had to cut just a small lock because it wouldn't hold much hair."

He slowly opened his mouth, for this was not the explanation he needed. At an amused glance from her mother, Sophie added, "This is my token to you. Papa gave permission for you to court me when you get back."

He gripped the locket, unable to respond. She instructed in a whisper, "Henry, you're supposed to put it on, but I don't want you kissing it in front of all these men."

He came to himself, draping the locket around his neck and hiding it under his sweat-stained shirt. "May I write to you?" he asked in a murmur.

Sophie looked inquiringly to her mother, who replied, "Yes. But send your letters to me, Henry. I will see that Sophie gets them."

Now Henry looked at Nicole to ask, "Will you write me back?" Personal letters to the men stationed at the outposts were rare and wonderful.

She smiled. "We both will."

Shortly, Nicole and Sophie had to leave in order to reach Westford before nightfall, as the barge trip upriver was much slower than that coming down. They sat huddled together in the cabin watching the poleman keep the barge away from the bank by means of a long pole. Nicole and Sophie's Lystran escort sat just outside the open door of the cabin.

The barge traveled upstream via cordelle—a thousand-foot-long rope attached to the mast and run through a ring on the bow. The far end of the cordelle was hooked to a team of plough horses on the towpath. "I feel so bad for Henry," Sophie murmured, head on her mother's shoulder. "And I would be mad at Bonnie, except I'm afraid of what Papa will do to her."

Nicole hugged her, pulling the warm fur tighter over her little shoulders. She glanced at the poleman's shouting at the patron (who stood at the rudder aft of the cabin) while he poled the barge around some obstruction in the water. "Papa loves Bonnie," Nicole reminded her. "He came up with a very good plan to keep her occupied for a while."

"What?" Sophie asked, sitting up. When Nicole told her, she contemplated the idea in wonder, then burst out laughing. "Bonnie will have fits!" she predicted.

Nicole smiled tightly. "She had better get used to it, because she won't be assigned another guardian until the spring."

"But she can't go out without a guardian," Sophie observed.

"That is correct," her mother said.

"Well—does that mean I won't be going out, either?" Sophie cried.

Nicole looked at her. "Where are you now?"

"Oh. Yes." Sophie snuggled her mother in satisfaction. A moment later she said, "I still feel bad for Henry."

Nicole looked out over the gentle waves of the waterway, crests glittering in the bright winter sun. "I would too, except . . . somehow, I feel this will be good for Henry. He had been getting very restless. He has never been away from Westford for any length of time, except when he was taken to Hornbound."

"Why would that be important?" Sophie asked.

"It amounts to . . . leaving the nursery, in a way," Nicole said.

Sophie protested, "Mama, he was sold into slavery! Wouldn't that count as leaving the nursery?"

"It was the beginning of his maturation," Nicole murmured, eyes across the water. "But more was needed. Henry wants honing, so it seems that God has put him to the whetstone once again."

When they arrived back at Westford, Sophie went straight to her friends to relate to them in detail her meeting with Henry. But she stayed away from the nursery, as she feared being conscripted to either assist or replace her sister.

By that time, word of last night's events had circulated to every corner of the palace. Ironically, the actions that had gotten Henry banished served to elevate him in the eyes of many courtiers, especially those with young daughters. They did not believe for a moment that Tobias had deserted his orders and secretly returned to Westford to simply speak to the Chataine. Giles, whose niece was a regular companion to the twins, was heard forcefully advocating a commendation upon Henry.

Upon returning to her rooms, Nicole checked with her

maid to make certain that she had no pending obligations, then she inquired after Ares.

The sentry reported that he was locked in what was certain to be a prolonged conference with Crescent Hollow's palace administrator Roerich and the Steward Giles over the escalating expenses of maintaining that luxurious habitation. Giles had offered it as a gift to Renée if she would only assume its maintenance; this she could not do, she purred, unless she had a husband to share it with. And that was probably the closest Giles had ever come to divorcing Genevieve.

So then Roerich had come up with the outlandish idea of turning the palace into an inn. The idea seized Giles by his imagination, but there were many questions to be settled and points to be clarified before a workable plan could be concocted. So while Giles and Roerich huddled over estimates and projections, Ares sat daydreaming about making love to Nicole. But his captors were holding the meeting in his receiving room, so there was nothing to be done.

Upon being informed of her husband's unavailability, Nicole hesitated only a moment before heading downstairs. There, she summoned a certain young man, a soldier of the Red Regiment, to an obscure storage room. He entered, then she entered after him and closed the door. And Twomey watched from around the corner with a very sad face.

At dinner that evening, Roerich was given the seat of honor next to Bonnie, so Vogelsong, Giles *et al* were again moved down a seat. But Giles objected none at all; as a matter of fact, he was bubbling in admiration of Roerich's revolutionary plans for turning a financial bog into a mountain of gold.

Ares and Nicole listened to the Steward's excited dissertation with divided attention as they studied the abnormally quiet child sitting between the Surchataine and Roerich. Her sister had been able to report only that Bonnie had also been very quiet dressing for dinner, and they hadn't talked at all.

"The rates for each room would depend upon the luxury of the furnishings and its situation, of course. For instance, a servant's room in the lower corridor with a straw bed and washstand would rent for two silver pieces, whereas a suite in the Surchatain's corridor equipped with a garderobe would rent for a royal a night.

"A visiting noble wishing the Surchatain's suite appointed with feather bed, tapestries, writing implements and servants would expect to pay three royals a night," Giles gushed. "Given the number of rooms, the palace could conceivably accommodate seventy persons at one time without seriously inconveniencing the upper-level guests."

"More, if the servants' building at the rear of the palace is improved," Roerich noted. He was an astute, good-humored man with a robust build and curly black hair.

"Yes, yes!" Giles agreed. "I believe the costs for renovation would be minimal."

"Especially with the cheap labor that abounds in the Valley," Roerich added. The Valley's acres of vineyards between Crescent Hollow and the Green Lady (the mountains in southern Lystra) required massive labor throughout the spring, summer, and fall, but especially at harvest. When the vigneron determined that the grapes were at their peak, usually in late September or early October, they had to be harvested within a few days to retain full flavor for the wines.

"Moreover—" Giles leaned over his plate of sausage and chestnut croquettes to make the crowning point.

But at that moment Bonnie, altogether oblivious to this conversation, leaned on her mother's arm to announce, "Mama, I want a baby."

The upper table stilled in shock; Nicole froze and Ares quietly choked. Giles looked baffled at how anything, especially babies, could be more interesting than making money. But Roerich, unflappable, laughed, "Goodness, dear, why? They are so messy and inconvenient."

"Oh, but they're so *cute*," she exhaled, turning toward him. "Little Tor is just the sweetest thing you ever saw. He's so pink and round, and he's just happy as can be cuddled in your arms. Oh! And he has the teeniest little— what do you call it?" She turned to her mother, who was so slow in responding that Bonnie turned back around to Roerich to attempt a description of Tor's little appendage.

"Bonnie!" Nicole exclaimed, but Roerich was laughing so hard that Bonnie didn't heed her at first.

Nicole was in the process of rising to remove her daughter from the table when Roerich said, "Forgive me, Surchataine; I led the Chataine into this transgression. I simply find her innocence refreshing, and of course the fact that she is being taught to treasure her eventual role of mother is highly commendable to your house." With that apology, he unwittingly killed any whispered indictments that lingered of Bonnie's purity in relation to her former guardian.

Sinking back down, Nicole murmured, "How kind of you, Roerich."

Sophie was staring at her sister as if she had just dropped out of the sky. Ares leaned toward Nicole to whisper, "Tell Bonnie that she shall not extract herself from nursery duty by making a spectacle of herself at table."

But Deirdre, Thom's wife and mother of Tor, was flushed with pride and beaming at Bonnie. Tor's father looked undecided as to whether he should be pleased or embarrassed. But he was vindicated in his inspired choice for nursery mistress.

As soon as cream scones appeared on the table for dessert, the guests were clamoring for Twomey, so Ares reluctantly sent for him. Accordingly, those at the upper table were dismayed when the sentry returned alone with a look of displeasure. He leaned down to Ares to whisper, "Surchatain, the jester says he is gravely ill and begs you to come to him."

"Oh, no!" Sophie breathed. "Papa, may I come, too? Please may I?"

"What? What is it?" Bonnie asked anxiously, and the report was repeated all down the table.

Ares rose, placing his napkin beside his plate. "No, Sophie. I will go see what Twomey's trouble is. Musicians." He gestured them forward to play in his absence. Accompanied by the sentry, Ares left the hall and went down the lower corridor where Twomey's room was located.

Opening the door, Ares regarded the jester lying on his pallet. As Twomey looked over dolefully, Ares remarked, "He doesn't look so sick to me. Tell the Surchataine that he will be out directly to entertain our guests." The sentry saluted and departed back up the corridor.

Closing the door, Ares came over to squat beside the pallet. "What is it?" he asked quietly.

"Oh, Surchatain, Twomey is sick," he groaned.

"You don't have an audience now, so dispense with the act and tell my why you summoned me," Ares said.

121

With effort, Twomey sat up to lean against the cold stone wall. "I am sick. I am sick at heart for what I have seen."

"What?" Ares asked in alarm.

He regarded Ares with watery eyes of hopelessness. "The Surchataine has been false to you."

"What?" Ares asked, uncomprehending.

"I saw her enter a storage room with a young man, a soldier. They did not come out for quite some time," Twomey related.

Ares stared at the jester's pinched, blotchy face. "No. I do not believe this."

"I tell you only what I see," Twomey said miserably.

Ares stood abruptly. "Our guests are expecting you. Come to the hall at once."

So Twomey got to his feet, donned his cap, and followed the Surchatain down the corridor to the banquet hall, where the guests sat waiting in suspense. When Twomey entered the hall behind Ares, a cheer went up from the table.

Transformed, Twomey bowed with sweeping gestures of the arms. "You are too kind to Twomey! What shall poor Twomey do for such good people?"

He looked around as some guests shouted, "Dance!" "Sing!" or "Tumble!"

Then he put his hand to his ear and said, "What? Riddles? Yes, Twomey will present riddles to such wise folk."

Meanwhile, Ares was reseating himself. His heart was pounding and his stomach a ball of lead. Nicole unfaithful? Never. He could never imagine it. But he could not look at her.

"Let Twomey begin with easy riddles, to give good

people practice." He strutted like a rooster, placing a thoughtful finger on his pointy chin. While there was some tittering at the table, most of the guests were silent in anticipation. "Here is our first!

> "Has fork and mouth
> but cannot eat.
> Forever runs
> but has no feet.

What is it?" Twomey cried.

Several voices responded, "The Passage!" or "A river!"

Twomey clapped his hands in joy. "Such wonderful people! Such quickness of mind!"

Ares watched him darkly. She would not. She couldn't. To think of her pleasuring another man—he gave a short, fierce shake of his head, and she glanced over at him.

"Another riddle for such wise people," Twomey declared.

> "Comes through doors yet leaves no tracks
> and passes the sun without shadow.
> Sifts your grain, stokes your fire,
> and chills you to the marrow.

What is it?" he demanded.

Again, a number of voices cried, "The wind!"

Sophie fretted, "Oh, I was about to say that!"

"Such knowing people, to see hidden things!" Twomey declared.

Ares took a gulp of wine, feeling himself sinking into a black morass. At a light touch on his arm, he looked into Nicole's questioning face—such a beautiful face that received no other kisses but his. Ares looked away, his heart hammering as if to break his ribs.

"Another! Perhaps a harder one?" Twomey posed, his face taking on a crafty look. The guests responded to this challenge vociferously. "Then guess this:

"The first letter a question eternally pending.
The second forms a line never ending.
The third: What I am called, but never me.
The fourth: Upon which a ball does perch for thee.
The fifth: What heaven and hell in common hold.
But, alas, the rub: This riddling grows old."

He looked around, and there was a space of silence. Guests looked questioningly at each other, and some stared off in concentration, mouthing letters without sound. While waiting for them to figure it out, Twomey marched around the table like a martinet.

Thom opened his mouth, but when he saw Sophie sit up in sudden apprehension, he closed it again. Uncontested, Sophie cried, "Youth! It's youth!"

The guests applauded and Twomey made an exaggerated bow to her. "The Chataine has been taught well! What all her mother must know!" he exclaimed. Nicole smiled and Ares looked at him as if ready to slay him on the spot.

Skipping lightheartedly back to the foot of the table, Twomey sang, "Another, another, let us give out another. Like this:

"Twin brothers we be,
and a burden carry we
by which we are bitterly pressed.

In truth we may say
we are full all the day
but empty we go to our rest."

Twomey looked around, but everyone was silent, with faces showing concentration. Some whispered back and forth in conference, so Roerich leaned over to whisper to Bonnie, who cried, "Shoes! Those are your shoes!"

The audience clapped and laughed, and Bonnie grinned. Ares watched Nicole smile at Roerich, and Ares wondered, *Who is it? Who is she meeting? Someone younger? Someone unscarred?* If Ares found out who it was, Tobias' death will have been merciful in comparison.

"Now Twomey is tired," the jester said, sagging as if on loose strings. "Twomey is sick at heart and tired. Let him go rest, please."

"No!" "Not yet!" "Give us one more!" "Just one!" the guests clamored.

"One more," Twomey straightened only a little, looking at the Surchatain. "Just this:

"The poor have it.
The rich need it.
It is greater than God.
It is more evil than the devil.
And if you eat it you will die."

A profound silence fell over the hall, which normally reverberated with every little sound. Standing at the foot of the table, Twomey looked from face to face. "Can no one answer poor Twomey? Does no one know?" Not a peep was heard in reply. No one was even whispering guesses to his neighbor.

Then Twomey looked at Ares at the head and said, "Can Surchatain Ares answer?"

Ares turned red eyes to him and uttered, "Nothing. It is nothing."

"Ahhh!" Enlightened, the guests applauded Ares' astute answer.

He looked at Twomey to say coldly, "You are dismissed." The jester bowed and dragged himself out, a pathetic, broken figure. Then Ares rose and left the hall without a word as Nicole looked after him in concern.

She bid goodnight to their guests, thanking Roerich for his kindness. When she kissed the girls goodnight, Bonnie asked, "Am I helping in the nursery again tomorrow?"

"Yes, after your lessons," Nicole said firmly.

Whereupon Bonnie turned smugly to her sister. "You don't have anything so important to do." Sophie eyed her, weighing whether Bonnie was trying to trick her into helping or genuinely puffed up over her duty.

Finally, Nicole was able to hasten up the stairs to the Surchatain's suite. Opening the door, she saw Ares leaning on the hearth, staring down at the fire. "My lord," she murmured, coming to twine her arms up under his shoulders and lay her head on his back. He shifted as if uncomfortable. "Ares, what is wrong?"

She felt his chest expand deeply. "Nothing," he muttered. "It is nothing."

"I think not," she sighed, but he did not respond. "I resent that matters of state steal away your peace of mind like this. Come, my lord, let us forget it for a while," she suggested in a low voice.

As her hand stole down to caress him, he suddenly pulled away. Astounded, she looked at his tight face and throbbing scar. "Ares, what is it?"

He tossed his head as if he were pinned under a great weight. "I will sleep elsewhere tonight."

This was so unprecedented that Nicole was struck speechless. But when he began to move toward the door, she hastened to place herself between him and it. "You will not, my lord, until you tell me what has happened to alter you like this." Even in her sternness, she looked so lovely that he turned away, groaning.

"Ares, enough riddles! What is it?" she cried. "You were fine when I left for the Harbor this morning. Tell me!"

"No, Lady; you tell me," he countered. "Tell me what you have done."

She stared at him, confounded. "What I have done? I have done nothing!"

"Nothing? Is that the answer to everything?" he laughed in pain, and she began to fear for his sanity. Then he sobered. "You were seen seeking privacy in a storage room with a soldier not your husband."

8

Ares watched his wife's face drain of color. "Who told you this?" she whispered.

"That is not important. The question is, have you—betrayed me?" His voice caught as if a spike had been driven through his throat.

Nicole staggered back, fortunately coming up against a chair that prevented her collapsing to the floor. Distraught and distracted as Ares was, he almost reached out to steady her, seeing that she was not feigning. She stared around the room without recognition of anything that crossed her view.

For she knew well enough that a Surchataine publicly accused of infidelity could expect banishment, at best—and a quick trip to the slave markets. As with her daughters, even the whiff of impropriety without any proof whatsoever would be enough to taint her.

Then she blinked and straightened with new composure. Turning abruptly to the door, she flung it open. Instinctively, Ares stepped forward to stop her leaving. But she was not; she merely said to the sentry outside, "Summon Pearcey."

The young sentry paused. "Forgive me, Surchataine—I do not know this person."

"He is in the Red Regiment. Captain Crager will call him out for you," she said impatiently. He bowed to her and quickly departed, the next sentry stepping up to take his place.

Ares watched as she closed the door and carefully walked around him, eyeing him, then stood over the fire to warm herself. Neither of them spoke, but he found himself suddenly calmer, almost rational for the first time since dinner.

The knock was long in coming—hours, it seemed—but when it finally sounded, the sentry let in a young man unknown to Ares. He wore a uniform with the insigne of the Red Regiment on his collar. He saluted Ares and bowed to Nicole, then stood at attention, waiting.

Again walking past Ares, Nicole said to the young man, "Pearcey, I want you to tell the Surchatain everything that has passed between you and me. Leave out no detail."

"Surchataine," he acknowledged. Without looking at Ares (which would have been presumptuous) Pearcey began, "The Surchataine summoned me about a month ago to express her concerns about the number of strange men that the Widow Renée has up to her chambers. The Surchataine did not want these men to have free run of the palace at any time. So she instructed me to keep watch on them after they had left the Widow's apartments, and make sure that they departed the palace directly.

"If they stayed the night, I was to keep watch to make certain that they did not leave her rooms at night. If they began wandering the palace at any time, I was to escort them out. I was also to report to the Surchataine on this matter whenever she required. But I was to operate in secret to avoid besmirching the Widow's—reputation."

As Ares gaped at him, Nicole turned to her husband. "Do you have any questions for the watchman, my lord?"

Snapping to, Ares sputtered, "Men? How many men come to her apartments?"

Pearcey gathered his brows, thinking. "If I remember aright, that would be five men making a total of twelve visits over the past month, Surchatain."

Ares looked aside, and his eye landed on the portrait of his family. "I see."

"Do you have any other questions of him, my lord?" she asked.

"No," Ares whispered.

"You are dismissed, Pearcey. Thank you," Nicole said. Once again he saluted Ares and bowed to her, then crisply exited. He left a heavy silence behind.

Gathering her soft skirts, Nicole curtsied deeply. "I ask your forgiveness, my lord, for my indiscretion in meeting with a servant in public view. It never occurred to me that anyone in the palace would attach such evil motives to my comings and goings. But since someone has expressed such a base opinion of me, it must reflect on you. I will not burden you further." Choosing not to wait to be dismissed, Nicole turned to leave.

She did not make it halfway to the door before he was in front of her, holding her arms. "Nicole, I. . . ."

"You thought me capable of lying with another man, to my death if I am discovered and to my damnation if I am not," she observed, white-faced.

"No," he whispered, closing his eyes and bowing his head close to hers. "I never believed it."

"Then who filled your ear with such slander of me?" she demanded.

He lifted up, sighing, "Twomey."

"The jester?" she said, stricken.

"He . . . sees much that happens around the palace, and tells me in secret. He was the one who alerted me to Tobias," Ares explained.

Her face smoothed. "So that is why he required your personal attention when he was summoned at dinner."

"He told me only that he saw you go into the storage room with the soldier. It was not his intention to slander you," Ares insisted. His memory led him astray on this point, but Nicole held a different opinion than what he stated.

"Why didn't you tell me about him?" she asked.

"I did not want to burden you, Nicole. But I could ask you why you did not tell me about Pearcey," he said levelly.

"I did not want to . . . burden you," she murmured. But that was only a half truth. The whole truth was that a tiny part of her feared that Ares might be one of those men visiting Renée's chambers.

It seemed to Nicole that the former Chataine—Ares' first love who spurned his offer of marriage—never gave up her attempts to seduce him. But every time Pearcey concluded his report and Nicole would ask, *"Was there any other man in her chambers?"* he would always answer, *"No."*

So when Ares whispered, "Nicole, please forgive me for doubting you," she could not conceivably refuse him, though her pride clamored to make him suffer for at least one night.

But when she looked up to the deep brown eyes that had seen years of suffering, she clasped him passionately around the neck to kiss him. He gripped her so tightly that she could not breathe, then scooped her up to carry her back to the sleeping chamber.

As he dropped her onto the bed, his ardor suddenly vanished. She sat up. "What—?"

Holding out a hand, he said, "Wait right there. I will return directly."

"Ares!" she exclaimed in frustration as he backed out and left their chambers.

Contrary to his frequent expostulations to others, he ran down the stairs to the chapel. Flinging open the doors, he entered the dark hall, lit by a solitary candle at the entrance. One candle was kept burning all night to provide light for midnight confessors.

Taking the candle, Ares went to a small side room and opened the door to throw feeble light on a figure huddled under a pile of blankets on a cot. With no fireplace, it was cold in here. Ares shook the figure in the area of his shoulder. "Father Birondo. Father!"

"Uhh?" The mound of blankets moved, then a hand reached out to grope for the spectacles on the side table. Sitting up like a mummy shedding its wrappings, the father put on his spectacles and blinked at Ares. "Surchatain?"

"Father, have you been praying for me? About the dream?" Ares demanded.

"Yes, of course, Surchatain—"

Agitated, Ares sat on the edge of the cot. "Well, it happened again tonight. Not the dream, but—pieces of it come to me as I am doing something ordinary in the day. Yesterday, it was when I was reaching for my woolen underwear. I remembered that from the dream.

"Tonight, it was as I was standing over my wife—I had the strangest sensation that that, too, was part of the events leading up to the white knight calling me out for combat. I am most anxious to know what this means," Ares said.

Father Birondo sighed. "I have importuned the Lord on this matter. All that comes to me is the question, 'What are you trying to teach me from this?'"

"That is not helpful, Father," Ares said almost resentfully.

"Then I shall continue to pray, Surchatain," he replied.

Ares exhaled. "Yes. Thank you. Goodnight." Taking the candle, he left the cubicle, closing the door behind him. When he opened the chapel doors and sconced the candle in its place, he glanced out at Twomey, standing beside the foyer fireplace as if waiting.

"Ah, Twomey. I trust you are feeling better?" Ares said cheerfully, coming over to him. Glancing around, he whispered, "All is well. Do not be concerned about what you saw—it is of no consequence. Good night." Ares slapped him genially on the shoulder.

Twomey bowed his head. "I am most relieved. Good night, Surchatain." But as he watched Ares ascend the stairs two at a time, he did not feel relieved. For the first time, the Surchatain had discounted his report. Worse—if the Surchataine discovered who reported her, then Twomey had just made a powerful enemy. This he must address. . . .

At Nicole's Harbor, the soldiers were bedding down after a full day of clearing roads of snow, scraping ice from slips, repairing docks, and loading and unloading cargo—for even in the winter, ships docked at the Harbor.

Bone-tired, Henry sank down on the hard pallet, heedless of the cold. All day long in the midst of labor, he had been reaching to the locket under his clothes just to feel it, to assure himself that it was real. Now, as he lay stretched out on his aching back, his hand rested on the pocket that held the letter . . . the one his father had written to Captain Yonge.

Bonnie's taunt came back to him almost audibly —*"Who do you think you are?"*—and he barely opened his eyes. Oh, he knew who he was: grandson of Talus the Usurper, son of Cedric the Stupid.

He tried to picture this Cedric, or remember anything he had said or done that Henry himself had witnessed, and not simply heard of later. But nothing came to mind. When Henry thought of this cursed ghost from his past, all he remembered, strangely, was a wooden eagle he used to have. He believed it got broken—he didn't remember how. But he remembered the broken beak. And that's all.

But memories of Ares ran deep and vivid. By far, they consisted of Ares' carrying him on his shoulders, on his back, in his arms—it seemed that Ares was carrying him around wherever he went. How large he seemed back then! Henry himself did not realize this, but when he pictured Ares in his mind, the scar did not appear. What was there was a strong, reliable presence . . . a shield and bolster. . . . Clutching the pocket with the letter, Henry closed his eyes and fell asleep.

The morning found Ares so preoccupied with various matters that he dispatched his early devotions a little too efficiently before turning to worldly obligations.

First, he requested that Nicole have her watchman continue his duties, except that Ares recommended she rotate the responsibility to a new man once a month. After that length of time, he explained, they got jaded or bored to the point of inattention, and so became useless.

When Nicole expressed fears that rotation would serve to spread word of Renée's activities, he assured her that all of the servants and most of the soldiers already knew.

Since the weather today was clear and slightly warmer than it had been, Giles came to Ares with the astounding request to accompany Roerich back to Crescent Hollow to begin implementation of the grand plan for the inn at once. Travel was not an issue, for the paved road between Westford and Crescent Hollow sustained traffic throughout the winter. Roerich himself had made the two-day trip almost comfortably in a carriage.

What was remarkable was Giles' willingness to leave the palace books in the hands of his assistant Stengi in order to apply his financial genius over a broader sphere. So Ares gave him leave.

Then Vogelsong came to Ares that morning to tell him, "Surchatain Fanchon's messenger requests an answer that he can take back to his lord, Surchatain."

Ares glanced at the young Counselor in amusement. "Oh, he does, does he? Where has he been staying these three weeks?"

"At the Dancing Bear, Surchatain, and he expresses concern about the level of his funds," Vogelsong said sympathetically. The Surchatain had kept the man waiting a long time.

Ares smiled, looking over another document. "So the messenger requires an immediate answer from the Surchatain because he has exhausted his travel allowance on ale and wenches," he said dryly. Vogelsong's mouth dropped open at the revelation.

Ares went on, "Well, kindly go to the Dancing Bear, and take a large purse, Counselor. Hire a private room and sit the messenger down with a pint that shall continually be replenished. Tell him that if he must take an answer back straightway, it will be 'no.' But if he will give us more time to investigate the matter, we may be able to supply him with happier words. Then let him talk, and keep his cup well filled. Be his best friend in the whole world. By the time you leave him, I want you knowing everything about Fanchon and the situation at Corona that this man knows, and that his mother, father, brothers, cousins, and casual acquaintances know."

Vogelsong uttered a sharp laugh. "I shall attend to this straightway. How very shrewd of you, Surchatain!"

After the Counselor bowed and hastened out, Ares, mindful of Carmine, murmured, "I learned from the best." Then he stopped and slowly raised his eyes to the bright window, glittering as if paned with diamonds. "*What are you trying to teach me from this?* I have been approaching it from the wrong angle all this time!"

Nicole also began her day thinking of Carmine. She had missed him mostly for her husband's sake, because she knew how dependent Ares had been, or considered himself to be, on Carmine's counsel. Now Nicole wished she had it for herself. She wanted to know what to do about the jester.

It seemed clear to her that this Twomey was attempting to gain favor and a certain measure of influence with Ares by first making himself indispensable, then alienating Ares from everyone else he was close to. This she would not allow. But as long as Ares found him useful, what could she do?

She threw on a heavy cloak to go out and walk the apple orchard to think. Even in the dead of winter, the bare trees were beautiful in their form, like works of sculpture. The orderliness of the rows was also comforting: they had been planted just so, each one receiving the space it required to be heavy with blossoms in the spring, verdant in the summer and productive in the fall. And when their arms cradled the previous night's snowfall, there were created art forms never seen by human eyes before.

Wearing thick leather boots, Nicole did not require the orchard paths to be cleared of snow before she walked. She rather enjoyed kicking the powdery stuff, crunching it underfoot, or tracing designs on its crystalline white surface with a twig. So for an hour or more, she walked, prayed and thought: What to do about Twomey when Ares did not consider him a threat?

She could plant false information for Twomey to report to Ares, thus discrediting him. But this could so easily be traced back to her that she would be the one discredited—and besides, Nicole resolved not to stoop to lies.

She could voice her concerns to Ares, but if he did not understand her, or disagreed, then the situation would deteriorate into a power struggle between her and a jester, which she found absurd—and risky. She could have him turned out of the palace for any number of reasons, but she was uncomfortable with such heavy-handedness, especially when everyone at court liked him so much. And no one knew anything about him! . . .

Nicole stopped then, looking up as the trees saluted this new line of thought. Twomey knew so much about everyone at the palace, while keeping his own background a deep secret. That must mean there was something about him worth knowing. But how to find it out? That is when she most wished she had Carmine's counsel, for he was gifted at extracting information from unwitting subjects. Alas, he was gone, but . . . he had left behind a protégé—and a skillful one, at that.

So Nicole promptly turned back up the path, sliding on icy patches under the crisp snow. But the fact that she didn't fall emboldened her to more deliberate risks, so that servants were peering out of windows at the Surchataine running and skidding on the slick path like an adolescent.

Back inside the palace, she shed her cloak and boots to don indoor leather shoes (fur-lined, for walking on cold stone floors). Then she went to Renée's apartments and knocked on the door. Eleanor, Renée's longtime maid, opened it, and smiled upon seeing one of her favorite people. "Surchataine! Come in."

"Thank you, Eleanor. Is Renée up?" Nicole asked, looking toward the closed bedchamber door.

"No, Surchataine, the Chataine has not risen for the day," Eleanor said clearly, then whispered, "I can make her rise, if the Surchataine wishes." Nicole's delicate brows came up, and she nodded. So Eleanor opened the wardrobe and began rifling it as though looking for something.

An instant before the bedchamber door was flung open, Eleanor closed the wardrobe and picked up the ewer. Renée appeared in the receiving room with a suspicious glance toward her servant. "Eleanor, go get my breakfast."

The maid curtsied. "Yes, Chataine. Excuse me, Surchataine." Nicole watched as Eleanor flowed out with the ewer, closing the door behind her.

Nicole turned back to Renée, who sniffed, "She's been trying to find where I have hidden the gold I inherited from Nicklos. But she won't."

Nicole protested, "Dear Chataine, she's been your personal attendant for—how many years? When has she ever taken so much as a copper pence from you?"

"This is different," Renée said, sitting at her vanity to scrutinize her face in the looking glass. Pretending that the tiny wrinkles were not there, she began applying a chalk-based makeup that accentuated those wrinkles. "What can I do for you, dearest?" she asked, glancing up at Nicole's reflection in the glass. As Nicole opened her mouth, Renée added, "Whatever it is will hinge on your removing that irritating young man you have spying on me."

Nicole closed her mouth, thinking fast. Then she said, "Darling, that is for your protection. If that nasty little jester sees one of your—guests roaming the palace, he is likely to tell Ares, and thus subject you to a very unpleasant questioning."

Renée looked up sharply. "Ares doesn't know about them, does he?"

Nicole glanced down. "I did not tell Ares when I set the watchman, and he reports only to me. I was concerned to protect you from gossip."

Renée warmed visibly. "Thank you, dear heart." Just as rapidly, her demeanor changed. "I hate that little fool, that jester."

Nicole pursed her lips, moving to Renée's other side. "I do not much care for him, either. The problem is, everyone else enjoys his performances so much, I cannot just order him away. I have noticed, however, that he is very close about his background. I think that must be because there are skeletons strewn along the path behind him. If someone could get him to talk, and find out anything about him—a family name, a town, a past master —then I could legitimately send out scouts to dig up whatever the jester is hiding."

Renée was watching her steadfastly in the mirror. "And you wish me to prime his pump."

Nicole shrugged. "I certainly wouldn't know how to go about it. But I have never known a man to refuse your attentions."

"True," Renée admitted, returning to her own reflection.

"So I suppose what you do depends on how many more times you wish to watch him perform the Wasserleben," Nicole observed.

Renée's vivid blue eyes glazed over. "I shall begin operations on him today."

"You are merciless." Nicole smiled, bending to kiss her cheek. At that time, Eleanor returned with a breakfast tray for her mistress, so Nicole bid them both good day.

Renée took her time preparing her toilet that morning in order to lay the groundwork for implementation of her plan. When primped and attired to her satisfaction, she sent Eleanor downstairs to chat with a silly, talkative laundry maid named Glinda. Eleanor had gleaned much useful information from this girl—for instance, she was the first to report that Melva, the former Chataine of Qarqar, had been spotted waiting tables at an inn in Eurus, looking hard and old. (Since Ares never heard anything directly from Melva, he did nothing to investigate these reports.)

Eleanor also learned from Glinda before anyone else of the impending marriage of Lady Vivian, Renée's mother, to Lord Notham. That union had taken place almost four years ago, and Eleanor kept Renée daily posted on the delightful battles Vivian was waging with her stepdaughter, the Lady Rhea.

Today, Eleanor's assignment was to gently probe Glinda for information as to the jester's daily habits. While Eleanor was gone, Renée spent a leisurely hour eating candied pansies and cracking open her colored stained-glass window (much more expensive than plain windows) to drip wine on the heads of unsuspecting victims thirty feet below. Since they did not know what substance had fallen on them from the sky, their efforts to remove it were usually quite entertaining and, in winter, innovative.

At length, Eleanor returned to report disapprovingly that the jester had taken to making himself such a shadow at all times except dinner that Glinda could not say for sure where he might be found at any particular time, except—

The jester had such an overwhelming fondness for mincemeat pies that whenever he got one, he would take it to a private spot to eat. This spot was always the same: off the north kitchen corridor was a room containing an abandoned well that had gone dry years before anyone's remembrance. The carved stone wellhead still stood guard over the useless hole (which, actually, may have found use as a receptacle for anything which someone wanted never to be found again). The point being, whenever Twomey received a mincemeat pie as a special treat, he would crouch behind the wellhead to savor it unmolested.

Upon hearing this, Renée went to her wardrobe to select a dull black woolen cloak, hitherto used solely for clandestine errands at night. "Does the kitchen have any mincemeat pies already made up?" she asked Eleanor.

"I'm sure they do, Chataine. They always keep a few on hand."

Throwing the cloak over her shoulders, Renée checked its pocket to make sure it contained a lacy handkerchief. As she did, she instructed Eleanor, "Then go ask Sophie's maid Menchal to see that the jester is given one in appreciation for his performance last night." This was another servant with whom Eleanor had developed a useful relationship.

"And, dear Eleanor, see that he is found and given it at once, for that old well room is cold and drafty and I don't want to be kept waiting there for an hour."

Eleanor curtsied. "Of course, Chataine," she said, and departed the room.

Renée paused to squirt a bit of perfume in her eyes, which immediately caused tears to gush forth. Raising the hood of her cloak, she proceeded downstairs to the old well room—cold, dim, coated with the dust of disuse, and presently unoccupied.

Brushing dirt from the edge of the three-foot-high wellhead, she peered down into the dark hole, about thirty inches across. For safety's sake, an iron grate had been bolted onto a narrow interior ledge running the circumference of the hole about eight inches below the top. Faint odors suggested that the well might have found occasional use as an emergency latrine, but hardly anyone in the palace would attempt such desecration when longstanding rumors held that the room was haunted.

With a hood covering her blond coif held in place by a golden tiara, Renée sat on the edge of the wellhead facing away from the door. She arranged her cloak around her in a dramatic swirl, allowing for enough fabric to cushion her derrière on the stone.

When she was all set, she began weeping in a quiet, dignified manner, daubing at her stinging eyes with the handkerchief. She was required to carry on like this for only a quarter hour before the sudden echoing patter of hasty feet was heard entering the room. Renée started and spun to the door, raising a hand in surprise to her throat. Equally surprised was Twomey, clutching the treasured mincemeat pie to his breast.

Neither spoke for a moment, then Renée lowered her reddened eyes demurely and made as if to leave. Twomey, dressed not in motley but a rather decent suit of wool, came out of his shock to bow and say, "Forgive Twomey for disturbing the beautiful Chataine."

"No, no." She waved. "The fault is mine. I shall leave."

"You are sad," he said, his face mirroring her sadness.

"It is of no import," she said, touching a corner of lace to her still-watering eyes.

He came toward her, the pie all but forgotten. "Can Twomey help? I can listen, if nothing else."

"There is nothing to say," she sighed, sinking weakly to the edge of the wellhead again. "I just feel so—useless, at times. Abandoned. With my dear husband Nicklos gone, and my darling Carmine gone—" She lapsed into bitter sobs.

Twomey set the pie on the wellhead to kneel at her knees. "Please, beautiful lady, don't cry. I cannot bear to see such lovely eyes disfigured. How can I comfort you?"

She smiled at him sadly. "Unless you can raise the dead, I don't see how you or anyone can help me." She expelled a great sigh, raising her eyes to the cobwebbed ceiling rafters. "Have you ever lost someone you loved, Twomey?"

"Oh, yes," he murmured meaningfully.

She looked at him with pleading in her bloodshot blue eyes. "Tell me."

He glanced warily at the corridor beyond the door, then said without a trace of pretense, "All right."

9

Renée allowed the jester to see a tiny spark of hope glowing in the ashes of her sorrowing widowhood. She did not use anything as clumsy as words to urge him on to self-revelation, but fixed her lovely if red-rimmed eyes on him in rapt attention. Again he looked cautiously at the door toward the little-used corridor; his sharp instincts were obviously howling discretion.

In a low voice devoid of the cringing jester mannerisms, he said, "I was in service to a great house, and became confidant of the lady of the house. Our friendship was pure and honorable, but the master of the house could not endure that the lady would enjoy any man's company other than his own. So she was . . . dealt with, and I . . . escaped with my life."

Dry-eyed, Renée evaluated him. "It is unkind of you to sport with me, jester, when I exposed myself to you in my grief." Greatly offended, she gathered her widow's cloak (which covered voluptuous skirts) as if to depart in a huff.

Twomey sprang up. "How have I given offense?" he demanded, shocked.

Renée's breathing deepened in indignation. "I have

traveled widely, all over the Continent. I have entertained visitors from every major city in every province south of the Ice Lands. I *know* all of the great families, but never have I heard such a tale as you describe. You are merely making it up to play with me in my grief." In her feigned passion, her eyes began to water again.

"No, Lady, I swear that is not so!" Twomey's own eyes were watering. "But Westford has had no dealings with Corona for many years, so you would not know them."

"Do not tell me that any noble in Surchatain Fanchon's court would stoop to such hard dealings with a lady's butler," she said, bristling.

"I was not a butler, I was—" Here his discretion won out. But seeing that she must have some token of his truthfulness, he admitted, "I must not utter the family name. But it was indeed a member of Fanchon's court—a high administrator, as a matter of fact. I escaped the night before I was to be sold into slavery, and wandered south, begging." His voice was gravelly with self-contempt.

Renée searched his face. "This can't have happened but most recently. You are too young to have borne such hardship for many years."

"It was only weeks before I came to this place, and my salvation," he said, breaking under her flattery.

Renée looked down pensively, then raised her lovely face, free of tears, to say, "Forgive my hasty impugning of your good word, Twomey. I do feel better, and I hope that I may have the pleasure of your company again." Rising, she leaned forward to place a kiss upon his bristly cheek. "Thank you, my friend."

"You are a thousand times welcome, dear Chataine," he said, enraptured.

So Renée left him to his pie and hastened upstairs as

fast as her unwieldy cloak would allow. Entering her rooms, she threw off the cloak for Eleanor to hang in the wardrobe. Then she began pacing in concerted thought. Turning on Eleanor, she demanded, "A messenger came from Fanchon of Seleca some weeks ago—is he still here?"

Eleanor's brow wrinkled thoughtfully. "I do not know, Chataine."

Renée threw up her hands in exasperation. "Then go find out, dear Eleanor!" With a curtsy, the maid departed to do this. While she was gone, Renée poured herself another cup of wine and stood gazing into the robust fire.

Shortly, Eleanor returned to report, "Yes, Chataine, Fanchon's messenger is at the inn in town. The Counselor Vogelsong is with him this very moment, pumping him for whatever information he can provide about his master."

"Drat!" Renée slapped the mantel in agitation, causing a crystal figurine to fall onto the hearth, shattering. She did not heed it.

"*But*," Eleanor added significantly, coming closer to whisper, "I also hear that the messenger is hurting for funds, which the Counselor has not been authorized to provide."

Renée drew in a breath. "Darling Eleanor, you never fail me! Summon Hauffe at once." Almost smirking, Eleanor curtsied and withdrew again.

Hauffe, gentle, worn, sorrowful, appeared with pathetic eagerness. Even Renée pitied him, for he had been Carmine's personal servant—the one to raise the alarm when his master failed to return to his chambers after what he promised would be a short errand. Only Hauffe had fallen asleep awaiting him, so it was morning before the alarm sounded, far too late.

Ever since, he wore his guilt like a hair shirt, and if he

could no longer serve Carmine, then he would serve the great love of Carmine's life. Before he arrived, Renée had plenty of time to access a secret place and extract a pouch of gold royals.

Escorted in by Eleanor, Hauffe bowed. "You summoned, Chataine?"

"Yes, dear Hauffe. I have an assignment of utmost importance that I can entrust to no one but you." Deliberately, she placed the pouch into his hand. Knowing what it contained by its weight alone, he quickly looked up at her.

She continued, "Even as we speak, little Counselor Vogelsong is at the inn interrogating a messenger from Fanchon of Seleca. Vogelsong is trying to get information for Ares, but I need information of a different sort. I need confirmation of a story given me."

She paused to see that he was attending her. "Here is the fairy tale: a certain nobleman of Fanchon's court dislikes the fact that his wife is getting too close to a male confidant who is attached to the family, so he discards her in some fashion and prepares to sell her confidant into slavery, but the man escapes the night before he is to be sold. This fairy tale actually took place, supposedly, last summer. Now, if this topic comes up in Vogelsong's interrogation of the messenger, I want you listening in. If it does not, then you are going to rescue the messenger from his money troubles in exchange for confirmation of this tale.

"Hauffe, darling, this is most important: do not simply tell him the story and see if he confirms it. Give him just a fact or two so he can recognize it, but make him tell you all the details *with names*. I want all the names. Are you with me, dear?"

"Certainly, Chataine." He bowed.

"Now, it could be that by the time the Counselor gets done with him, he will be in no condition to remember his own name, much less someone else's. If so, you must stay the night and talk to him tomorrow, when he has sobered up enough to remember just how bad his money troubles are. Can you do that for me, dear Hauffe?"

"Yes, Chataine," he said firmly.

"If you bring back information that proves useful to me, then I shall not require the return of anything in that pouch. Understood?" she asked. He could only nod dumbly —the pouch was full. "Then go."

After waving him out, she paused to savor the thrill of the game. It had been a long time since she had played a worthy opponent, but this jester might prove more entertaining than even he thought himself. "Now, Eleanor. Summon Nicole."

"Dear Chataine, I cannot simply summon her. She is the Surchataine," Eleanor demurred.

"Oh, you know what I mean! Tell her that I need to speak with her!" Renée said crossly. Eleanor bowed on her way out, having made her point.

In short order, Nicole was at Renée's door. "Did you talk to him?" she asked in an excited whisper.

"One moment," Renée said stiffly, then turned to Eleanor. "You are dismissed." Eleanor curtsied and let herself out. "You know how servants gossip," Renée said darkly.

"Yes. Now, about Twomey?" Nicole said anxiously.

Renée exhaled in exhaustion. "I tried, dearest. I did talk to him, but the man's like a live clam. He wouldn't open a crack."

"Oh, dear." Nicole drooped in disappointment.

"However," Renée said thoughtfully, and Nicole looked up in hope. "I have the feeling—no, it is more than that, it is a distinct premonition—that the jester is on the verge of doing something just offensive enough to Ares to get himself kicked out of the palace."

"You think so?" Nicole asked.

"Yes, I do. I can't quite put my finger on it, but he seems to have developed the kind of attitude that gets people in trouble with your husband. So, dearest, I'm sure it would be best for you to simply do nothing, and let Twomey hang himself," Renée said.

Relieved, Nicole said, "Yes, you're absolutely right. Oh, Renée, thank you."

"If you want to thank me, then call off the spy," Renée reminded her.

Nicole paused uncomfortably, because Ares had directed her to do otherwise. But since Pearcey had been relieved of duty this morning and his replacement for tonight had not yet been appointed, she said with drawn brows, "Chataine, no one should be watching you at this time."

Renée's eyes widened, and she murmured, "Oh, really? Then someone else has gotten into the little game."

"Perhaps it would be safer for you to meet your—callers somewhere outside the palace, dearest. In disguise. You know how servants talk," Nicole muttered, with a glance toward the door.

The idea caught Renée's fancy. "Perhaps you're right."

"Thank you for trying with Twomey, anyway." Nicole leaned forward to kiss her cheek.

"I shall keep trying. Therefore, don't be surprised when you see me being affectionate toward him at dinner," Renée told her.

"I understand. Thank you again." And Nicole departed.

"You're welcome. No need for you to interfere in a game so far beyond your skill, dearest," Renée murmured, pouring herself another goblet of wine. Holding it to her lips, she paused to regard the shattered figurine on the hearth. "How playthings do get broken." And she took a large draught in satisfaction.

Since Nicole was so near the library, she stopped to look in on the twins at their lessons. They were just being let out for the day. After a light midday meal, they would go about their separate business: Bonnie to the nursery, and Sophie to recreational classes with her friends. Children of administrators and courtiers who were not interested in being certified in Roman's Law took winter classes in literature, Latin, astronomy, needlework, or games.

Sophie preferred additional classes to boredom, while Bonnie, on previous days, had found more inventive methods of occupying herself. Today, she hung around her mother outside the library in some reluctance. "Mama, do I have to go to the nursery today?"

"I thought you enjoyed it," Nicole said.

"I do." Bonnie fidgeted while Sophie watched. "It's just . . . a lot of work."

"True. But think how disappointed the little ones would be not to see you today after playing with you all of yesterday. Can you imagine poor little Tor crying at the door, looking for you?" Nicole asked. Of course, Tor was too young to know who took care of him yesterday . . . perhaps.

Bonnie wavered. "He is a little angel," she admitted.

Nicole gestured to the nearby sentry while telling Bonnie, "And he will be so happy to see you again today. Chataine Bonnie is ready to go to the nursery," she told the sentry. He bowed to them, and Bonnie went with him willingly, if not eagerly.

When her sister was out of earshot, Sophie turned to her mother. "How long will she have to work in the nursery?"

"As long as she is a help and not a hindrance," Nicole replied, putting an arm around her daughter's shoulder to walk with her down the corridor.

"She'll get tired of it," Sophie predicted.

"Probably. But she may prefer it to her new schedule."

Sophie stopped. "What schedule?"

"Bonnie will not have the free time she has enjoyed in the past. She will have a choice of activities, but there will not be quite as much opportunity to—toy with young men," Nicole replied.

"How? What do you mean?" Sophie asked.

"Your father and I are discussing the particulars," Nicole said. "Now, what class are you off to?"

"Roux and I are learning All Fours," Sophie said.

"This is a card game?" Nicole asked.

"Yes. It's very tricky," Sophie said smugly.

"Very good," Nicole laughed. "Perhaps you can teach it to me."

"Oh, I'd love to, Mama!"

Nicole leaned down the few inches necessary to receive her departing kiss, then Sophie skipped on down the corridor to her receiving room.

Nicole turned downstairs to head for the kitchen. She rarely interfered with Georges' handling of the dinner menu, but he insisted on her approval of it in advance, for form's sake. This she was happy to give, although by the time she usually got around to doing so, it was too late in the day to change it.

As she was entering the kitchen corridor, she was startled by the sudden appearance of the jester, bowing low. "How can Twomey serve the beautiful Surchataine?" he asked in his ingratiating manner.

"I want nothing from you," she bristled.

That told him what he needed to know. Cringing, wringing his hands, he pleaded, "Forgive Twomey, Surchataine. Please forgive Twomey for speaking to the Surchatain. I only say what I see."

Nicole evaluated him for a moment, then said *sotto voce*, "You appointed yourself Ares' spy for your own reasons, so you tell him whatever you think will further your designs. You chose to slander me to my husband—for what purpose I do not know yet, but I am confident that it will soon become apparent. Although you may be a useful source of information to him now, he has many sets of eyes in the palace. But there is only one person he chooses to sleep with." With that, she lifted her soft skirts and walked around him.

While the weather was bright in Westford, just a few miles south a sudden winter squall sent walls of snow, sleet, and rain crashing into Nicole's Harbor. Crews were barely able to secure the few ships in their slips before the storm made it impossible to see, much less work. So the men hustled back to the cold barracks to cluster by the central firepit.

Henry, being one of the last ones inside, glanced at the crowd around the meager fire and bypassed it to sit on his pallet against the wall. He shed the wet cloak, hanging it on a nail to drip away from the pallet, and wrapped himself in the thin blanket. He started to lie down, but finding it a half-degree warmer to stay sitting up, he leaned against the wall and closed his eyes. He thought about Westford—every spare moment, he comforted himself thinking about home. That was the only thing that had kept him sane in Hornbound before Ares came to rescue him.

Now, Henry thought about his friends Hoose and Scroggs and Captain Crager, who had been greatly instructive; he thought about pranks pulled on the night watchmen and hot pies stolen from the kitchen. He thought about Nicole, who had always been a loving, warm presence. Strange that he didn't think of her as a mother like he thought of Ares as his father—she was more like a sister, moreso than Renée ever was.

He suddenly opened his eyes. Who was his mother? Her name was. . . . He couldn't remember. She left the palace because. . . . He didn't know.

Shrugging, he wrapped himself tighter in the blanket and closed his eyes again. Truth be told, all he knew was that she left because her son was not important enough for her to stay. So, truth be told, he didn't care about her, either. He had more pleasant things to think about. And lately, he had been thinking a lot about Sophie.

A clattering. "Dogs! No trouble beating that!" someone at the firepit groaned in disgust. Henry barely opened his eyes. The clattering sounded again.

"Vultures!" exclaimed someone else amid supporting cheers. With the temporary respite from work, the men around the firepit had brought out the knucklebones. There was rowdy cheering and cursing at the luck of the roll, what with the copper and silver pieces bet on the outcome.

One fellow was having singular luck: "Senio!" he roared over the losers' groans. "Second time straight!"

"I'd think the die were shaved, were they yours," someone else grumbled.

"Aye, but they're Rupe's, and he's lost worst than anybody today," another replied.

The winner of this roll collected the bets. "What? Is this all you got? What's this? It's just old twisted iron." He began playing with it, twirling it.

The loser replied, "That's a leper's brand, fool. It's what they use to brand lepers."

"Yeah? Huh. Don't look like it's worth much," the winner scoffed, eyeing it in condescension. He savored his luck over the soldiers because he was not even a member of the Lystran army, but a workman who had finagled his way into the barracks because soldiering fascinated him.

He then glanced at Henry sitting apart on his pallet. The workman also knew something about the different regiments, and had heard about Henry. The fact that a Blue had been dispatched to Nicole's Harbor en route to Odea aroused some curiosity among the men, as those of the Blue Regiment usually enjoyed far more prestigious assignments.

Given the rumors that this particular Blue had killed a fellow Blue over a girl, his relocation seemed downright punitive. So the knucklebones winner felt entitled to address the aloof soldier with sarcasm: "You! Hey, Father! You won't lose your salvation gambling a piece or two!"

Henry, too tired to take offense, only muttered, "I haven't anything to bet."

In his desire to get everyone involved in the game, the winning fool shifted toward him. "Sure you do! You got something on that silver chain there—"

Henry came directly awake. "Come closer and I'll kill you."

The other raised his hands in mock terror. "Hey, now, all in fun." But he did back away, and Henry realized that he had to stop the telltale fingering of the treasure under his shirt, else it would get stolen while he slept.

After Ares had cleaned up from his afternoon drill with the Greens, Vogelsong was waiting in his receiving room. He had much information to impart to Ares, but the meatiest morsel came first: "Surchatain, it seems that your caution is justified. Fanchon's messenger is terrified of what will happen to him, or his family, should he fail to return with good news. For not only does the slave trade continue to thrive in Corona, but Fanchon and his administrators use it to dispose of enemies and unsatisfactory friends."

Settling into his chair behind the table, Ares observed, "You mean, they sell them into slavery to get rid of them."

"Exactly, Surchatain."

Ares nodded. "All right, then, tell me everything you know." And Vogelsong leaned forward to relate his conversation with the unhappy messenger in detail, which amounted to trivial gossip.

When he had concluded, Ares commended him, "Very good, for your first contact. But I want more details about Fanchon's overtures to Qarqar. Since they are governed by a citizen council, I want to know who has received Fanchon's messages. So I want you to pay another visit to the messenger tomorrow."

Vogelsong hesitated. "As you wish, Surchatain. But . . . there is still the issue of his sore lack of funds—"

"Then take a purse with you," Ares conceded. "Offer him no more than five royals, but you may spend up to twenty."

"Thank you, Surchatain. This should be interesting," Vogelsong said.

Evening descended on Westford; the chandeliers in the great hall were lit; the tables drawn together and set with pewter; the guests arrived in great good spirits, and Ares and Nicole were announced as they took their places at the head.

Oyster quenelles on bean soup, marrow and liver balls, and roasted guinea hen came out of the kitchen in pleasing presentations, so talk was high and happy. Sophie leaned across the broad table in an attempt to whisper to her sister, "Did you hear the rumor?" Her parents were immediately attentive, though neither looked up.

Bonnie came out of a tired stupor. "What?"

"Twomey is doing something special tonight!" Sophie said.

Several people heard. Ares glanced toward Nicole without turning his head. Vogelsong asked Sophie, "What is he doing?"

She turned to him. "I don't know, but Roux says she heard it's going to be wonderful!" Courtiers' children who were not at table were usually allowed to watch entertainments from the doorways.

"This I'd like to see," observed Thom, to whom Ares told everything.

The news spread quickly down the table until the guests were talking of nothing else. Ares glanced at Nicole, then leaned close to her. "I will do whatever you require, Lady. If you do not wish to see him, I will not allow him to perform. If you want him gone, I will command it."

But Nicole would in no way deny Renée the opportunity to work on Twomey. Goblet at her lips, she murmured, "It makes no difference to me, my lord. Why should I deprive everyone of entertainment? As long as I have your regard, let him do as our guests desire."

He exhaled, "My regard? Lady, you have my utter devotion."

When he lifted her hand to kiss it, she glanced toward Renée, who returned a secret wink. "Actually, I am rather interested to see what he will do," Nicole admitted. Ares was raising a hand to summon him when she interjected, "After dessert, as usual, my lord. Let us give the kitchen their due for such a feast."

Apprehending the latter end of this conversation, Bonnie began shoveling food into her mouth with such haste that her mother reprimanded her. But the rest of the table took their cue from Bonnie to clean their plates with the speed of beggars.

Other than Thom and Ares, who set their own pace in any activity, only Doctor Savary refused to be rushed. When goaded teasingly by Soucie, he grumbled, "Hasty eating interferes with proper digestion. Besides, I'm tired of the fool."

He was roundly booed for such an opinion, but Ares eyed him with fresh respect, and a little pain, as the doctor was beginning to sound more and more like old Doctor Wigzell . . . one of a growing number of people whom Ares missed sorely.

At last, not soon enough for the bulk of the table, the apricot preserves had been sufficiently appreciated and Ares called in the jester. Nicole's side of the table eagerly turned their chairs, which were beginning to show wear on the carved feet from such energetic use.

The moment Twomey entered the hall with a lute slung over his shoulder, he was greeted by thunderous applause and astonished murmurings.

Instead of the motley, he wore a very fine suit of red wool with black stockings, silver buttons, a dashing black cape, and a tasseled hat that could have come from the shop of Lord Preus.

The jester had also taken pains to shave his face and apply a little perfume on the handkerchief tucked into his cuff. All in all, it was an appearance that might have made Giles jealous, were he here to see it.

With the white lacy corner peeking out correctly from the sleeve, Twomey held the lute out of the way to make a flourishing bow to the head of the table. "Surchatain, thank you for the honor of your summons. I shall endeavor to entertain all as expected, but I have a favor to ask of your greatness." He spoke straightforwardly, with no fawning or idiot talk.

The guests looked at each other as Ares said dryly, "Go on."

"Thank you, Surchatain. I ask your gracious indulgence to allow me to direct a song to one person at this distinguished table," Twomey said.

Ares looked reflexively at Nicole. "This is your choice, Lady," he said under his breath.

"Who could refuse such a heartfelt request?" she murmured back. Both believed that Twomey intended some kind of performance toward her, in apology or appeasement.

"This is granted," Ares said.

Twomey bowed again with extra flourish, and the guests applauded eagerly. Then with graceful strides, he walked around to Ares' side of the table and knelt behind Renée so that she had to turn in her chair to look at him. The other guests craned their necks to see.

Shrugging the lute into his hands in the manner of a practiced musician, Twomey began to strum and sing with straightforward, aching sincerity:

"You have bound me with your thighs,
I am captive to your wiles;
Your jeers rend my heart
You are such a tart
To me, my dove, my love.

"If I loved you on a bet,
Would you love me better yet?
For that love of mine
Was bought as it is
Now, my dove, my love.

"What then shall I do
To get such a maid as you?
Is there hope for me
To every touch your
Parts, my dove, my love?"

He finished on a lingering note, gazing lovingly into her limpid blue eyes as she smiled down on him. There was stark silence in the hall for three heartbeats—and then stone-rattling laughter.

10

At the raucous, unrestrained laughter, Twomey dropped the lute to look around in shock, his jaw hanging slack. All around the table, whichever way he looked, the guests were laughing so hard that they had to hold their stomachs or wipe tears from their eyes. Ares was staring at him in bewilderment and Thom eyed him in contempt. But Nicole saw what had happened.

Twomey had sung a venerated old love song which everyone here knew, as it was recorded in Roman's Annals. However, Twomey's version, wherever he had learned it, was a crude, stupid corruption of the original. This he did not realize when he endeavored to sing it straightforwardly to Renée.

She, however, reacted with complete aplomb, accepting his song in the spirit in which it was intended. Radiant and smiling, she bent forward to place a kiss on the top of his tasseled hat, bringing her chestly assets tantalizingly close to his face. Following this intoxicating gesture, she whispered, "Meet me in the well room after dinner."

Had she just proclaimed him Surchatain, it would not

have had a more profound effect on him. He leapt up in joy, seizing his hat and flinging it upward with a mighty cry. Then he threw himself into an exuberant series of turns, leaps, and somersaults in complete disregard of the dignity of his new suit.

The table responded with wild applause, upon which he bowed low to the head of the table and bounded out of the hall like a hart in spring. The guests sprang to their feet to send him out with a standing ovation.

Still seated, hand at his mouth, Thom leaned toward Ares to mutter, "He's gone mad."

"He's in love," Ares countered, watching Renée. Twomey was a man in love, and she was encouraging him—after expressing such clear disdain for him previously.

Before Renée could catch Ares watching her, he redirected his attention to finishing his apricot preserves, all the while thinking hard. If she had a sudden interest in Twomey, it could only be because she had discovered something useful about him that she was now endeavoring to turn to her own ends. This made him immediately useless to Ares.

With a mild sigh of regret, he drained his goblet and turned to his wife. Fortunately, the jester was expendable. Others were not. When she turned her sultry green eyes to her husband, he said, "Shall we retire, Lady?"

"Whatever my lord desires," she murmured, and he smiled.

While Ares was escorting Nicole upstairs, Renée went into the chapel to pretend to pray. Going upstairs and then coming down again would attract too much attention, but she did not want to go directly to the well room.

First, it was imperative to make Twomey wait, and sweat, and wonder if she would come, only to be overwhelmed with joy when she finally appeared. Second, there was too much traffic in the corridors around the well room immediately after dinner. Those servants needed to clear out to their own drinking holes before she would condescend to enter the lower corridor.

After the lapse of almost an hour, during which time she had to fend off Father Birondo from attempting to counsel her, Renée finally rose from the hard bench and entered the foyer. It was suitably deserted, so she progressed noiselessly (as much as rustling silks would allow) to the darkened corridor close to her destination. Here, she was forced to take a candle from a wall sconce to see by.

The moment she entered the well room, there was movement from a dark corner. Twomey, obviously waking, sprang up unsteadily, blinking in the light of her candle. "Am I dreaming?"

"Am I?" Renée countered, sitting delicately on the edge of the well head. She positioned herself with her back to the doorway to hide the candlelight from view of the corridor while she listened for any movement behind her.

He staggered toward her. "Beautiful lady! Is there any hope—can a mere jester hope to court such a one as you?" he pleaded.

She lowered her eyes demurely. Hauffe had not yet returned from his assignment, so, not knowing how successful he would be, she determined to make the most of any opening given her. "A mere jester, no." She paused. "But something tells me that you are no mere jester, Twomey."

He opened his mouth, mute as the struggle between discretion and lust waged mightily within him. Slowly, imperceptibly, the scales began to tilt. "I am not," he said in a whisper of substance, even power. "I have been both priest and Counselor."

"Oh, Twomey!" She leaned toward him with shining eyes. "My first love was a Counselor. But—tell me your true name. The name that I breathe into my pillow at night must be real."

He opened his mouth to obey her command, but—wretched happenstance—a pair of feet passed close by in the corridor outside, entering the storeroom next to the well room. While the lovers were not driven from their concealment, it jolted the jester back to reality. Wincing, he whispered, "In due time, Lady. Let me find a way back into the Surchataine's good graces before I bare all to you."

Renée arched a brow in mild interest. "My lovely Twomey, you jest. What could you have possibly done to fall out of favor with sweet Nicole?" *That is why she came to me expressing disdain for him!* she thought with mounting excitement.

His face took on a sniveling expression that she studied with detached interest, and he shrugged. "The Surchataine had met a young man privately, of which I informed the Surchatain."

Renée's mouth dropped open in delight. "Dear, virtuous Nicole has been naughty?" she whispered in glee. "And you told Ares? What did he say?"

Pleased to have her conspiratorial approval, he said disparagingly, "Unfortunately, the Surchatain did not seem to place much credence in my report."

"Of course he wouldn't," Renée chortled. "He would never believe ill of his sainted wife. Tell me—who is the man?"

"I do not know his name," Twomey said in disappointment. "He is a young soldier, tall and handsome."

Either because of his coloring of the matter or her readiness to jump to conclusions about Nicole, Renée did not apprehend the man's obvious identity as the soldier who had been assigned to spy on her. "Oh, that's just rich," she said in delight.

Being drunk with love robbed Twomey of common sense as effectively as any liquid could. So he proposed, snickering, "Should I whisper news of the meeting to a talkative maid or two?"

Renée eyed him. She had no interest in betraying Nicole, but the fact that Twomey suggested it opened the door to numerous ways she might exploit him. "I don't know. It would make Ares very angry," she replied watchfully.

Twomey leaned on the well head in nonchalance. "Don't worry about him, my love. I have him wrapped around my little finger."

Renée's eyes glowed in admiration. "Oh, my! In such short a time since last summer? What a master you are at this game! One would think you played with Surchatains like dolls!"

"I have had a match or two," he acknowledged, glancing shrewdly aside.

"Oh, darling Twomey, do tell me! Leave out names if you must, but give the poor little dog a bone to gnaw on," she begged.

He shrugged, now completely helpless in her grip. He did not even glance out to the corridor as he said, "One lady of a certain court used to come to me for confession, though that was not even my office. But I had her confidence so completely, she preferred talking to me than to the priest, even with the obscuring curtain between us— she could not see me, you know. So I listened, and gave her such wise counsel that all went well for her when she heeded it.

"But over the weeks she grew so enamored of my voice, and so eager to see my face, that one day during confession she reached out and tore the curtain from the window between us! Thereafter, I allowed her to confess with the curtain open—though of course, the iron latticework remained between us.

"Soon, her desire was to remove that, as well. But— that was impossible," he laughed. "However, the planking below the window was unstable, so I was able to pry off a board so that she could thrust her little foot through the opening into my lap. I then could remove her silk slipper and caress her soft foot." He closed his eyes, shivering in delight at the remembrance.

It was all Renée could do to keep her face impassive, for what he was describing was beyond improper, it was obscene. Had he attempted to stroke her bare foot, she would have crammed him headfirst down the well, grate or no.

His face changed, and he opened his eyes. "The priest was jealous, and began watching me, looking for a way to bring me down. So when he saw her tying her shoe back on in the confessional, he went poking around it and found the loose board. He brought charges against me to the Surchatain, but—" here he laughed wildly—"I turned it around on *him!* All this time I had made sure that the lady had not got a clear view of my face, for those confessional boxes are dim, you know. During the trial, I so convoluted his accusations and her statements that by the time it was done, *he* was sold into slavery along with her!"

This so stunned Renée that she momentarily fell out of character. "You allowed the lady to be sold into slavery for the pleasure of being stroked by you?" she asked quietly.

He quickly descended from his euphoria to correct his misstep. "No, no!" he laughed nervously. "That was her sentence, but I would not allow it. During the night, I bribed her keeper to let me in, and aided her in escaping out the window to a friend. The last I saw her, she thanked me with tears."

Renée did not doubt that the last he saw the lady, she was in tears, but not from gratitude. So it was with redoubled adoration that Renée breathed, "Oh, Twomey, how wonderful of you. I feel I know you better every moment"—which was true, at least. Glancing out at the dark, quiet corridor, she said, "I must go. Will you meet me here again tomorrow night?"

In response, he grabbed her head and brought his stinking mouth to hers. Renée pulled away with a strength that startled the weaker man. Only her supreme gamesmanship allowed her to smile coyly at his black-toothed grin. "Later, darling," she murmured, then betook herself into the corridor.

Hastening up the stairs by feeble candlelight, she fiercely wiped her mouth with the back of her hand. "It will be a great joy to make you writhe, you disgusting little man," she uttered. Rushing into her chambers, she demanded of Eleanor, "Has Hauffe returned?"

"No, Chataine," she replied. "Is my lady ready for her bath?"

"Yes. But first get me the paste so I can clean out my mouth," she said, spitting into the fireplace.

Deep in the night Ares awoke, sweating in the chill of the bedchamber. Once again, the white knight had rammed his sword into Ares' chest, uttering his profane benediction.

But tonight Ares lay still, concentrating all his mind on the invisible Immortal who alone has authority over life, death, and dreams. *What are You trying to teach me in this?* he asked silently. *What are You trying to teach me?*

He waited breathlessly, sternly focused, until he was finally forced to take a breath in disgust. Nothing! Nicole, tucked in close beside him, stirred. He kissed the top of her head, exhaling tiredly. It was just a dream. It had neither meaning nor purpose; it was just—a random nightmare passing through.

He closed his eyes again. Just a dream. Then his eyes opened to slits to watch the hazy orange shadows of a dying fire. It was a dream that should have passed through, but seemed to have found a home in his head. If God revealed no meaning in it to him or Father Birondo when they had both been asking relentlessly, then why should it continue? Why couldn't he make it stop?

Ares pondered this. How does one stop a dream? He might as well hold back the wind. Or . . . redirect it? Suppose he should concentrate on redirecting it? For instance, have himself put on armor in the dream?

Wide awake, Ares stared up at the white plaster dimly visible in between the ceiling beams. No—putting on armor probably would not answer the problem, which seemed to go deeper than clothing choices.

He was then sidetracked by an auxiliary line of thought, intriguing in its implications: When he deliberately chose the cotton underclothing instead of the wool, he did not dream about putting on the woolens again. When he went downstairs to the priest instead of flinging himself on Nicole (as he had in the dream) then that did not repeat itself, either—not yet, at any rate. When he chose not to allow the dream to dictate his waking life, his will prevailed. The question was: could he make his will prevail in the dream?

So Ares devised a test based on the most singular feature of the dream—that of the knight's growing a new head. Ares decided he would attempt to redirect the dream: instead of cutting off the knight's head, Ares would demand *à parler*.

This was conventional wartime protocol and certainly within Ares' control, normally, as opposed to how many heads his opponent could produce. Therefore, as Ares closed his eyes to go back to sleep, he envisioned himself over and over riding out to meet the white knight, dismounting, and calling for *parler*.

Some minutes later, he opened his eyes again. Now he was so agitated and restless that he couldn't go back to sleep. Sighing, he shifted toward Nicole again. All he had to do was reach for her and she embraced him in her sleep. So for now, he put the matter of the white knight out of his mind.

The following morning, Vogelsong's various duties prevented his going to the inn first thing, which did not worry him. Conscientious as he was about fulfilling his responsibilities, he knew that the messenger would not be awake or coherent at first light, given the hospitality he had received last night, courtesy of Vogelsong's purse.

So the young Counselor took his time in seeing to other matters, especially certain expenses posted by Giles' assistant, Stengi, in his absence. Vogelsong was most curious as to why these expenditures had waited until Giles' departure to be brought out for approval.

So it was almost noon, cold but clear outside, when the Counselor finally bundled up to set out for the Dancing

Bear. As it happened, on his way out of the courtyard in the throng, he unknowingly passed Hauffe on his way in. The servant strode through the dirty slush, up the icy steps, and into the great foyer as if he was on a mission of great import.

Brushing aside lesser servants who did not do their jobs so well, he hauled himself up the long, curving stairway as rapidly as his old, stiff knees would carry him. Then he stood at the Chataine's door and knocked.

"Who is it?" she asked irritably. When he identified himself, the Chataine Renée herself flung open the door and dragged him inside. Her maid was absent, obviously attending to the Chataine's business elsewhere in the palace.

"Dear Hauffe, how good to see you. Tell me that you have profitable news to share with me," she said. That she was still in her nightrobe did not seem to trouble either of them, what with the greater matter at hand.

He bowed in self-satisfaction. "Your servant strives to please, Chataine. As you predicted, the man was out cold in a private dining room when I arrived yesterday, so I had him taken up to his room and laid on his bed. Then I waited through the whole long night until he began coming to just an hour ago.

"He expressed great alarm at the presence of a stranger in his room, and informed me that he had nothing of value to steal. I reassured him that my intent was only friendly, which I proved by ordering him breakfast and stiff tea. When he had eaten his fill, and was most appreciative of it, he expressed curiosity as to my purpose.

"I then explained to him that a certain noble of Westford had encountered rumors possibly concerning someone in Corona. This noble, whom I would not name, wished these rumors to be investigated, but knew no one who might have witnessed the events in question except the man to whom I was speaking. These rumors, I told him, involved a lady of Fanchon's court who had been sold into slavery as punishment for too close a friendship with an administrator, or noble, of that court—

"That was all I was able to say before the messenger interrupted me in great excitement to ask if I knew the whereabouts of this administrator, for there was a large bounty on his head. I told him that I was not privy to everything my master knew, but if he would tell me all that he knew of the matter, there would be great reward in it for him. Thereupon, I drew out the purse you gave me and placed a royal on the table before him. 'If you recognize this affair, then tell me all of its events,' I said.

"This he was only too eager to do, especially when I laid another royal before his eyes. And this is what he related to me: In the spring of last year, a monk came to the court at Corona to act as tutor to the ladies who desired learning, if their husbands permitted. My messenger did not know how it was that the monk arrived—whether he was summoned or simply appeared—but nonetheless, he proved to be such a popular teacher that a number of the courtly ladies began studying under him in various subjects: music, literature, dance.

"For a while all went well. But then a few husbands began to hear whisperings that this monk was exercising a little too much familiarity with some of the prettier ladies; specifically, he was said to touch their hands or their hair. In one instance, he was accused of kissing a lady on the cheek. But as she strongly denied it, and no one would come forward to present the accusation formally, the controversy died down. Until . . . Fanchon's wife, the

Surchataine, began taking classes from the monk."

Renée did not interrupt, so Hauffe continued, "She took only a few classes in poetry, then stopped coming. But then, all of a sudden, she began going to confession, which had never been a habit of hers in the past. Yet, beginning in mid-summer, she began going every day, sometimes twice a day. Stranger still, the priest in charge of hearing confessions was often known to be gone from the palace at the very times that she was said to be at confessional.

"This went on for only a few weeks, for the priest became suspicious upon hearing about comings and goings during his absence from the chapel. So one day he made as if to depart on one of his usual errands, but hid near the confessional box in the chapel. Shortly, the Surchataine came for her confessional. And sure enough, the priest watched the monk enter the box to hear her. While she was within, the priest heard giggling that was most uncharacteristic of such times.

"Then, when the Surchataine was ready to depart, she opened the door and reached down to replace her slipper on her foot! The priest watched her leave, and the monk leave. When both were gone, he himself entered the box and began investigating it. The first thing he saw was that the curtain had been ripped down and rehung on splinters, to be easily removed again. And when he began going over the structure of the box, he discovered a loose board merely standing in place in the partition beneath the window.

"Deducing what had been going on, the priest took the board to show the Counselor, who immediately brought charges of seduction and licentiousness against the monk. He was brought to trial before the Surchatain that very evening. But as no one had seen the monk in the confessional other than the priest, and the lady strongly denied everything except going to confessional with a man she assumed to be the priest, it was decided that the priest himself was the guilty party, and that upon imminent danger of detection, he had brought charges against the monk to deflect suspicion from himself.

"So this is what Fanchon ruled: the priest was sold into slavery that very night, but the Surchataine and the monk were held in their quarters to be interrogated again in the morning. All the court agreed that, most likely, they two would share the priest's fate on the morrow.

"However, during the night, the Surchataine, in fear or shame, stabbed herself to death. Her maid, discovering the act only moments after it had happened, raised such a cry throughout the palace that it was turned upside down. By the time anyone thought to look in the monk's cubicle, he had escaped and disappeared.

"Therefore," Hauffe finished, "there is now a bounty of one thousand royals for the return of this monk to Fanchon dead, and two thousand royals if he is returned alive."

II

After a moment of reverential silence, Renée said with glistening eyes, "Dearest, darling Hauffe, my precious Hauffe, you are as faithful and good a servant as there ever was."

"Your servant thanks you, Chataine," he replied, bowing.

"One more detail, darling. Do we know this monk's name?" she asked.

"Symon, Chataine. He was known to Fanchon's court as Symon," Hauffe replied as the crowning touch to his report.

Turning toward the brilliantly colored stained-glass window, Renée closed her eyes, inhaling the sweetness of victory. "You are almost done, dearest Hauffe. I want you to return to the inn. You are not to speak to the messenger, however; you are merely to sit in the common room and listen. Stay to yourself, stay quiet, and listen, for if the messenger is the kind of man I think, he will not be content telling this story to only you. You may leave when the inn closes, then come tell me anything interesting you have heard."

"Yes, Chataine," he replied.

She uttered, "You are dismissed, darling."

He bowed and withdrew as Renée stood gazing at the window. In an unprecedented act of gratitude, she unlatched it and threw it open. Braving the icy air, she stood at the open window and whispered to the cottony clouds, "Thank You, thank You. How unutterably kind of You. This is so much fun."

When Eleanor entered and saw this, she rushed forward with motherly scoldings to close the window again. Renée only looked at her with full eyes. "We have much to plan, my darling Eleanor."

On the other side of the palace, someone else was standing at an open window. Ares was looking out over the silver-white fields, concentrating on the image of a white knight. Over and over in his mind, Ares made himself dismount and call for parler. He did not draw the sword. *Do not draw the sword or you will use it. Call for parler. He is a knight; he must parler if you demand it.*

At the knock on his receiving-room door, Ares reclosed the windows and turned. "Enter!" To his great surprise, a sentry dragged in a cringing, crying Twomey. "What is this?"

"Surchatain, pardon, but this rat was caught in the act of eating a currant pie meant for the Surchatain's table tonight. The dinner master is fit to be tied, and demanded that he be brought to you for punishment," the sentry said with a little shake of the culprit.

"I will see to it," Ares said, bemused. After the sentry had left and shut the door, Ares asked Twomey, "Have you lost your mind?"

"Surchatain, forgive me. Forgive me," Twomey said, tears in his eyes. Crouching almost to the floor, he went on,

"Punish me as you will—it does not matter. My eyes are my undoing."

"What are you talking about?" Ares asked.

"I will be whipped for it. I do not care. All that matters is saying what I have seen," he groaned. But seeing Ares display impatience, Twomey whispered in agony, "I saw the Surchataine come out of a storage room with the same young man. Only, as she was leaving, she had to stop to retie her slipper onto her foot. And that is what I saw. My life is over."

Ares paused. "When did you see this?"

"Just now, Surchatain. In the lower corridor where she met him the first time," Twomey sighed.

Ares studied him for a few moments, then went to the door to open it. He told the sentry outside, "Escort Twomey to his room and post a guard. He is under confinement until further notice. And tell Georges that we will devise a way for Twomey to work off the pie he ate."

The sentry saluted and Twomey bowed to the floor to kiss Ares' boots. "You are most kind to poor Twomey, Surchatain. Kind Surchatain." Ares merely gestured to the sentry, who hauled the jester out by the back of his overlarge shirt.

They had been gone for several minutes when Ares, brows knit, finally moved from that one spot to sit behind the correspondence on his table. But the moment he was seated, he had to rise again because the door to the bedchamber opened. Nicole emerged, smiling and sleepy-eyed, though dressed for the day.

Ares went over to take her in his arms. "I've rarely seen you sleep so late. Everyone knows that you are downstairs conferring with Georges by this time," he murmured.

"I've seldom been so tired," she smiled, stretching. "But I'm so glad you woke me last night." She brought his head down to kiss him with lazy sensuality.

"Don't," he said, and she opened her eyes. "Vogelsong tends to rush in unannounced, and he would faint dead away to see this."

She laughed, pulling out of his arms. "Then I will make you wait until tonight for anything more, beast."

"You are cruel," he said, smiling.

She sighed, smoothing her skirts. "I must have lost half the day. Was someone here just now?"

"No one important," he said. "But Sophie was here earlier, looking for you. Seems there's a game you promised to learn from her."

"Oh, I promised? Well, I had better go make good on my word. Good day, my lord." She curtsied deeply to him, and he nodded.

He returned to sit at the table, but did not look at the correspondence. Instead, his eyes fixed on the middle distance. "*Why . . . ?*"

A hasty knock barely sounded before Vogelsong did indeed rush in. "Surchatain!"

"Counselor?" Ares said, brows lifted.

"Surchatain, the most amazing thing has happened!" Vogelsong insisted.

"Sit and tell me," Ares said, waving him to the chair.

He did sit, blurting, "I went to the inn to speak with the messenger again—and lo and behold, he is in fine spirits, entertaining a woman in his room, eating dainties, happy as can be!"

"Really," Ares said, intrigued. "So, somehow he acquired money between last night and this afternoon."

"Yes. And most amazing, the moment he saw me, he

demanded to know if we have seen Symon," Vogelsong related.

"Symon? Who is this Symon?" Ares asked.

"That is precisely what I asked, Surchatain. So he told me a most amazing story." Whereupon Vogelsong related to Ares everything that Hauffe had just finished telling Renée.

Ares listened impassively, as he did when he was concentrating, but even in the excitement of the narration, Vogelsong noticed something in his face change when he heard the part about the Selecan Surchataine's redonning her slipper in the confessional.

When Vogelsong had finished his account and sat breathless, Ares was quiet. Then he asked, "Do we have any idea who it was who came to the messenger this morning?"

"No, Surchatain; he gave the messenger no name," Vogelsong said firmly. "He said only that he represented a Westfordian nobleman who wished to confirm the major points regarding this Symon's treachery."

Ares looked thoughtfully to the window. "So Fanchon's wife committed suicide? I heard nothing of this."

Vogelsong shook his head energetically. "All I heard, Surchatain, was that she had been deposed."

"Her name was. . . ."

"Conteria. Surchataine Conteria. A great beauty, from what I was told," Vogelsong said. When Ares was silent, he went on, "This nobleman must have encountered a wandering monk who raised his suspicions. But how he got wind of such goings-on, I cannot imagine."

"Fanchon would not want it widely known, for several reasons," Ares mused.

"Certainly not! It would undermine all his efforts in reestablishing trade with Lystra," Vogelsong said, affronted.

"Two thousand royals for Symon's live return," Ares muttered, fingers at his lips. "Fanchon seems most desirous of putting hooks in living flesh."

"Who would not be wroth to discover that his wife had been patsy to this fool, and died for it?" Vogelsong said indignantly.

"Indeed. Well. For now, Counselor, we need to know if our mysterious nobleman's servant visits our messenger again. So have Thom select two men to place at the inn disguised as merchants," Ares instructed.

"Good plan, Surchatain!" Vogelsong enthused.

"I am glad you approve," Ares said wryly. "You are dismissed."

When the Counselor had left, Ares went back to the window to open it. His joints protested the sudden onrush of cold air, but his mind needed its clarifying effects. Leaning on the windowsill, he looked up to the clouds to say, "Thank You. I appreciate this enlightenment, at least." Then he looked out over the countryside to think over numerous questions here raised:

Had Twomey—or rather, Symon—been setting Ares up all this time to make a play for power? That is what it seemed. Or had he hoped to blackmail Nicole into submission, to use her as he had used Conteria? These questions Ares acknowledged, but set aside as irrelevant at this point, and moved on to other questions, such as:

What nobleman knew enough to pump Fanchon's messenger for the circumstances of Conteria's death? It must be someone at this palace, certainly someone who was at the dinner table. This question was relevant, because the man was obviously pursuing an agenda that could conflict with Ares' purposes. Nonetheless, Ares could not even guess who it might be, so that question was laid aside as well.

The most important question, and the one to which Ares bent his mind, was: How might he use this new information against Fanchon? For since it had been confirmed that Fanchon continued to patronize the slavers —and lie about it—Ares had lost interest in trade with Seleca. Now, he only wanted to interfere with Fanchon's support of slaving.

So Ares spent the next hour trying to conceive a way to manipulate Fanchon's desire for revenge against him. Finally, after much concerted thought, Ares gave up. He could devise many ways to irritate or anger Fanchon, but not loosen his ties with the slavers.

So, reluctantly, Ares turned to a consideration of war against Fanchon. Ares dreaded war—a month of battle could wipe out a hundred years of progress in a province, inflicting as much suffering as slavers did. But Ares and his officers had long been perplexed over the tenacity of the slave markets. Now he knew why he could never uproot them: Fanchon's sponsorship. As long as a Surchatain as powerful as Fanchon remained to protect the slavers, they would continue to thrive.

When Ares turned to his honeycomb to pull out the map of routes into Seleca, he suddenly saw the white knight before him, challenging him. As Ares had been practicing, he mentally left his sword hanging by his side and called for parler. Over and over, he called for parler until the image faded. But the sudden apparition during daylight troubled him. That had never happened before.

He brought out the map and unrolled it without seeing

it, for Twomey filled his mind's eye. He was the key piece, somehow, and as such, he must be totally contained. The mystery nobleman must be allowed no access to him. "Sentry!" Ares called. The soldier opened the door and stepped in, saluting. "Summon Doctor Savary," Ares instructed, and immediately the soldier was gone again.

Minutes later the doctor was escorted into Ares' receiving room. "Have a seat, Doctor," Ares instructed, and the physician dropped into the chair across the table from him. Savary was a busy man who worked long hours attending patients and researching cures, and had little patience for conferences. Only his respect for Ares modified his obvious impatience.

"Doctor," Ares began, tapping his fingers on the table, "I wish you to go find something wrong with Twomey."

"Surchatain?" Doctor Savary lifted his brows in question.

"I want him declared to be ill with—something, anything—so that he is not able to leave his room or receive visitors. I wish him confined to quarters without raising suspicions as to why."

"So he can't perform tonight?" the doctor asked hopefully.

"That is correct," Ares confirmed.

Savary stood. "I'm sure I can find something. He's not in the best of health, anyway."

Ares called the sentry back in to instruct him, "Escort the doctor down to examine Twomey. Doctor Savary is the *only* one who is allowed to see him, and no communications are to be passed to or from the jester without coming to my hands first." This the sentry acknowledged before departing with the doctor.

When they had left, Ares sat back in his chair with only

partial relief. There was something more . . . something that he was missing. . . .

So he summoned Commander Thom and Counselor Vogelsong. After a moment's reflection, he also summoned Nicole. He had gotten himself into grave trouble attempting to shield her from unpleasantness before. Now, he would not repeat that mistake.

They all arrived at almost the same moment. Curtsying to Ares, Nicole said, "My lord, Sophie will be requiring an explanation as to why she has been deprived of her pupil."

Ares smiled thinly. "I will give you an explanation, Lady, but as to whether you should pass it on to her, you decide. Sit, all of you, please."

As Vogelsong, Thom and Nicole took seats opposite the table from him, Ares leaned back in his chair and took a breath. Then he began telling them everything that he knew: first, he had Vogelsong repeat to the others his conversation with Fanchon's messenger. Then Ares related to them Twomey's accusation against Nicole this morning, and the implied identification of Twomey with the fugitive Symon.

He explained to them how he had asked the doctor to order Twomey confined to quarters for safekeeping, and he finished by saying, "Since it is evident that Fanchon is personally supporting the slave trade, I see no way to sever that connection but by going to war against him. I would do anything else first, but I cannot see what that would be. Hence, I ask you all for your counsel: Should we make war on Fanchon to end the slave trade?"

Ares looked at them one at a time. To his great surprise, Thom appeared reluctant. "Surchatain. . . . We don't know anything about Fanchon's numbers, yet, our province is so large, and our numbers comparatively few, for the area involved. . . . We are stretched thin just defending our borders and fending off the slave traders. However, if you believe that this is the only way to rid ourselves of them, then I am with you. It is true that we have tried everything else—we have tried trade inducements, and bounties, and raids against the camps. But as long as they have him to hide behind, they will continue to feed on us. If you judge that a preemptive strike against their master is called for, then so be it."

Ares acknowledged this, then looked at Vogelsong. "Counselor?"

Vogelsong hesitated, then said, "I must agree with the Commander. Fanchon has proved his deceit and brutality. We cannot continue to sit within our borders while his slavers slip across wherever they can to steal away our people. If he will not respond to reason or humanity, he must be addressed with force."

"Well said." Thom nodded.

"Quite," Ares agreed, then looked at his wife. "Surchataine?"

She looked uncomfortable. She was used to giving him private counsel, but seldom had been asked for her opinion in front of his administrators. "I know nothing of war," she murmured. "I cannot tell you whether you should attack Corona or not. But. . . ."

Because Ares waited silently for her to shape her halting thoughts into words, neither Thom nor Vogelsong dared interrupt. "It only seems that Twomey has been given us for a reason—"

"That is what I thought," Ares interrupted. "But I cannot see what that is. Can you tell me how to use him?"

"No," she said, downcast. "Renée had hoped to find something—"

"She just enjoys playing with him," Thom snorted. "Pathetic little man."

Since Nicole declined to say anything else, Ares said, "Well, for lack of a better alternative . . . war it is. We will begin strategy meetings in the morning," he directed Thom. Ares dismissed them with thanks, but Nicole left with a troubled face.

Evening fell over Nicole's Harbor before it reached northeast to Westford. On the coast, the storm had finally abated, but there was no point in going out to work in the darkness, so the men stayed put in the barracks.

After a meager dinner of mush and hard brown bread, they were then expected to retire quietly to their pallets in anticipation of a long work day tomorrow.

But they were bored and restless. The knucklebones winner wanted to play again; when he could find no takers, he began toying with the leper's brand he had won. It was an evil-looking thing, a thin iron rod twisted into a serpentine shape with a wooden handle. He sat by the fire to rest the brand in it, watching spellbound as it grew red hot.

Henry had no difficulty falling directly asleep. Like most experienced soldiers, he knew to take what rest he could, because he never knew when he might be required to go without it for days. In his sleep, however, he forgot his earlier determination to keep from betraying the presence of his treasures.

While he was unconscious, his hand crept up to clutch the locket through the blanket. He was dreaming pleasantly: There was Nicole in her floppy hat, laughing at him; there was Hoose crawling through the loose boards in the barracks with purloined apples; there was Sophie watching as he played chess. Then there was a searing blast of pain unlike anything else he had ever felt.

Screaming, he bolted upright, reflexively knocking away the unknown torment. Other shouts answered his, and the dark barracks was immediately in upheaval.

Henry knew nothing but the imperative of relieving the agony. Leaping up from his pallet, crashing through the door, he fell into the snowdrifts that lay up against the barracks and plunged his right hand into the deepest part of the drift.

Behind him, torches flared, shouts resounded, and someone went running past him down the path toward the officers' barracks. All the while, Henry was aware of nothing but the fiery throbbing of his whole arm.

Momentarily, someone came out to kneel beside him, and others followed to stand around them. "Come, son, let's have a look at ye." Henry blinked at the speaker—one of the older soldiers in the barracks. "Come, let's see," he urged again.

Henry resisted the man's efforts to pull out his arm, which was buried elbow-deep in the snow. It hurt too much. But then other torches appeared, and by their light Henry looked up into the grim face of Captain Derrick. "What's happened?"

The solder beside Henry replied, "I'm trying to see, Captain."

Derrick ordered, "Stand up, Henry."

He obeyed. Trembling in pain, he got to his feet. The other men crowded around as Derrick lifted Henry's right hand. There, on the back of his hand, were the fresh raw burns of the leper's brand. Henry stared at his hand as if it belonged to someone else, and the first thought that crossed his mind was, *I'll never be able to marry Sophie now.*

Derrick began calmly, eloquently cursing before he

stopped to ask, "Who did this?" As soon as he released Henry's hand, Henry dropped back to his knees to plunge his arm into the melting snow again.

Weeping, the knucklebones winner was pushed forward to face the Captain, and the brand, still red hot, gingerly handed over to him. Derrick stared at the man as he tried to cover the right side of his face. "Let me see your face," Derrick ordered.

The man covered it yet more firmly. When others pulled his hand away, they saw an oozing red burn scoring the right side of his face. Henry suddenly looked up at him. *Like Ares, but not like Ares,* the thought streaked across his brain. Preoccupied with his own pain, Henry lowered his head again.

"What the devil did you do?" Derrick shouted.

The knucklehead could only cry, so the elder soldier replied, "Far as we can tell, Captain, this idiot branded the boy in his sleep. Henry here came awake and knocked the brand back into his face."

Three or four witnesses standing around solemnly affirmed that this was so. In response, Derrick raged at the knucklehead until it became apparent that the man was absorbing none of it for his blubbering. The Captain broke off to eye him in disgust, then waved. "Turn him out! Get him out of my sight! He's never to show his face in my outpost again!"

While the knucklehead was led away, the Captain scowled at the instrument of torture. "And throw that into the Sea." It was gingerly taken away.

Composing himself, Derrick knelt beside Henry to lift his red, swollen hand from the snow and examine it again. It had no fat to prevent the hot iron from damaging the veins and sinews just under the skin. "Move your fingers,

Henry. Can you form a fist?" Henry obediently worked his hand, trembling.

The Captain blew out a breath of steam on the frosty night air. "Well, you'll be hurting for a while, but it's a clean burn and will heal. Get back to bed, Henry."

He got to his feet and turned back into the barracks. In the doorway, he stopped to raise his throbbing hand to his chest. The locket was still there, as was the letter, so he went on in.

Derrick briefly shook his head, then told a subordinate, "Send a messenger to the Surchatain in the morning to tell him what happened. Sad thing, that. The boy won't ever be able to walk among the living without being harassed for the rest of his life."

Barely an hour before dinner was to begin at Westford, Hauffe returned to tell Renée all that he had seen and heard that afternoon. So she was forced to radically alter her plans, sending Eleanor on a flurry of errands before her mistress was due to appear at table.

At the commencement of dinner that evening, as soon as Ares and Nicole were seated, the Surchatain raised his hand for silence at the table. "I am sorry to tell you all that Twomey has been taken ill, and will not be able to perform for us tonight. I now regret that I forced him to perform the other night when he was obviously beginning to falter."

Bonnie almost burst into tears. Sophie asked in grave concern, "What's wrong with him, Papa?"

"Well . . . Doctor?" Ares looked to the physician.

Doctor Savary cleared his throat. "The jester is suffering from the accumulated effects of black humors in his body, and requires rest and periodic purging to restore the correct balance of bodily humors." He used such obtuse jargon whenever he was required to make an authoritative pronouncement about something when there was nothing he could say.

The guests responded with a unified groan of disappointment. Renée studied Ares suspiciously, but he didn't even glance in her direction. So her eyes went to Nicole, who leaned toward Bonnie to hear her complaints. Just to be thorough, Renée checked Thom as well, but his face never told her anything. Had Ares discovered something about her plaything? She desperately hoped not.

Tossing her head, Renée said, "Poor fellow. I shall go to him straightway after dinner to offer consolation."

Now Ares looked at her. "You may give any message you wish to the sentry at his door, Chataine. But you may not see him."

Surprised, she asked, "Why not?"

Ares glanced at the doctor again, who sat at Renée's right. He paused for the wine steward to fill his cup, then cleared his throat. "Lady, your presence would *not* facilitate the balancing of any man's humors."

A titter went around the table, and Renée sighed in acknowledgment of this fault. Sophie said, "Then I'll go to him and try to cheer him up."

The table smiled on her, and Ares said, "We'll see." He waved for the serving to begin.

Following dinner, Ares explained to Sophie that since the doctor was not sure yet what all was wrong with Twomey, she could not see him. So she composed a note of encouragement which Ares did allow to be delivered to the sad little man.

Deep in the night, when almost everyone in the palace was asleep, Renée rose from her bed. Stepping over

Eleanor, asleep on her pallet on the floor, Renée lit a candle from the fireplace and retrieved her black cloak from the wardrobe. She quietly donned the cloak, placing in its large pockets a few items that Eleanor had purloined earlier in the day.

Then Renée slipped out of her chambers. The one candle made for a feeble light in the dense darkness of stone corridors, but she could walk them blind.

Silent as the dark stone walls encompassing her, she proceeded downstairs until she came to the lower corridor. One branch housed Twomey's cell; the other led to the corridor off the well room. Renée turned down the latter corridor and entered the well room.

She stood over the well head, setting the candle on the edge of the well to illumine the grating. Then she withdrew a wrench from the cloak pocket and applied it to one of the bolts that held the grating in place. But it was unyielding, having rusted in place after so many years.

So Renée wrapped the wrench head in a corner of the cloak and brought it down forcefully on the bolt, which readily broke away. There were three others that had to be removed in the same manner, then she was able to heft the grate from its narrow shelf (with some effort) and look down into the black abyss.

"That will do," she murmured. She then examined the grate to determine that the rust on it was merely superficial, and that it was still structurally sound. It was also quite heavy.

Setting the grate up against the well, she knelt before it and removed a coil of rope from her cloak, also procured on the sly by Eleanor. Renée tied one end of the rope securely to the grating, then let the rest—about twenty feet —hang free.

Grunting, she maneuvered the heavy grate back in place on the narrow shelf inside the well with the rope dangling down. After seeing that all was satisfactorily in place, she emerged from the well room with her candle, tossing the wrench into a store room.

Then, wiping rust from her hands, she turned down the corridor housing Twomey's cell. There was a sconced torch by the door, and a solitary guard leaning up against the wall beside it, sound asleep.

Renée approached the door, eyeing the sentry, who was a young member of the Gold Regiment. She tapped him once on the shoulder; when he did not wake, she poked him more forcefully.

He startled awake: "Wha—! Uh—Lady, the jester may have no visitors," he blurted, blinking at her.

She drew up close to him to whisper, "What is your name?"

"Efrain, Lady," he said, sweating.

"Well, Efrain," she said, toying with his collar, "I have come only to offer a few words of consolation to the poor dear man within. Should you allow me this, then some night when I am lonely, and in need of consolation myself, I will know who to summon to my chambers."

He opened the door for her and stood back out of the way. "Thank you," she breathed. Then she entered and closed the door behind her.

The flickering candlelight revealed the jester curled up on the pallet, cloak wrapped tightly around him. She stood over him to nudge him with her foot. "Twomey. Twomey!" she hissed.

He jerked upright, gazing around, then looked up to see her face illumined by candlelight. "Am I dreaming?" he murmured sleepily.

191

"No, dearest Twomey; it is I. Are you awake? Two-mey, darling, are you fully awake?" she asked, holding the candle down to his face.

He turned his face away from the flame, but struggled up to his feet. "Yes, beautiful Lady, I am awake."

"Good," she said, her voice harder, though just as quiet, "because I have something to tell you, Symon."

12

Twomey sank back against the wall, his next words forming an involuntary wail: "What? What did you call me?"

"Keep quiet, you despicable worm," Renée hissed, glancing at the closed door. "Yes, Symon, I know your whole sordid tale, and I would be pleased to hand you over to Fanchon to be drawn and quartered for another two thousand royals in my petty cash drawer."

Grabbing at his short, bristly hair, Twomey began running in desperate circles around the cell, stumbling over the pallet, knocking over the washstand. He was wild as a newly caught ferret. "He knows! Surchatain Ares knows, and he will give Twomey up!" he cried in a strangled voice.

"No, Symon, Ares does not know yet. I have not told him," Renée said imperiously.

He stopped in his tracks, gazing at her, then threw himself at her feet. "Anything. Twomey will do anything for the lady if she will not tell." He began kissing her feet in a manner that quickly transmuted from servile to lustful, so she kicked his face. He landed against the wall looking dazed and hopeful.

"You have the right idea, dearest Twomey. As long as you do exactly what I say, I will not tell Ares anything," she purred.

"Yes, yes," he gulped, nodding.

"The problem is, Ares has this irritating habit of finding out things that I would rather he not know. If he finds out who you really are, he will certainly spoil our fun in one way or another, the beast. So our first order of business is to get you out of the palace," she said.

"Yes!" Twomey cried, and she had to hush him again.

"This is what you must do," she whispered. "Tomorrow morning at exactly ten of the bells, ask to be taken to the latrine. I will have someone around the corner here, waiting to distract the guard. When he lets go of you, you must run immediately to the well room. I have unbolted the grating over the well and fastened a rope to it. Lift the grating, tie the rope around you, and lower yourself into the well. You wait there until I can come retrieve you. Are you following me, darling?"

"Yes, Lady," he said reverentially.

"Listen, Twomey: the grate is heavy, but you need only lift its edge to give you enough room to drop down in the well. Then the grate will fall back in place over you. Even if someone looks in the well room for you, they will never see the tiny bit of rope on the grating, or you in the well."

"Wonderful, beautiful Chataine," he murmured in ecstasy.

He tried to take her hand to kiss it, but she pulled away. "Another thing, dearest: Don't ever touch me again. Tomorrow at ten," she said, then turned back to open the door. The sentry glanced around nervously when she emerged, but relaxed upon receiving her lingering kiss on his lips. "Thank you, dear Efrain."

"Anything, Lady," he said with a grin. With that, Renée betook herself in satisfaction up to her chambers and undressed herself for bed.

In the dead hour before dawn, Ares lay writhing and sweating on his bed, for in his mind, he is riding out to battle. As every time previously, he is wearing only his dress blacks when he comes upon the white knight, whose polished armor gleams in the sunlight. The knight's crown is prominent; his double-edged sword formidable. "Parler, parler," Ares muttered in his sleep, but Nicole was too deeply asleep to hear him.

As Ares rides forward, his challenger strides eagerly to meet him on foot. The knight wants this battle badly, so he calls out a ringing challenge. The words? Ares is never sure of the words, except that they are an invitation to die.

The mocking, disdainful challenge stirs his anger, so Ares dismounts, putting his hand to the hilt of the sword. But for some reason he pauses—or is held back. There is something he must do; he feels it. An eternity seems to pass while the knight waits for him to make his move the knight must wait for Ares to strike first, so Ares struggles with something he knows he should do. And that is to . . .

"*Parler!*" Ares shouts in his dream. "*I demand à parler!*"

The knight seems to waver in disappointment; he does not wish to parler, so he does not respond. But as Ares comes forward, for the first time he sees the crest on the knight's shield. It depicts a gryphon.

The mythical monster appears to come to life, turning its bloody beak toward Ares and stretching lethal claws toward his throat. Ares springs back and draws his sword, but he does not attack the beast emerging from the shield.

Aiming instead for the knight's neck, Ares lops off his head.

But another springs up in its place, and while Ares watches in amazement, the new knight rams his sword into Ares' unprotected chest. He falls to the ground, feeling the hard earth become a tomb beneath him. All the land around him turns into a cemetery, and as he lies dying, his enemy leans over him to utter, *"The righteous shall die by his faith."*

Are bolted up in bed, breathing hard. The black room reeled as if on its own path through the heavens. "I know what it means now," he gasped, heart pounding. "I know what to do!" Turning back down to his wife, he gripped her head and kissed it. "Oh, my dove, you were right!"

"Um hmm. Later, my lord," she mumbled, and rolled over.

Laughing, Ares scrambled off the bed and ran out to the receiving room in his woolen underwear. He opened the door to the sentry outside, who jumped upon seeing him. "Summon Counselor Vogelsong and Commander Thom to me at once. And Father Birondo!"

"Surchatain!" He saluted.

Ares shut the door and hastened back to the bedchamber to grab his dress blacks, socks, and boots, which he carried out to the receiving room. While he yanked on his clothes, he paused periodically to laugh and mutter to himself. "It was the timing. I merely had to wait for the events themselves to reveal the meaning of the dream!"

Thom appeared almost immediately, obviously newly wakened but alert. Father Birondo showed up shortly thereafter. "I know now," Ares told them. "Wait." He was brimming with the news, but would not begin until everyone was present. Except Nicole—she needed her rest. He would tell her later.

It took a few minutes longer for the Counselor to arrive. While waiting for him, Ares paced the room in excitement and Thom put a few more logs on the low-burning fire to brighten and warm the room. Father Birondo made heroic efforts to stay awake until the Counselor was shown in, disheveled and weaving.

With his top administrators gathered in attendance, Ares said, "I now know what the dream means."

Two of the three glanced at each other. "What dream, Surchatain?" Vogelsong asked, but the priest straightened, now alert.

"God has been warning me that Fanchon wants to lure me into war. He is ready for war, whereas I am not. He expects to despoil and impoverish us to enrich himself and his friends in the slave trade. I might kill him, but another just like him would spring up to take his place. In attempting to do what is right, I would bring ruin on myself and my province. So God has sent us a better way." Here Ares threw back his head and laughed again.

"How so, Surchatain?" Thom asked carefully. The Surchatain's behavior was almost unprecedented.

Ares looked at him. "Which slave traders do you most want in your hands right now?"

"Oh, well. Dorn. Saracini. Urias. Ticzon. Ransweiler," Thom listed off.

"Morguloff," Vogelsong added, intrigued.

"What would you give to have Dorn, Saracini, Urias, Ticzon, Ransweiler, and Morguloff in your grip? Two thousand royals?" Ares asked.

"If I had it," Thom slowly replied.

"Twomey," Vogelsong breathed.

"Twomey!" Ares laughed. Then he turned deadly serious. "Counselor, I want you to write out this message immediately and take it to the Dancing Bear to give to Fanchon's messenger: I have Symon, and I will deliver him alive into his hands if he will deliver to me Dorn, Saracini, Urias, Ticzon, Ransweiler, and Morguloff. I will accept neither gold nor terms other than these. If Fanchon is not interested in the trade, I will put Symon on a ship and send him across the Sea. Do you have it?"

"Yes, Surchatain!" Vogelsong replied in delight.

Ares looked at Thom, who admitted, "Clever, Surchatain."

"It was not my idea," he sighed, shaking his head. "Thank you, Father Birondo. You told me exactly what I needed to hear."

"For that, I am deeply gratified." The priest bowed while the other two studied him.

Then Ares looked at the young Counselor. "Why are you still here?" Whereupon Vogelsong jumped to his feet and rushed out of the room.

Ares looked back at Thom, who saluted, saying, "I will go see that the jester is secure. It would not do to have him escape at this point."

"Good," Ares muttered. "You may go back to bed, Father," he added, suddenly drained. But with sunrise breaking over the horizon, there was no point in going back to bed himself. So when his priest and Commander had left, he sent down to the kitchen for some breakfast.

Vogelsong returned within two hours to report that Fanchon's messenger had so readily accepted the urgency of delivering the sealed letter that he departed early, taking advantage of the unseasonably mild weather. However, he left his lady friend asleep in bed, so that the Counselor was compelled to pay not only her wages, but the messenger's outstanding bill for room and board. This Ares approved after the fact.

When he realized that Nicole was awake, he went in to her while she was getting dressed to tell her of the plan that had been revealed to him by his dream.

As sure as he was that the revelation was from God, he was therefore surprised by her subdued reaction to it. She said nothing as she sat at her mirrorless dresser to absently pick up a hairbrush. "Would you rather we went to war?" he asked, almost offended.

"No, of course not," she said, then paused in brushing out her rich chestnut tresses.

"Well?"

"Well, I care nothing for Twomey, of course, only . . . you will be handing him over to unspeakable torture. That is why Fanchon wants him alive. What Twomey has done is evil—I certainly would not defend him—only, to give anyone up, knowing what will be done to him. . . ."

"I will think on that," he quietly agreed.

Shortly after nine of the bells that morning, Ares received a messenger from Nicole's Harbor. The soldier entered his receiving room, saluting. Given permission to speak, he told Ares, "Surchatain, I have a report from Captain Derrick. Last night there was an altercation in the barracks. One of the men—not a soldier, it turns out, but a laborer—had come by a leper's branding iron. For some reason, he waited until Henry was asleep, then . . . branded his hand with it. Captain Derrick wanted you to know that the young man now carries a leper's brand on his hand."

Ares absorbed this blow silently. The mark was not only permanently disfiguring, it would make Henry unwelcome in any social setting or court—anyplace where he might be required to show his hands. It would disqualify him from setting foot in shops, inns, markets, fairs, churches, homes—even Westford, but by special provision from Ares himself. Henry's life and future had been radically altered by an unfathomable act carried out in an instant.

"So?" Ares asked.

The soldier stammered, "Well, Captain Derrick wanted to know—what you wanted to do about him—"

"The Captain knows that Henry does not have leprosy. He is to be dispatched to Odea as I originally directed, but Captain Derrick may wish to send a letter with him stating the circumstances of the leper's brand," Ares said.

"Yes, Surchatain." The soldier saluted and began to turn out.

"I haven't dismissed you," Ares said.

He made a quick about-face, paling. "Surchatain."

"I have a message for you to give to Henry," Ares said.

"Yes, Surchatain."

"Tell Henry I said, 'Now you carry proof that you are my son.'"

The soldier gazed at the man who had borne a disfigured face since childhood. "Yes, Surchatain."

"You are dismissed."

After the man had left, Ares sat staring at the closed door. A look of mingled sadness and purpose crossed his face, and he murmured, "Now we will see what you are made of, Henry."

Then he momentarily covered his eyes in dismay—but there was no putting off what must come next. He had granted Henry permission to court Sophie when he returned to Westford. Given these new circumstances, Sophie had to be allowed to withdraw that, should she choose.

So he reluctantly summoned her from her lessons. But he took care to tell the sentry, "Only Sophie is to come, not Bonnie, but I do not know what they are wearing today."

"That information is not required, Surchatain," the sentry replied, saluting, and Ares, for once, was pleased. This sentry just happened to be observant enough to know that Bonnie had been working the nursery these past few days, wearing requisite nursery-attendant clothing.

When the young soldier came and pulled Sophie alone out of the library, Bonnie was incensed—and curious. So, disregarding the tutor's admonitions, she left the library after them, watching from a distance as Sophie was escorted to their father's receiving room. Feeling excluded and a little fearful, Bonnie hung in the corridor, watching for her to come out.

When Sophie entered, she curtsied. "Good morning, Papa." But upon seeing his face, she asked, "What is wrong?"

He leaned forward in his chair to clasp his hands on the table in front of him—an action that opened floodgates of anxiety within her. "Sophie, I received a message from Nicole's Harbor this morning—"

"Is he dead?" she cried, rushing the table. "Papa, is Henry dead? Is he dead?" she screamed. She pounded her fists on the table, screaming the question over and over.

Ares jumped up from his chair to round the table and grab her little hands. "No! Sophie, he is not dead. Sophie! Calm down and listen. Listen to me."

She fell silent, trembling, while he held her hands and spoke in a low voice. "He—was injured last night. For some reason, he was branded with a leper's mark last night. He now carries a leper's brand on his hand, though he is not sick. But . . . I wanted you to know, so that you could withdraw your permission for him to court you, if you wish. You need not be bound by that now."

With eyes rendered unseeing from shock, she gazed at his black jacket. She remembered when she was little, how she would fall asleep in his lap, resting her face on that jacket while he was working at his table or presiding at council meetings. (Yes, the Surchatain had allowed his young daughter to quietly play at his feet or sit on his lap during meetings.)

Then he would waken her when he had to get up, and she would be left with the indention of the brocade on her cheek. She used to run to the mirror to study it, and wonder what it would be like to be marked for the rest of her life. No parties. No fancy dinners. No courtly honor. Only the knowledge that a mark on her skin did not define who she was inside.

He waited now while she stared blankly into space, then he gently began, "Sophie—" She looked up at the scarred face that she loved, then pulled away from him with a groaning sob and ran out of the room.

Bonnie watched her sister flee in tears down the stairway, and followed her. Darting through the crowded foyer, Sophie ran blindly from one lower corridor to another, simply seeking somewhere to grieve. But there seemed to be servants everywhere who stared at her when she passed.

Finally, she came to a place where there weren't so many people. She stopped in a corridor near the well room and leaned against the wall to cry.

The bell tolled ten. Twomey made a request of his jailer, who began to escort him down the corridor toward the latrine outside. At the head of the corridor, they heard a sudden feminine cry: "Oh!"

Both Twomey and the guard stopped in their tracks to see Glinda limping around the corner. She looked up pleadingly. "Oh, I fell from the step and hurt my ankle. Can you see if it's broken?" And she lifted her skirts to reveal a tantalizingly bare ankle.

While the guard gaped at her ankle, Twomey made a sudden break for it, dashing down one corridor and up another. "Stop!" the distracted guard shouted, but Twomey had disappeared.

Mistakenly thinking he had run outside, the guard ran out to the rear quadrangle, where uninterrupted work was in progress. He scanned the courtyard in mounting panic. The laundresses working at the large wash basin here—Purdy spreading hay for his sheep there—the farrier leading out the horse to be shod over there—deliverymen waiting at the back gate and soldiers carrying gear out to the armory—he saw all this, but not his prisoner.

At this moment Twomey was approaching the well room corridor at a frantic run, almost tasting freedom. But suddenly there loomed in his path Sophie, of all people.

She turned toward him, startled by his sudden appearance. He drew up in a dead halt to stare at her. Brushing tears from her eyes, she attempted to smile. "Hello, Twomey. Are you feeling better?"

With a guttural cry, he rushed her, knocking her to the stone floor and stumbling over her on his way to the well room.

13

Bonnie arrived at the head of the corridor in time to see the jester stop, stare at her sister, then knock her down and run over her.

The shock of seeing such a thing happen paralyzed her until she looked at Sophie crumpled on the floor, crying. Then Bonnie was filled with a righteous rage that propelled her down the corridor toward them.

Not seeing her, Twomey darted into the old abandoned well room. With a scream, Bonnie followed him. "Beast! You beast! How dare you!" She hardly perceived his standing over the well with the grating in his hands before she was upon him, beating, scratching and kicking.

The grate bounced off the well head and dropped clattering to the stone floor, leaving the mouth of the well standing open. Bonnie's surprise attack was momentarily effective, but Twomey, however small, was still a man fighting for his life.

He intercepted one small fist and struck her in the face once or twice to forestall further scratching. Then he gripped her by the neck and hauled her, twisting and struggling, up onto the edge of the well head.

At that moment Sophie rushed to the door. Upon seeing her sister being hoisted over the open well in the dark room, Sophie began screaming so as to rouse the dead. She stepped back into the corridor to scream there, where her voice would carry farther.

Bonnie, meanwhile, had no intention of being thrown down the nasty old well. She twined her feet around Twomey's legs and scratched his face viciously with her one free hand. Closing his eyes against the onslaught, he was rendered momentarily immobile. But she was weakening, as he was squeezing her neck very hard.

The fight was soon interrupted by a half-dozen servants and soldiers rushing past Sophie into the well room with lights. While one wrenched Bonnie from Twomey's grip, two more lifted him by his arms off the floor. "Goin' to drop the Chataine, little funny man?" one whispered. "Let's see how you do down there."

"Yeah!" "Dunk him!" came the cries. Bonnie, set down on her feet, rushed to Sophie, who ran forward to embrace her. Pushed into a corner of the room by the sheer number of people squeezing inside, they held each other tightly, crying as they watched the mob take charge of Twomey.

The guard who had been stationed at Twomey's cell pushed past onlookers at the door, shouting, "Stop! Don't! Stop it!" But his expostulations were drowned out by their laughter and jeers, for Twomey, now a rag doll, was being thrown from one burly set of arms to another over the well, each time a little closer to the yawning black hole. Everyone who had resented his favored status wanted a hand in this new game.

Two men had Twomey hoisted head down over the mouth of the well when there was a sudden shrill whistle. All motion stopped and laughter subsided; bodies at the door parted like wheat for Thom to pass through, with Ares behind him.

By the light of three or four torches, they regarded with steely eyes the now-docile mob. Then the Surchatain said quietly, "Put him down. I need him alive." This order was complied with instantly. Twomey, crying, collapsed in a boneless heap on the floor.

Ares glanced at the crowd in the room. "Does no one have any work to do?" They bowed to him and quietly filed out—all except the guard, who stood dejectedly with a torch beside Twomey's formless lump at the well. Thom, appropriating another torch, walked over to pick up the grating with one hand and examine it.

When enough people had cleared out, Ares saw his daughters huddled in the corner. His lips parted in surprise, then he extended his arms, and they rushed to wrap themselves up in him, crying afresh.

At that time Nicole suddenly appeared at the door, winded and flushed, and Bonnie reached out to her with one hand while still clinging to her father. "Bonnie! Sophie! Whatever has happened?" Nicole gasped.

Sophie lifted her teary face, scratched and slightly bruised from landing hard on the stone floor. She began, "Um, Papa told me about Henry [Nicole glanced in alarm at Ares, who could only shake his head] so I ran down here crying, and I saw Twomey rushing up, and he just pushed me down and ran past me! And then Bonnie—"

But Bonnie was desirous of telling this part herself. "I saw him push her down! And it made me so mad that I ran in here after him! But then he started trying to throw me down the well!"

Nicole sank back weakly against the wall, seeing the red finger marks on Bonnie's neck that were already starting to bruise. Ares turned his scar to the guard, Jared, who shook under his hard stare. "Yes?" Ares uttered, waiting.

The young man raised his hands. "Surchatain, he—asked to be taken to the latrine. I was taking him, but one of the maids fell and broke her ankle, and—he lit off! He disappeared! I couldn't see where he'd gone!"

"It was planned in advance," Thom said, hefting the grate. Ares gently untangled himself from his daughters, who then rushed to their mother. He went over to scrutinize the grate that Thom held up. "The bolts were broken off," Thom pointed out. There was no need to explain the purpose of the rope tied to the grate.

Lowering the grate, Ares murmured, "I have a dangerous adversary under my roof. Someone wishes to have my pawn for his own use."

They both looked at Twomey on the floor. "We can interrogate him to find out who it is," Thom suggested.

Ares agreed. "Take him down to the dungeon and have at it. Just don't kill him."

Thom took one step toward Twomey and he began wailing, "The Lady Renée! She promised to get me out! She did all this to help me!"

Ares and Thom looked reflexively toward Nicole. "Why would she do this?" Ares said, hoisting the grate.

Nicole shook her head numbly. "I cannot imagine. Only . . . I am sure that her intent was not to help him."

Bonnie turned on her mother to angrily demand, "*Aunt Renée* took the grating off the well so that I might fall down in it?"

Open-mouthed, Nicole looked at her daughter, then her husband. "I do not know. Why is everyone requiring explanations from me for what Renée does?"

"You are quite right, Lady. I will seek that information from the source," Ares said. He looked past her to gesture to a sentry outside, who entered, saluting. "Summon the Chataine Renée." When he had moved off and the next had taken his place, Ares told him, "Get Coyle or Godbold in here to reset this grating in concretus. It will not be removed again."

"Surchatain!" He saluted before sprinting away.

Curious, Thom leaned over the well and deliberately dropped his torch down it. They watched it grow dimmer until it disappeared with a faint thud. "Ironic that the well went dry with all the underground streams around this place," he muttered. "Just wondering why."

Ares held another torch down to study the outside of the well head. "I wonder if it was ever a well." Thom looked at him, brow raised, and Ares pointed at the rim of the well head. "Do you see any rope grooves?"

Thom studied it. "No."

The girls promptly lost their fear to come over and look. Even Nicole edged closer as they all began studying the old well head. "Look at the carvings all around it," Nicole said.

Ares held the torch lower to get a good look at the figures carved into the stone sides of the well. They were all naked people in postures of agony, with upraised faces that were eternally, silently crying or screaming. "Those are awful!" Bonnie said indignantly.

Sophie clutched her father's hand. "Papa, what do they mean?"

"I'm . . . not sure," he said, though he was beginning to develop an idea.

At that time, Renée was escorted into the well room. "Ares, really, this is so irritating. What is it now?" she asked coolly. She was dressed in silken finery, as usual, with mounds of petticoats that spread her skirts so far out, she had to hold them in to keep them from brushing against dirty stone in the narrow lower corridors.

Bonnie confronted Renée, hands on her hips. "Do you know that Twomey almost threw me down that old well?"

"How inconvenient," Renée said, frowning.

"Chataine, I need to know why you were helping Twomey escape," Ares said. His voice was level, not threatening in the slightest—in short, the tone most likely to elicit something approximating the truth from her.

"Helping him escape? I was doing no such thing," she scoffed, with a disparaging glance at the jester.

"Oh, but she did!" Twomey cried. "She came to me last night late, and told me to ask to go to the latrine at ten of the bells, and she would distract the guard, and that I must run to the well room, and she would hide me in it until she could get me out of the palace!"

Everyone looked at Renée. Rolling her eyes, she said, "Ares, you are so helpless, it's infuriating. I don't see how Nicole puts up with you. I'd certainly cheat on you. Come with me."

Despite the fact that it sounded much like a command, he followed when she turned out of the well room. As a matter of fact, everyone but Twomey and his guard Jared— Ares, Nicole, Thom, Bonnie, Sophie and several sentries— trailed Renée as she went down that corridor and up another, finally coming to a long, narrow side room that faced the back quadrangle.

Positioning herself carefully so as not to be seen from outside, she peered out a narrow arched window. "Do you see the man with the bone cart by the gate?" she asked Ares. Once large animal bones were scraped of meat and emptied of marrow for kitchen use, they were sold to the bone man to be ground into feed meal for poultry and swine.

Ares craned his neck to get a view of the person in question. The others behind him could not hope to crowd close enough to see, so listened as he said, "Yes."

"He is not here for the bones. He was hired at the inn last night to steal Twomey this morning and sell him to Fanchon for two thousand royals. My darling Hauffe overheard the whole plot yesterday. I don't know where *your* men were at the time, but they should have been in the next booth, listening as well," Renée lectured.

Ares glanced back at Thom, who countered, "If your man Hauffe hadn't pumped the messenger for the story, he wouldn't have been spreading it all over the inn."

Renée tossed her golden ponytail impatiently at him. "If my darling Hauffe had not drawn the story from him in the first place, you never would have known about it. *I* can't help that your follow-through was less than satis-factory."

Thom pursed his bristly lips, at a loss for a rejoinder. But he jerked his head at a sentry. "Go hold the bone man for questioning." (Later, he denied any knowledge of or involvement in any plot to steal Twomey. However, he was not the regular bone man, but a stranger, and had ten gold royals in his pocket—an astounding sum for a bone man. Before he could be questioned further, he somehow escaped.)

Ares turned back to Renée. "Then why did you put Twomey in the well room?"

She studied him. "You don't know what it's for, do you?"

"What? What is what for?" he said.

"Must I explain *everything* to *everyone*?" she fumed in superior tones, flouncing back up the corridor. They all followed her back to the well room like a group of school children. From his seat on the floor, Twomey looked up in the vague hope that she would receive some measure of punishment to alleviate the suffering coming to him.

"Pay attention, please," Renée said when they had all gathered in the small, dark room. "Torch, please." She gestured at the sentry to hold it over the well, which he did.

Then Renée said, "This is not a water well. It was never meant for drawing water. My horrid but imaginative grandfather Talus had it dug for different purposes, as you should have been able to guess from the charming carvings along the sides. This was the dangling well." She looked at them meaningfully, and Ares lifted his chin in recognition.

"What do you mean, Aunt Renée?" Bonnie asked in a small voice.

Renée looked at her fondly, then waved to the sentry again. "Hold up the grate, darling." With the torch in one hand, he used the other to hoist the grate to an upright position on the edge of the well head. "Do you see the marks on this old iron?" She pointed.

"Rope grooves," Thom muttered.

"How bright of you, Commander," she said, her voice tinged with sarcasm. Then she addressed Bonnie again: "When horrid old Talus wanted to punish someone in a special way, he would have one end of a rope tied to the grating here and one end tied around the person who had been bad. Then he would dangle them down in the well and bolt the grate in place . . . and leave them there. I heard that some would hang on for days, even weeks," she said in dry amusement.

"Then, you . . ." Ares began, glancing at Twomey.

Renée turned to eye the little man in contempt. "My aim was to use the well in the manner for which it was intended. Once he had inserted himself into it, why in the world should I get him out again?"

Ignoring Twomey's sudden wail, she bent to her protégé. "It displeases me that you were inconvenienced by this nasty little man trying to throw you in, as if he *could*," she snorted. "And I am sure that you made him very sorry for trying."

She paused to deliver a smirking glance at Twomey's face, covered with bleeding scratches. "You did well, darling. Certainly better than some of the men here," Renée added caustically.

"Thank you, Aunt Renée," Bonnie said, beaming. Then she glanced at her sister. "Sophie did well, too."

"That's right," Sophie said quickly. "I stood right here and screamed so that everyone came running."

"You both make me proud of my sex," Renée said regally, and they squeezed each other's hands in congratulation, giggling. Ares and Nicole looked at one another while Thom, thoroughly beat, stood with drooping head.

Renée then turned to needle Ares a little more. "How could you have served under my grandfather and not known what the dangling well was for?"

"I was only a lieutenant, usually stationed away from the palace," he said defensively, then mused, "I do remember hearing about people being 'put in the well,' but never connected it with this, until now. Your father, Cedric, did not use this," he added almost as praise.

"No, he just chopped their heads off and was done with it," Renée said in a hard voice. "My father was too pragmatic to use the well—it brought work to a standstill while all the servants listened to someone cry for days on end. They said you could hear their cries echo throughout the palace, and that even after someone had let go and died, or died and let go, you could still hear their cries at night."

"How d-did you know ab-bout it, Aunt Renée?" Sophie asked through chattering teeth.

"The old servants remember, dearest," she whispered. "They remember, and they talk."

Godbold the engineer came hesitantly to the well room door. "You summoned me, Surchatain?"

"Yes," Ares sighed. Jerking his head toward the well, he said, "I want this well head taken out and destroyed, and a solid plate of iron set in concretus over this hole. But first . . . have Father Birondo come say a prayer of absolution and peace over it. And as for the jester—" He suddenly looked at Thom and waved. "You know what to do with him."

Thom turned vehemently to the sentry. "I want him in the lower dungeon with four guards at the door. No one other than the Surchatain or myself is to speak to him. And if this woman"—he pointed to Renée—"comes within a mile of him, then—then—"

"Stop stuttering, darling, it's so unattractive. I certainly won't set foot anywhere near that stinking hole," Renée sniffed. The guard saluted to the Commander and Surchatain before hauling out the unfortunate Twomey.

As Renée was moving toward the door, Ares raised a hand. "Chataine, the next time you have information of such—importance, would you consider simply telling me?"

She looked appalled. "Why, Ares, what sport is there in that? I would have told you where he was, eventually." She added to Nicole, "I simply don't know how you put up with him. You must be a saint." Without waiting to be dismissed, she walked out, skirts rustling around her.

With the spell of Renée's presence lifted, Ares directed his family out of the well room so that Godbold would have room to work. They made their way up toward brighter rooms, and Nicole paused by the kitchen. "Bonnie, see what Veola has for you to eat, then . . . your babies will want to see you."

Nicole deliberately chose not to make a further issue of what might have happened in the well room. Her daughters must be strong to survive in the world with virtue and honor intact. Since they had evidenced some strength in this conflict, Nicole would not nullify that with tearful coddling. At any rate, it would not serve as an excuse for Bonnie to get out of nursery duty.

Sophie squeezed her sister's hand. "I'll go with you, Bonnie."

"Oh, that would be fun! You'll adore little Tor," Bonnie promised.

While they were heading toward the kitchen, Sophie paused. Turning back to her father, she said, "I've decided what to do about Henry, Papa."

"Yes?" he said.

Only minutes later, a messenger arrived at Nicole's Harbor from Westford. He gave the Surchatain's reply to Captain Derrick, then went to seek out Henry. Upon inquiring, the messenger was directed to a group of eight soldiers on the docks who were repairing rigging and sails. They were actually huddled just beneath the docks, seeking shelter from the cold, blustery wind that whipped around them while they tried to work.

Approaching, the messenger spotted Henry sitting and sewing a patch on one edge of a canvas sail. Gripping a needle and thread with cold fingers was hard enough, but Henry was also hampered in using his left hand, because his right was swathed in dirty bandages.

"Henry," the messenger said, and he looked up. "I delivered Captain Derrick's message to the Surchatain about what happened to you, and the Surchatain said you're to be sent to Odea as planned." Henry nodded and bent over the stitching again. "He also had a message for you."

"What?" Henry looked up again.

"I said, the Surchatain had a message for you. He said, 'Tell Henry I said, Now you carry proof that you are my son.'" The messenger paused to make sure Henry heard him, but when he did not respond, he walked off.

Henry stared off into the middle distance for a moment, then his eyes widened and he leaped straight up from a sit, pumping his fists high in the air. "Yes! Yes! Hahaha!"

The other soldiers momentarily regarded him as a lunatic before returning to their work. But Henry continued to jump up and down, inadvertently destroying the newly patched sail beneath his booted feet while he laughed and pounded the air with his fists until the bandage tore away from the wound. Then he stopped to examine the fresh bleeding. "Ow."

14

Over the next few weeks, life slowed to the most basic level of subsistence in Westford as winter dug in for a last, prolonged thrashing. Ares could only hope that Fanchon's messenger made it back to Corona safely, as there was no knowing one way or another. Giles, also, would have been unable to return from Crescent Hollow had he desired, but the consensus at Westford was that he was probably having too much fun planning the conversion of the money-sucking palace into a profit-making inn.

Even commerce between Westfordian merchants and the palace slowed as the stakes that marked the roads got buried or blown down, and merchants whose suppliers had been thwarted by the weather had nothing to deliver to the palace in return. The kitchen staff were unable to get to market for days at a stretch, and even Lord Preus sent an abject apology to Renée that he had been unable to acquire the fabrics needed to provide her with samples of new spring gowns when promised—the first such appointment he had missed in many years.

Georges, however, was unflappable. His astounding 27 years' experience in setting food in front of royalty every single night served him exceedingly well. At such times that lesser men were driven to offering salted meat and brown bread to their masters, Georges' true genius and foresight shone with dinners of fresh venison, larded grouse, pickled pigs' feet, and many other such wonderful dishes, all arranged to perfection on polished pewter platters. On certain nights Ares was compelled to bring Georges to the hall to be applauded by the dinner guests. And every waking moment he wore around his neck a large gold medallion Ares had cast in commemoration of his twenty-fifth year of service.

Sophie sent a message to Henry at that time, but the barge was not running, so her letter, along with several others, had to be carried on horseback. But when the horse stumbled off the snow-blanketed road and fell atop the rider, his pouch was torn open and letters scattered. He gathered the letters back up as best he could and remounted with a broken leg to eventually make his delivery, but Sophie's letter was left buried under muddy snow. She hardly gave a second thought to the fact that Henry did not reply to it.

Due to the harsh weather, some guests were unable to appear for dinner, but those absent were few. Dining at the palace was such a coveted honor that guests risked life and limb to attend. More frequently, however, they simply stayed on at the palace for days on end, and Ares did not object. These were loyal friends and supporters who had earned a measure of accommodation. A number of them also brought their children, who alleviated winter boredom for his own.

In compensation for Twomey's absence, as he still resided in the dungeon, heavily guarded, other entertainments were devised (by whom was a question of debate for a long time). One of the most popular was a game called "Rabbits in the Hole."

In this game, a group of chairs was set out on the floor, the number of which was one less than the number of people desiring to play. A moderator, chosen at random, stood with his back to the chairs while the participants (the "rabbits") circled the chairs.

Whenever the moderator called out, "Fox!" the rabbits were required to scurry to safety to their "holes" (the chairs) and the one rabbit left out in the open was caught by the fox. The number of chairs was accordingly reduced by one and the game repeated. The winner—the last person with a chair—was then allowed to choose the hat from any man's head and wear it for the rest of the evening.

This reward was as entertaining to the guests as the game itself, in that many men were vainly reluctant to show off their bald heads, and the sight of a man with two hats, or a woman with a man's hat atop her cap, never failed to amuse. Incidentally, neither Ares nor Thom—nor anyone in the military, for that matter—wore a hat indoors. But since they did not play this game, it made no difference to those who did.

Another popular entertainment was when one or another of the guests proposed to sing or dance or recite a piece for the pleasure of the others. If they were good, the audience determined their reward, and if they were awful, the audience also determined their punishment. Again, the determination of rewards and/or punishments was often more amusing than the piece itself. Ares and Thom never participated in these games, either, but everyone else did. Even Nicole could be persuaded to join Rabbits in the Hole, though she never won, even when others cheated in her favor.

The most ridiculous standoff ever occurred when, by conspiracy, Nicole and Evangeline were the last two rabbits standing. When Thom, his back to them, called, "Fox!" both women paused beside the lone chair, waiting for the other to sit and win. The other would not sit, so they both hovered over the chair while the audience groaned and laughed.

Finally, Ares got up and put a second chair beside the first so both could sit and allow the evening to move on. Both were also rewarded with men's hats.

On another evening, while a winter storm raged outside, the guests were comfortably chatting and laughing by warm candlelight over nesselrode pudding when Renée suddenly stood. In Giles' absence, Bonnie had entreated that Renée sit next to her. To accommodate her, Vogelsong graciously moved down one place to Giles' seat. Wagers were then placed as to the chances of Renée's hanging on to that seat after Giles' return. The interest in the wager and the possible outcomes thereof was compounded by the fact that Vogelsong made a much pleasanter dinner companion for Genevieve than her husband did.

At any rate, on this evening when Renée stood, all conversations ceased and all eyes turned to her, as she intended. She was glowing and beautiful, as always, in a fabulous low-cut gown (which some of the women were beginning to wear again, growing tired of Nicole's modesty).

Renée announced, "I desire to entertain this worthy audience tonight, but I require the assistance of a man." She looked down the table as if weighing selections, but Ares sank imperceptibly in his chair and Thom raised two fingers to cover his smiling lips. "May I?" she demanded sweetly.

"Yes!" "Of course!" Mostly male voices answered her, as those who did not know her well vainly believed themselves in the running to assist her. Ares did not speak, but Nicole glanced at him, smiling.

"Then will I have the assistance of the man I choose?" she asked. She stepped away from her chair to walk down the table as though about to tap someone at the lower end.

"Yes!" the uniformly male chorus responded.

"Very well." She turned on her heel to face the head of the table and said, "I require Ares to assist me in dancing the Wasserleben."

Laughing encouragement rose from the table while everyone pivoted in his chair to look at Ares. He eyed Renée a moment, then dropped his hand in resignation, pushed back his chair, and stood.

Sophie led the clapping and cheers while Bonnie watched with slight jealousy: she and Henry had danced the Wasserleben perfectly well, thank you, but their performance was about to be eclipsed by the two best dancers at Westford right now. Bonnie suddenly thought she might like to take dancing lessons again.

Reluctantly, Ares walked onto the floor as Renée gestured to the musicians. He bowed slightly to her; she curtsied and he took her hand. The musicians began to play, and the audience watched intently while two superb dancers performed the elegant piece.

Nicole followed them with her eyes in admiration—without question, they were splendid together. She began to feel rather small watching them, though neither envy nor jealousy appeared in her heart. She just felt . . . small.

Then the unthinkable happened. Toward the end of the dance, Ares stumbled over one of the more complicated steps. In so doing he almost brought Renée down, and she dropped clear to her knees. He was able to haul her up only far enough to get his foot caught in her skirts, whereupon a clear ripping sound was heard over the viola. Ares added an extra few steps to the Wasserleben in order to get off her dress and get her to her feet—and so the dance ended in a jumble.

A few of the more polite members of the audience, or those anxious not to offend either performer, attempted to applaud. However, Bonnie issued something between a snort and a chortle, and the table collapsed in laughter. Nicole only smiled, but Thom had to hold his head for laughing. The shrieks resounded off the stone as Renée turned furiously to Ares. "You did that on purpose!"

"Surely you jest. I am not Twomey," he said in composure, but then turned his eyes to her meaningfully. She regarded him suspiciously, with nothing else that could be said. Nor did she ever demand that he dance with her again. And when Bonnie sought punishment for the pair's performance, her mother quickly nixed it.

When Bonnie grew weary, as expected, of working in the nursery every single day, she was offered the same classes that the other girls attended. She did attend a gaming class once or twice, but refused to apply herself to learning the rules, so found it boring and stopped going. The first day that she rebelled at going to the nursery or to class, she was in for a surprise.

Sophie had gone to rope-knotting class. ("A rope-knotting class?" Bonnie had snorted. "Yes, we learn to tie knots like real sailors!" Sophie had explained, which sent Bonnie into such fits of laughter that Sophie marched off to class by herself.)

In Sophie's absence, Bonnie determined to investigate some of the goings-on in the lower corridors which she had overheard some of the maids snickering about. Opening the door to leave her quarters, she was momentarily startled by the presence of a sentry directly blocking the doorway, his back to her. She attempted to push past him, but he wouldn't budge. So she snapped, "What are you doing? Get out of the way!"

"Pardon, Chataine," he said, still facing away from her. "I have been commanded to guard the doorway, so that I will do."

She blinked at his broad, high back. "Are you an idiot?"

"No, Chataine; I am following orders."

"Oh! This is absurd." She attempted to push him out of the way again, but he was not moving an inch. Stamping in anger, she demanded, "Take me to Papa!"

"Yes, Chataine." She was gratified that he moved aside to escort her the short distance down the corridor to her father's receiving room. Her sentry then told the sentry at the door, "The Chataine requests an audience with the Surchatain."

Whereupon the sentry at the door replied, "The Surchatain is in conference and left orders not to be disturbed. However, he indicated that if there was a problem with the Chataine Bonnie [her ears pricked up in alarm] she may address that with the Surchataine, who is in her receiving room."

So the sentry took her the few steps to Nicole's receiving room door, where (according to form) admittance was again requested. This time it was granted, so Bonnie was shown in to her mother, who put down a book upon her entrance. "Hello, dear," Nicole said, looking not surprised.

"Mama, that horrid guard wouldn't let me out of my

room!" Bonnie vented, pointing outside to where the villain stood.

"I see. So you did not go to the nursery today?" Nicole asked.

"I needed a day off," Bonnie sighed as if exhausted.

"Nor to a class with the other girls?" Nicole continued.

"They bore me," Bonnie sniffed.

"I'm so sorry," Nicole said. Picking up her book again, she called, "Guard!" He entered with a bow. "The Chataine wishes to return to her room."

"No, I don't!" Bonnie said, glancing at the sentry in alarm. "I want to go—someplace else."

"I'm sorry," Nicole repeated without a shred of sympathy, "but your father has directed that if you do not go to the nursery, and you do not go to class, then you stay in your quarters. Escort her out," Nicole ordered, returning to her book.

"No, wait!" Bonnie said desperately. The guard paused and Nicole looked up. "Mama, that's just—mean! Sophie doesn't have a guard standing over her all the time! I can't —" And she burst into a flood of tears.

Raising the book once more, Nicole told the guard, "You have permission to carry her back to her room if she will not walk." To Bonnie, Nicole said, "You are dismissed." Then she turned a page and fixed her eyes on it.

"Don't touch me!" Bonnie shouted as the guard loomed over her. Teary and furious, she stomped out as hard as she could in soft leather shoes. As there were people in the corridor, she raised her face and walked decorously to her chambers, taking care to slam the door in the guard's face once she was within.

But the next day, she chose to go to class with Sophie.

And on succeeding days, she worked in the nursery whenever Sophie would help her, and on other days went to one of the gaming classes. In this manner, she discovered that she possessed a natural talent for bocce ball that earned her considerable respect among the regular players—that is, she could throw the ball hard and still aim well.

So the days crept by until mid-March, when the snow suddenly stopped and the sun came out. Winter was by no means over, but at all once roads were clear and the barge was running again. And Captain Derrick decided that it was time to send a fresh set of men to Odea.

Sitting on the westernmost point of the Pervalley Highway before it crossed the border into Eugenia, the outpost was the major checkpoint for legitimate traffic seeking entrance into Lystra. It was also the hub for scouting operations to control the illegitimate traffic. Both kinds of traffic increased exponentially in the spring. So early in the morning, Henry and twenty other men boarded a carrack bound for Mcelyea.

This was a port town west of Prie Mer, just at the eastern edge of the Green Lady (the small mountain ridge so named because of its resemblance to a woman lying on her side—to sailors, at any rate). Given good weather, the ship could sail along the coast in about sixteen hours. After debarking at Mcelyea, the men would then have a day's ride (again, given clear weather) to Odea.

With no gear but the clothes on his back, Henry boarded the boat. Along with the letter to Captain Yonge from Ares, Henry also carried an open letter from Captain Derrick explaining that the brand on his hand did not signify leprosy. All of his traveling companions had heard of the incident, so had no fear of him, but Henry knew that this letter would carry no weight beyond Odea.

Sitting on the gently rolling deck of the small ship, looking out over the green, choppy waves, Henry wrapped the cloak tighter around himself and inhaled the salty sea air. Strange that he didn't feel sad. He was tired, and his hand was still sore—he looked down at the tender pink skin where the scabs had started to fall off. But he didn't feel cheated or abused. If Ares truly regarded this as a mark of sonship, then it was worth it.

He studied the ugliness of the brand in admiration for a moment. When he was too young to understand how these things worked, he sometimes used to fantasize that something would happen to him to scar him just like Ares, so that anyone who looked at him would know that he was Ares' son. Now that it had actually happened, he was a little awed by it.

He watched a few more men board, and his hand crept toward the locket hanging from his neck. Sternly, Henry brought the hand back down. He would master this; he would break this habit of constantly seeking reassurance in the treasure hidden under his clothes over his heart. He knew that the locket was there; that was enough "You, boy! Get off your arse an' get your back into it!" the ship's pilot yelled.

The Surchatain's son got to his feet in private satisfaction. "I've not sailed much. Show me what to do."

Shortly after the ship had set sail, one of the workmen clearing the road between Westford and Nicole's Harbor saw the edge of parchment sticking up from the melting snow. Upon investigating, he discovered the letter with the Surchatain's seal depicting the lion and the cross.

The intended recipient's name at Nicole's Harbor was smeared but legible, so the conscientious workman put the letter in his pocket. About four hours later, when a wagon rolled by on the newly cleared road bound for the Harbor, the workman handed the letter up to the driver.

Upon arrival at Nicole's Harbor some hours later, the driver unloaded his cargo of dried beef, treacle, flour, and lard, then remembered the errant letter in his pocket. This he delivered to a sentry, who in turn took it to Captain Derrick.

The Captain looked at the smeared lettering on the side opposite the royal seal. "Huh. Well, he's sailed, and another ship won't follow for weeks yet. Suppose I'd best just hang on to this in the meanwhile." And he put the letter in a corner of his quarters for safekeeping, where in fact it was almost guaranteed to be forgotten.

The carrack bearing Henry arrived in the middle of the night at Mcelyea, where the men sleepily debarked and bunked down for a few hours' rest. At the first light of dawn they were roused again to load up pack animals, as well as their own horses, for the ride to Odea.

As it happened, only six of the men, including Henry, had orders for Odea. So those six rode out, leading two additional horses laden with supplies for the outpost. As cold as it was, all of the men wore gloves. Fingers frozen stiff were useless in controlling a horse.

Nestled between the Green Lady and the Poison Greens, the valley they were crossing enjoyed milder weather than Westford. There was very little snow on the ground, and while the road was not paved, it was flat and frozen hard. So they were traveling at a good steady gallop, aiming to arrive at the outpost before nightfall. Being on the western edge of many acres of vineyards, the riders had the long rows of brown skeletal vines on their right and grassland gradually yielding to rocky terrain on their left, toward the Eugenian border.

Early midafternoon, they were far enough north to have passed most of the vineyards that covered the valley floor. This area, with poor, rocky soil, seemed to be the depository for stones cleared from the vineyards over centuries of cultivation. The farther one got from the eastbound road, the more numerous the rocks that lay scattered about.

On the riders' left, toward the west, stands of gnarled trees—a mix of barren oak, stunted ash, beech, and scrub brush—crept to within five feet of the road. There was little to allay the monotony of the ride until all at once they were startled by the abrupt appearance of a second group of riders out of the trees, eleven in all, only ten yards ahead.

The two groups reined up in mutual surprise practically face to face. Then the leader of the trespassers sneered at the soldiers, and Henry got a good look at the red scar that traversed his forehead. Before the Lystrans could react, he spurred across the road toward the east. He was followed by a scraggly group of brigands, heavily armed. "Dorn!" Henry exclaimed. "I know him! That's Dorn! After them!"

When he started to spur in pursuit, one of his group said, "Why?"

Henry wheeled his horse. "Because if you don't, I will come back and beat the devil out of you." Without waiting to see if any of the five would follow, Henry reined back around to give chase to the slavers. He gained them quickly because they heard him coming. They had time to stop and form a line to await him, grinning.

But as he approached, he held the reins in his left hand to take the glove off his right with his teeth. Whether they expected him to stop and turn tail, or stop and talk, or stop and draw a sword (which he did not have), they were unprepared for what he did do.

Singling out Dorn, Henry rode straight at him, shucking his feet up out of the stirrups. By the time the slavers realized that he was not going to stop at all, they had no time to do anything but get out of the way—all except Dorn.

Henry's horse swerved instinctively to avoid a collision at the last moment, and he leapt out of the saddle right into Dorn, knocking him off the horse to the ground with a solid thud. Dorn grunted as he landed on his back with Henry atop him. "Ungh! Get off me!" shouted the slaver, his right foot caught in the stirrup. Henry rolled off him just before Dorn's horse reared and took off running through the field of stones, dragging the man along.

Henry scrambled to his feet while the other mercenaries dismounted to gather in a circle around him. A few drew their weapons, but most wanted the satisfaction of blood forcefully applied to their hands. Henry thrust his right fist up, shouting, "Leper! Unclean!" And he hit the nearest man in the face with that fist.

The rest of the mercenaries fell back, dropping their swords and scampering to their horses in a blind panic. By this time Henry's companions had caught up to them, and managed to catch two of the escaping brigands before the rest thundered away.

At this point, the reluctant member of Henry's group, seeing that he might actually make it back to beat the devil out of him, hastened up to insert himself into the fray as if he had been there all along.

"Don't worry about them," Henry panted, glancing at the brigands in flight—as if anyone was about to go racing after them—"Ares will see to them. Dorn's the one I want."

Looking for Dorn's fleeing horse, Henry climbed back into his saddle, never noticing the broken chain and locket at his feet. While hampered in having to take care for the stones, he rode in pursuit of the escaping horse until he saw that it had calmed enough to slow to a trot. There was nothing hanging from either stirrup.

Henry scanned the ground between himself and the horse, finally spotting a small mound. Approaching it, he dismounted to look over Dorn's barely recognizable body, head bloodied and lying at a most unnatural angle to the shoulders. So, satisfied that Dorn's slaving days were concluded, Henry loaded up the body on the slaver's horse and remounted to rejoin his companions on their way to Odea.

That very day Ares received a message from Fanchon of Seleca accepting his proposal of a trade: Symon for the slavers.

15

The problem was, Fanchon said in his message, he doubted that he could locate all the slave traders Ares had demanded. But if Ares would give him a month to search, he would collect all those he could. In a month's time, how many would Ares accept in exchange for the monk, Symon, alive?

Ares sat with Thom and Vogelsong in his receiving room to debate this question. "Getting only two or three will do us little good," Thom argued. "Others will simply jump right into the gap, and appreciate our clearing out some of their competition."

Vogelsong asked, "Can we secure some kind of oath from Fanchon that he will desist from patronizing the slave trade?"

Ares shook his head. "He will swear to a life of piety and total submission—anything—to get what he wants. In actuality, we will get nothing but what we wrest from him at the moment of trade."

The three sat in contemplative silence. "If we specify a number less than six, he will give us that and no more," Thom observed.

"But it is unrealistic to expect that he could produce all six of them. If we demand all or nothing, then we thwart ourselves," Vogelsong countered.

Ares leaned back in his chair with a slight groan. "It all seemed so clear when I first got the idea."

There followed another silence, then Thom shrugged. "Throw it back on him. Tell him to produce however many he can in a month, and we'll then decide if that's acceptable."

Ares studied him. "That is rather a good idea."

"It would keep him in a state of uncertainty, rather than ourselves," Vogelsong admitted.

"It would insure that we continue to have the upper hand in the negotiations," Thom said.

Ares grunted in conviction. "That is what we'll do, then. Write that out for the messenger to carry back at once," Ares instructed Vogelsong, then paused. "Where is the messenger?"

"I believe that he is still in the foyer awaiting instructions," Vogelsong mused.

Something like fear crossed Ares' face. "Set a guard on him at once, before anyone else can talk to him. Feed him and house him—guarded—in the lower corridor tonight. We'll send him off with our reply in the morning."

"At once, Surchatain." Vogelsong rose to bow, then departed to see to the messenger.

Thom continued to sit with Ares while he looked contemplatively toward the windows. Even when they were closed, Ares tended to look to them when in thought. He was instinctively drawn to the light.

"What word is there of Henry?" Thom asked.

Ares glanced at him with an expression that might have indicated gratitude. "Captain Derrick shipped him off to

Odea as ordered. I've not heard from Captain Yonge regarding him." He added in a low voice, "I miss him."

"What, can no one else run down corridors?" Thom asked wryly, and Ares grinned.

"I sometimes wonder . . . if I did enough," Ares murmured, and Thom eyed him in surprise. Ares inhaled. "For what he will be facing, I wonder if I did enough to prepare him. I did not know at the time what—trials he would be facing." All the administrators knew of Henry's branding.

"Would you really want him to grow to manhood without such trials?" Thom asked.

Ares leaned forward abruptly. "Your perception is sometimes irritating, Commander. You are dismissed." To his credit, Thom stood and saluted without a hint of smugness.

But he paused before leaving, and Ares watched him. "If I may irritate you further, Surchatain . . . I request that you come observe the swordmaker's daughter."

Brow creasing, Ares stood.

First the crocuses appeared, and Nicole was spotted lying flat on her belly in the garden admiring them. Then people started going outside without heavy cloaks, and Lord Preus brought a stunning array of new spring gowns to the palace in a determined attempt to recapture some of the business drawn away by that upstart Tailor Gathing.

Then the hordes of jonquils at Willowring Lake burst into bloom, and suddenly there were baby birds cheeping and apple trees awash in blossoms and sunshine glinting off dewy green grass. The world came alive again.

Regular messages resumed between Nicole's Harbor, Mcelyea, Odea, and Westford, though Captain Derrick did not remember the smudged letter in his safekeeping. The swordmaker and his daughter received a series of interviews with the Surchatain, and Ares was satisfied with everything he saw and heard.

Giles returned from Crescent Hollow towing cartloads of architects' drawings, lists, price estimates and a bound volume of the proposed plan of converting the palace to an inn. Ares took one look at the stacks of written materials and promptly conferred upon the Steward carte blanche in the matter.

Giles walked around the rest of the day in a golden glow before hastening back to Crescent Hollow again, leaving Stengi in charge of the books, Genevieve with her preferred dinner companion, and Renée in the seat next to Bonnie.

The twins clamored to go on outings to the lake, to town, to everyplace on the Continent (it seemed). This meant that Bonnie would require a new guardian.

Accordingly, she came to Ares with a list: "Papa, I've made up new questions for interviewing guardians. I've decided that my guardian should know something about my favorite shops and treats. I've also come up with a written test for them to take in case I can't make up my mind about which one to select."

Seated at his table, he glanced at the long sheets of parchment she held. "That's very industrious of you, Bonnie, but I have already selected your new guardian."

"What?" She lowered the parchment in disappointment. "I thought I got to choose!"

"You did, for the last one. You chose Henry, and he did well. Now it's my turn," Ares said, looking back down at the *short* summary he had requested from Giles.

"Well, who is it? Is he cute?" she asked. When her

father returned a brief look she amended, "I mean, is he nice? What is his name?"

"Riley," he replied.

Bonnie was eager to test out this new guardian without delay. "Well, Mama said that Sophie and I could go to Tailor Gathing's to look at the new fabrics he just got in, so if you've already picked a guardian, can we go this morning? Oh, please, Papa? Please?" she pleaded as if her life hung on it.

Ares hesitated. "Riley hasn't taken the vow of guardianship at open audience yet—"

"Oh, he can do that any time," she said, waving it off. "And this will be a good time to see if we get along. Please, Papa?"

He evaluated her. "All right." While Bonnie jumped up and down clapping her hands (leaving parchments scattered on the floor) Ares called in the guard to instruct him to summon Seane and Riley to the foyer to escort the girls into town. The sentry saluted and departed; Bonnie flew to her father to plant a grateful kiss on his cheek before sailing out to find Sophie.

In short order, the girls were traipsing down the stairway in great excitement, carrying lightweight woolen cloaks—Bonnie's was deep blue, with a gold "B" embroidered on the shoulder, while Sophie's was a rich magenta with an "S" in similar silver lettering. "I know! Let's change places to fool the new guardian! That's a good way to break him in!" Bonnie suggested, thrusting her cloak at Sophie.

"Won't do any good, silly!" Sophie brushed it away. "Henry taught Seane how to tell us apart, remember? Besides, I want Tailor Gathing to call me by my right name. I like talking to him." Scanning the crowded foyer, she exclaimed, "Oh, there's Seane! I can't believe we finally get to go out again after so long!"

They gained the bottom of the stairway where Seane met them, smiling confidently. "Good afternoon, Chataine Bonnie. Chataine Sophie." He made a point to address them separately—and they didn't even have their cloaks on yet. "Are you ready to go?"

"Where's my guardian? His name is Riley," Bonnie said, glancing around.

Seane replied, "Yes, I know. Chataine Bonnie, meet Riley." Seane extended his hand to his right.

Bonnie blinked, looking all around. "Where?"

"Right here, Chataine," Seane laughed.

Sophie said, "Oh, my," and started laughing.

"What's so funny?" Bonnie turned on her. "Where is he?"

"Chataine, I am Riley," a voice beside Seane said, and Bonnie focused her attention on the face that was speaking. It belonged to a tall young woman who wore a split riding skirt, a short cloak, and a wide-brimmed hat.

"Isn't she great?" Seane enthused. "She's the sword-maker's daughter, and when she came with her father to the palace yesterday, the Surchatain watched her present arms and offered her the job on the spot. And I can tell you, she's been teaching me a thing or two!" The young man related events as they appeared to him, not knowing the depth of research the Surchatain had invested in the new guardian.

"Can you teach us swordplay?" Sophie asked in awe.

"If your father permits, Chataine," Riley said. She had a strong, confident bearing, and was fully head and shoulders taller than the girls. She then directed her attention to Bonnie, who was still staring at her in shock.

"Are you ready to go, Chataine Bonnie?"

Bonnie snapped out of it. "You can't protect me!"

"Not if you won't let me," Riley agreed.

"But what if a man tries to snatch me?" Bonnie asked.

"Then I will kill him," she replied. Flipping the edge of her cloak back, she exposed a mid-length estoc sheathed at her side.

"I saw her demonstrating it on a straw dummy when Captain Crager proposed a real-life test," Seane confided to the twins. "And let me tell you, she had him hopping. All the Blue were sitting down watching like a bunch of Greens."

A whole range of new ideas began to play in Bonnie's mind. Taking Riley's hand, she headed vaguely toward the great double doors. "You are very interesting. Have you ever killed anybody? I almost killed the jester when he tried to throw me down the well. I didn't have a sword, but I made him sorry he tried, didn't I, Sophie?" As Bonnie talked on, Riley glanced back at Seane, winking.

That evening, Renée was less than thrilled to discover that her coveted place next to Bonnie at the table had been usurped (for tonight only) by her new guardian. The whole palace had talked of nothing else after the open audience in which she was sworn in to her duty.

Back in her old place at Doctor Savary's left, Renée watched Bonnie enthrall the table with a recounting of their adventures in town: "Then while we were getting out of the cart at Tailor Gathing's, some stupid man I'd never seen before starts fawning over me—'Oh, two pretty little girls who look just alike, and your name must start with a "B"'—then he leaned down and tried to PET MY HAIR like I was a dog, or something, so Riley pushed him away. He looked so surprised! 'Well, excuse me,' he said, all offended. 'I was just talking to the little girl here.'

"And Riley said, 'She didn't give you leave to talk to her. Back away, sir.' And she tossed back her cloak to show him the sword—Papa, can we take sword lessons?" Bonnie suddenly interrupted herself to turn on her father.

Ares swallowed his mouthful. "Bonnie, I can hardly think of anything more dangerous than you with a sword."

"That's right!" she exclaimed, beaming up at Riley.

Amid the chuckles, Renée tossed her head preparatory to speaking. In her view, Bonnie's worship of this idol had gone on long enough. "Well, it is certainly wonderful that Bonnie receives the benefit of a variety of talents from so many different kinds of people. Tell me, Riley, do you dance?"

"No. Do you fight?" Riley answered amiably, clearly recognizing the challenge that had been issued.

"Not as such," Renée laughed.

Before she could continue the thought, Thom interjected, "She merely incites her adversary to place himself in torture devices."

"Really?" Riley chuckled, and Renée glanced at the Commander, whose remark seemed most uncharacteristic of him. "Then I perceive you have little need of a sword, being fully armed already," Riley added.

Some listeners' heads ducked at this apparent reference to Renée's tongue. "Me?" she laughed, with a glance at Thom to insure his silence. "No, no. I merely enjoy little games now and then."

"Games are a child's way of dealing with the world," Riley observed.

The table fell silent at this astute blow. "Why, you make too much of an innocent pastime," Renée purred. "Everyone plays at something. Even Nicole plays games."

"Leave me out of this, please," Nicole said sweetly, accepting the strawberry mousse from the servant's hand.

"Is it time for our game this evening, Ares?" Renée asked. He returned a clear warning look to her. Heedless, she went on: "What shall we play? A guessing game, perhaps? Oh, so many topics to choose from! Let us try this, as I am good at children's games: What is small, and pink, and round—?"

"I have had a baby out of wedlock," Riley said. "My aunt is raising him."

The guests went motionless in shock, then as if compelled by a silent command, they all looked at Renée. Sophie breathed, "Aunt Renée, that was just mean!"

Renée's decorated mouth dropped open slightly. "I had no idea," she protested, and no one believed her in the slightest. "I was referring to hollyhock."

Breathing out in exasperation, Ares said, "You are all dismissed." Summarily deprived of dessert and entertainment, the guests rose sulkily to bow to Ares while casting dark glances at Renée, the cause of their banishment.

She also eyed Ares sidewise in the knowledge that he was bringing the force of the table's disapproval on her to squelch her gaming instincts. "Spoilsport," she muttered.

On their way out of the hall, Bonnie was heard to tell Riley, "You should bring your baby to the palace nursery. Can I play with him sometime? Mayra says I'm gifted with the baby boys."

Springtime in Odea meant a doubling of the work load for the soldiers stationed there. So, despite the coolness of the morning, Henry and sixty-odd other men were in their shirtsleeves sweating over a marked plot in the field next to the barracks. They were harvesting stones from the field and road and piling them according to size near the outline of the building that was to be constructed from these stones. Dropping the fortieth stone on a pile, Henry lifted his arm to wipe sweat out of his eyes.

A fellow nearby stopped in his tracks. "Leper," he whispered in shock.

Henry glanced up. "You stupid piece of horse manure, are you the only one who hasn't heard how I got branded?" Captain Yonge had taken pains to circulate Captain Derrick's letter regarding Henry all over camp, but there were still the obnoxious few who liked to pretend that they didn't know in order to wring some entertainment from harassing Henry.

At first he treated it as a joke, but the more they persisted, the less tolerant he grew. A few days ago, someone had even found a leper's costume—a hooded white sheath—to lay out on Henry's pallet. He had tossed it into the fire, along with the offender's best jacket.

Still, there were new men arriving at Odea all the time, and the letter could only go 'round so many times. No one could even say who had it now. And, actually, this man did look new. "Leper! Leper!" He backed away, raising the alarm.

Most of the other men around waved him off, but a few paused uncertainly. There were always a few who really didn't know, and their look of repulsion and fear was beginning to rankle Henry deeply. No handsome young man could easily endure being treated like a loathsome freak.

"Shut your face!" Henry shouted. When the fellow would not, Henry made a diving leap for his legs and brought him down. He sat on him to stuff grass into his mouth, but he spat it out and kept hollering, raising his voice to a fever pitch.

Henry was yanked up by his shirt collar and thrown onto his back. From the ground, he looked up at Lieutenant Moeck. "Henry, the Captain wants to see you," Moeck said tiredly, as if repeating himself.

Henry hopped to his feet, shrugging his shirt back in place. Then he trotted to the main building, mounted the steps at a run, and entered Captain Yonge's quarters without ceremony, which would have added monotony to this oft-repeated exercise. When the Captain looked up from his correspondence, Henry did salute. "You summoned me, sir?"

Yonge exhaled. "Henry, if the Surchatain hadn't been so explicit in his praise of you, you'd be in prison for all the fights by now."

"They won't leave it be," Henry muttered, glancing away.

"No, and they won't ever, so don't you think you need to find a better way to deal with it? When you leave Odea, are you going to go around thrashing everyone who really thinks you're a leper?" the Captain asked. Henry, still looking aside, did not reply.

"Well, letter or no, you're a hindrance and a nuisance," the Captain went on, and Henry blinked. "So I am going to offer you a choice: You can sit in prison for the next six weeks, or you can ride patrol—"

"I'll patrol," Henry said.

"Just listen, Henry. It's high-risk duty. You ride out at sunrise and stay out on the border all the time. You only come back every few days to resupply and report."

"I'll patrol," Henry repeated.

"All right," the Captain said. "It's better with a partner

—d'you know of anyone who'd be willing to ride with you?"

"No," Henry said.

"All right," Yonge sighed. "Go—bunk down. You're out tomorrow. Dismissed."

"Sir." Henry saluted. Descending the steps outside, he unconsciously reached a hand to his chest before he remembered, again, that his treasure was gone. The empty space where the locket should have been taunted him daily, reminding him of everything that he had lost, and the bitterness welled up in him.

Before dawn the next morning, Henry packed up basic rations, rope, and a flint box in a blanket, then strapped a long sword on one hip and a hunting knife on the other. He went out to the stables and selected the best horse he could find, which happened to be Lieutenant Moeck's. Then he rode south from the outpost to begin his solitary patrol.

16

As the sun rose in its radiant warmth, Henry rode over rough terrain along the border amid scrub oaks, nettles and weeds. Because of the numerous gullies and rock outcroppings, the soldiers were never able to construct the stone wall along the border that Ares had desired. As a result, there were long stretches where the border was marked by nothing but a periodic trench and a few signposts. Unscrupulous traders and slavers had found such easy access into Lystra south of Odea that rough roads appeared in areas that would not accommodate an outpost. Hence the necessity of patrols.

So Henry rode aimlessly, seeing nothing but images in his mind of people he would not see again for a long time. The bitterness rose up strong and deep in him. How unfair that he should be banished for his obedience, and branded for no other reason than someone else's stupidity! He felt like a piece on a giant game board, being moved around simply for a greater power's amusement. And that was what rubbed him raw: the utter capriciousness of it all. He had been cast off for no fault of his own.

"It's just a game to You, isn't it, God?" he shouted,

causing the horse beneath him to flatten its ears. "What have I ever done that You should make me forsaken and hated? What?" he demanded.

He certainly wasn't expecting an answer. But Bonnie's question, *Who do you think you are?* seemed to float back to him. This time, Henry sensed no contempt; it was a real question, somehow, compelling him to pause in his rantings to think.

"I am Ares' son," he said, and while the concession was made that this was true, it was also pointed out to him that this was not his doing. It was Ares' faithfulness and compassion that had made him so. Without Ares' obedience to his vow before God, Henry would not even be alive to complain about his current condition.

He continued to ride blindly along the border while he struggled with these concepts of destiny and choice. It was so much easier to languish in self-pity than apply his mind to such issues that he refused to think at all for a while. Instead, he mindlessly watched the horse's hooves plod over grey dirt beneath him. He rode in disregard of his mission—a Blue on border patrol!—and disdain of himself. All the while that he sat slouched in the saddle enjoying moroseness, the issue waited quietly for his attention.

When he finally consented to open his mind again, the question was posed to him, What event had made Ares acknowledge Henry as his son? Henry looked down at the brand on his hand—but that actually wasn't the impetus for Ares' saying it the first time. He had said it after rescuing Henry from slavery in Hornbound. So the question arose, Why had Ares been prompted to reaffirm that after his branding?

Henry thought hard about this as he dismounted to walk the horse up an unstable incline, causing dirt and pebbles to cascade down from their path. He knew that it wasn't due merely to the physical disfigurement; in that case, Ares would have acknowledged as sons all those imposters who had vainly cut open their faces to impress him.

Or, Ares would have insisted that Henry's disfigurement, while appalling, did not count because it was on his hand and not his face. Remembering the knucklebones winner who had inadvertently caused himself to be branded with an eerie likeness of Ares' scar, Henry rejected any kinship between the two men. So if the family trait was not physical, it must be spiritual.

When the sun reached its apex, Henry stopped by a twisted old oak to drink from his water skin and eat some dry bread from his pack. He poured a little water in a pan for the horse to lip, then stroked its nose, smiling. Good, sturdy animal. A roan. In admiring Moeck's horse, Henry tried to forget the issue for a little while, but everywhere his mind turned, he found the question staring him in the face: what constituted sonship?

Sighing in frustration, Henry leaned back against the tree while the horse nosed among its roots for edible grass. To be like Ares meant thinking like him and acting like him, Henry conceded. The idea of Ares' picking fights with everyone who made fun of his scar caused Henry to snort. Ares would never do that. It was beneath him.

Remounting, Henry continued to ride as he thought about Ares' attitude toward his scar. He was so indifferent to it that eventually it ceased to be an issue to anyone, except those seeing it for the first time. Henry remembered trips into town where people stopped on the street to stare as Ares walked by. Some, to be rude or malicious, even made comments in his hearing about how ugly it was. Ares never reacted. Whether such comments hurt him or not, Henry never knew. They simply drifted by his ears and died for lack of response.

Henry studied his hand as it rested on the pommel. Scar tissue of puffy white flesh had filled in the burns so that the brand stood out in stark relief to the tanned, smooth skin around it. There was no hiding it. He looked around the rugged landscape, inhaling.

Ares never tried to hide his scar, not even by growing a beard. The few times Henry saw him with a beard, he noted that it did obscure part of the scar—certainly made it less noticeable. But for whatever reason, Ares shaved the beard off. It was almost as if—he would make no concessions to the scar. It would control nothing that he did.

Ares used it, though. Whenever he wished to present the most formidable appearance possible, he simply displayed his scar to the viewer's eyes. He didn't thrust his cheek out, or anything so obvious—he would just turn his face ever so slightly so that the scar was fully in view. It was almost as if he was saying, "*You think to intimidate me when I have mastered something such as this?*" It was highly effective, given Ares' strength and self-discipline.

Henry dismounted at a meager stream to wash his face and hands, and let the horse drink. Sitting back on his heels, he watched the water run off the brand into the new bracken growth at his feet. This being Ares' attitude toward his affliction, how could Henry emulate it to prove himself his son?

The answer was not long in coming. The first order of business was to accept the brand as a gift of sonship, a visible mark of his spiritual relationship to Ares—that's what Ares meant when he said it was proof. Henry had understood that instinctively in Nicole's Harbor; he just forgot it when he had to deal with the idiots who saw it differently. Captain Yonge was quite right: he had to accept it and figure out how to live with it. No—more than that, he had to figure out how to make best use of it. He had to treat it as a gift to be put to use.

At this point, a boulder of reality crashed into his fragile house of thought. This "gift" had deprived him of Sophie. Realistically, Henry saw no way that Sophie could accept a husband with a leper's brand, even if she wanted to. The man she married would be Surchatain, expected to appear at palace functions, to meet with heads of provinces, to entertain dignitaries from across the Continent. Repulsive as Ares' scar was, it did not signify a dreaded, infectious disease.

The impossibility of effectively explaining to everyone from here on out that the brand was the result of a mindless prank drove Henry back into despair. "You've taken Sophie from me, too," he murmured, crushed.

So? The question was not taunting, just . . . to the point. Once again, Henry was directed to Ares' life for instruction. Henry knew the details well: how Ares, when he was a young boy, had been grabbed up by his father to run for their lives when Henry's grandfather, Talus, went on a murderous rage to gain the throne.

In one horrible night, the little boy was deprived of his father, his uncles, his grandfather, his rulership, and his normal appearance. For unfathomable reasons, God had deprived Ares of everything meaningful to a human except life itself. Ares always acknowledged the one saving angel God had sent that evening in the form of Reynard, Talus' brother, who prevented him from killing the child.

Now, all these many years later, look at what Ares had become: a respected and effective Surchatain with greater power and wealth than Talus ever had. And it could possibly be that, because of the remembrance of the terror of that night and Reynard's part in saving him, Ares had saved Henry's life.

Henry watched the sun descend on the horizon as the realization spread over him that Ares had saved Henry because of what the scar had done to him. The grandson of the murdering usurper should have died when Ares was restored to the throne, but God used Ares' suffering to save Henry. In God's harsh dealings with Ares, He was playing no game, but laying the foundation of Henry's whole life.

The sense of humility and profound gratitude engendered by this apprehension drove Henry to his knees by the horse. Bending his forehead to the rocky earth, he whispered, "Then let it be. Take it all from me, if You will use me as You have used Ares."

His offer was accepted. Henry remained on his knees out of weariness for a while—after all, he had been engaged in this particular struggle all day long—then got to his feet and remounted. Evening was approaching; he was hungry and tired, so he looked ahead at a stand of stinted oaks that would provide wood for a fire and shelter for the night.

As he was riding toward the stand, his senses suddenly went on the alert before he saw anything. He smelled smoke. He heard the snorting of a horse. Henry stopped, staring ahead, then perceived the flickering of firelight through the trees. Someone was already camped there.

Henry quietly dismounted and tied the horse to a scrub brush. Then he stealthily crept up to the trees. From the shadows, he peered into a small clearing where three men sat around a campfire, their horses tethered nearby.

They were laughing and joking, in high good humor.

Large, roughly dressed, coarse, filthy men. Henry studied the orderly rows of chains and shackles that one fellow was rearranging in a pack—he was counting collars to see how many they had room for.

Shifting his gaze, Henry regarded their weapons: long swords at their sides, hatchets in easy-to-reach shoulder sheaths. Slavers liked hatchets because they were good for a number of jobs—chopping firewood, cutting tethers, severing limbs from resisting captives.

The fellow counting collars turned to his companions to grin, gap-toothed. "Say, I count forty! We can take forty, you think?"

"Easy as cradle-robbing!" another snorted. "They see ye coming and stare—jest stand there and let ye take 'em. Easiest work ever done. But say, Urias, where do we meet t'others?" Henry noted that he and the one with the collars wore their hatchets while the third, Urias, did not. Therefore, those two must be dealt with first, because a hatchet could be thrown, as well.

Urias replied, "We're to meet them at the Poison Greens ten miles west of Crescent Hollow—it's marked by a burned-out house from Ticzon's last raid." The subtlety of the location was acknowledged with appreciative chuckles from the other two.

Urias went on, "All together, we'll work our way south through the vineyards—lots of able bodies working in small groups, hardly none of 'em armed. The few soldiers tain't near enough to hold off all us at once. When we've filled our collars, we'll herd them back up through the Poison Greens to Ticzon's camp. As long as we stay clear of Crescent Hollow, we're good."

"You're a master, Urias, you are," the cradle-robber lauded, raising his cup in homage. The other seconded this, and the head slaver grinned as he gingerly peeled the roasted rabbit off the spit over the fire. Cradle Robber tipped up his hatchet to hack the rabbit into chunks, and they set to dinner.

Henry backed away to strategize. He wished now that he hadn't burned the leper's shroud, but—he'd have to make do without it. Taking care to make no noise, he removed his military cloak and the Blue insigne from his collar. He unstrapped his sword belt and placed that on the ground with his cloak. Then he shifted the sheath of his hunting knife around his belt until it hung directly down his backside. Taking a deep breath, he paused to whisper, "Make me like Ares," then he shuffled toward the campfire.

The slavers heard him coming, and started up as he came into the light. He dragged himself along in the manner he had seen the very sick do. While the three stared at him, trying to assess what threat he was, he extended his right hand toward them, moaning, "Leper. Unclean. Unclean!"

When the slavers jumped up with hoarse cries, Henry fell upon them. Whipping out his knife from the sheath with his left hand, he slit the throat of Cradle Robber and wheeled to plunge the knife into Collar Counter's gut. But by the time he had extracted it and come around to face the third, Urias, the man was waiting for Henry with drawn sword.

The two faced off for an instant. With the shorter blade, Henry was at a severe disadvantage. So before Urias could act on the advantage he possessed, Henry flipped the knife to grip it by the slippery blade and throw it straight into the slaver's chest. Even as hard as Henry threw it, it would have bounced away had it hit bone, but it found clear passage beneath his ribs. Urias fell down writhing. With the slaver's own hatchet, Henry stilled him.

A little dazed, Henry looked around, then sat to help himself to the slavers' last meal.

When he returned to the outpost late in the night leading three horses with bodies tied on them, the first thing he did was properly groom and stall Moeck's horse, stealing the oats from the Captain's horse's stall for it to enjoy.

Then he went to the barracks, candle in hand, and woke his worst tormentor. "Do you have another leper's shroud? I need it now," Henry told him. The man blinked at him as others raised themselves up on their pallets nearby.

"Well, if you come across another, give it to me," Henry said, turning out again while the man stared after him. Only then did he go to Captain Derrick's quarters to hand over the bodies and make his report.

Three days later, Lieutenant Alphonso rode into Westford with an urgent message from Captain Yonge at Odea. When Ares read it, he collected Thom, Vogelsong and Alphonso in his receiving room to cover it with them. Sitting across from them at his table, Ares leaned forward, folded his hands, and said, "Captain Yonge tells me that Henry has killed Dorn and Urias."

"Henry? Alone? Killed two of our most wanted slavers?" marveled Vogelsong.

"Henry alone killed two of our most wanted slavers," Ares confirmed.

Thom asked, "Then what are the other nine hundred men at Odea doing?"

Alphonso snorted and Vogelsong said warmly, "I knew he would make you proud, Surchatain."

"He's off to a decent start," Ares allowed. "But he also reported hearing about a meeting of slavers to take place imminently, south of the Poison Greens. Alphonso passed the spot on the way here." Ares nodded to him.

"Yes, Surchatain, two days ago. It's a wee hamlet that was burned out by Ticzon on a raid last summer. According to what Henry heard, all the big 'uns are to meet there again to go on a rampage collecting bodies for the market, then transport them through the Poison Greens to Ticzon's camp in southern Qarqar." Alphonso, bearded and stout, leaned back in his chair.

"When is this meeting to take place?" Vogelsong asked in alarm.

"Don't know. They could be gathering there now, Counselor," Alphonso said with a shrug.

"But no one was there when you passed?" Vogelsong asked.

"Not that I saw, Counselor," Alphonso replied.

Ares looked at Thom, who read his face. "The Blue and the Red? Or more?"

"There might be several hundred, with their armed guard. So let's take the Blue and the Red to meet them," Ares said. This amounted to approximately 3500 men.

Vogelsong and Thom looked at each other. Since the Counselor hesitated, the Commander spoke: "Surchatain, you gave your word that you would not ride out against slavers any more."

Ares opened his mouth but Vogelsong added sternly, "You gave your word in front of the Surchataine. What are we to tell her if you go? That you changed your mind? That it doesn't count?" The young Counselor took such personal offense at Ares' vacillation that Thom had to bite his lip to not smile.

Ares looked away, muttering under his breath while Alphonso studied the rug at his feet. Then the Surchatain leaned forward to tell his Commander, "Have Paramore and Crager head up their regiments. I want not a single slaver escaping. And there will be no prisoners taken. The mercenaries who choose to sell their services to the slavers will die with them." His officers agreed.

So Ares instructed Alphonso, "Ride back and tell Captain Yonge what we are doing. Tell him to issue Henry a commendation. And . . . tell Lieutenant Moeck that if he's upset about his horse being taken, he needs to provide Henry a good animal so that he won't be driven to stealing one."

"Surchatain!" Alphonso stood, saluting with a grin. "Good lad, that Henry," he was heard to murmur on his way out.

But once he had reclaimed his horse and departed the palace, he groaned at the thought of making that long ride back to Odea. He wasn't as young as he used to be—he was tired, and he sure could use a shot of good ale before setting out. Leaving at this time of the day, though, would guarantee he'd be sleeping on the ground for the next three nights.

Sitting on his horse while traffic flowed around him, Alphonso then glanced down the southbound market road. Say, how long had it been since he'd broken bread with good ol' Derrick?—who was stationed at Nicole's Harbor. Alphonso considered that if he rode down to Nicole's Harbor and stayed there tonight, he could hop a ship to Mcelyea and be at Odea just as quickly, with far less discomfort. Cheering considerably, he turned his horse south.

It was just about dinnertime when Alphonso arrived at

the outpost in Nicole's Harbor. He greeted the sentries with a roar and a wave, almost smelling the cod baking over hot coals. Night at the Harbor was a time of feasting on the day's catch, rowdy dancing, ample drinking, and lots of laughter—maybe even a pretty woman or two. Alphonso had many friends at every outpost, and they were always glad to see him. So he was ushered into Derrick's quarters with much backslapping and immediate calls for refreshment.

While they were seated at table with pints in hand, Derrick inquired after Alphonso's mission. So Alphonso told him of the unholy convocation about to convene south of the Poison Greens, and the fact that it had been discovered by young Henry. (Like many adults who watched children grow up, Alphonso had difficulty regarding Henry as an adult himself now, especially since Alphonso had not seen him recently—or thought he hadn't. He had actually passed Henry on his way out of Captain Yonge's quarters, but hadn't recognized him.)

"Henry?" Derrick paused, a strange look crossing his face. "Oh, for pity's sake. I forgot all about it." He then rose to retrieve the forgotten letter from its niche. "I got this letter for Henry about a month ago, just after he sailed for Odea himself."

"Well, hand it over, Captain; I'll deliver it," Alphonso said, reaching out, and Derrick put the letter in his hand. He tucked it into his shirt pocket, then hoisted his pint again and they talked of many other things late into the night.

That evening, as Ares was sitting to dinner with his guests, he received a messenger from Fanchon. Ares excused himself from the table, pulling Thom, Vogelsong, Rhode and Oswald out likewise, though he instructed his guests to continue with dinner in their absence. (It was rude enough for all of them to leave; Ares would not provoke Georges with the sight of guests' sitting motionless over hot dishes prepared to perfection.) Then they closed themselves in Ares' receiving room as he broke the seal and unwrapped the letter.

Ares glanced over it while the others waited. Then he looked up. "Fanchon says that he has captured all six of the slavers I desired, and proposes to meet in Eurus to trade the slavers for Symon, alive."

17

Ares' officers looked at him in amazement. Vogelsong voiced the obvious: "But—Fanchon can't have all six of them when we know that Henry killed two!"

"And the others should be meeting on the plain west of Crescent Hollow," Oswald added.

"It appears that Fanchon is playing with you, Surchatain," Rhode said quietly.

"He's looking for an offense to draw you into war," Thom said. "If you do not accept his word of honor that he has found the slavers you demanded, and refuse to hand over Symon, he will take it as a pretext to attack."

"Well, I have no objection to giving him Symon *after* we see what transpires on the plain," Ares said, brows raised. "Let us agree to a meeting with Fanchon in a fortnight. If that does not give us enough time, we will ask for more. Any objections?" he asked, looking around.

His officers shook their heads or remained silent. He already knew that they would have no objections. He had deliberately not consulted the one person who would have objections.

So Ares dismissed everyone to return to dinner.

Fanchon's messenger was fed and housed in the lower corridor (under guard), and promised a letter to take back on the morrow. When all was arranged, Ares returned to dinner, which had progressed in his absence. While his guests finished off sugar brittle in cream, Ares bent over a plate of boiled haddock.

He was still eating when his guests, like spoiled children, began murmuring for the evening's entertainment. Renée, back in the seat beside Bonnie, said to her, "It's a pity that your father doesn't allow you and Sophie to take dance lessons anymore—I learned the most amusing dance today at the estate of a friend. It is very easy and riotous fun. Would you like to try it?"

"Oh, yes, Aunt Renée! May we, Papa?" Bonnie said, turning to him. Sophie looked up eagerly.

"Of course," he said, breaking off bread from the loaf on the platter in front of him.

"Come then, everyone." Renée stood, pushing back her chair, and a great host from the table followed her. Renée swept to the center of the floor and took Bonnie's hand. "This is how we begin: everyone hold hands in a line. Sophie, take Bonnie's hand. Dear Genevieve, take Sophie's. There we are," she said encouragingly as the dancers formed a chain.

"Now, as the musicians play a rollicking tune, the leader of the line begins any step she wishes, and the rest of the line must do it just the same. After eight measures, the leader breaks off to join the end of the line, and the next person becomes leader. Just so."

Renée gestured for the musicians to play, then she began a lively but simple side step to the music. All the dancers, thirty by now, had to dance the same step while still holding hands. Renée then changed to a sliding step, and there were bursts of laughter and more people joining the line as all attempted to keep up with the new step. Meanwhile, Renée led the line in snakelike undulations around the floor, dancing.

At the correct measure, she released Bonnie's hand to circle back to the end of the line, and Bonnie become leader. She hesitated for a moment, then began hopping. So all those in line behind her, almost sixty people by now, were hopping up and down.

It was screamingly funny to see well-fed and well-dressed nobles huffing and puffing, trying to keep their hats on or their necklines decent while exercising so vigorously. Children who had been watching from the doorways rushed to join in. Thom's captains were in the line because the Commander had waved them to the floor, but they kept a disgruntled eye on him.

The only people left at table were Ares, Nicole, Vogelsong, Thom, Oswald, and Rhode. All these except Nicole were still eating. Ares glanced at his wife. "You may join the entertainment, Lady."

"Thank you for your permission, my lord," she replied. But she did not rise.

Vogelsong, still preoccupied with everything he had heard today, leaned toward Thom. "How soon will the Blue and Red be dispatched, Commander?"

"Tomorrow morning, Counselor," Thom replied.

Thom hesitated, about to say more, but Vogelsong asked, "And how long will the march to the meeting place require?"

"About two and a half days. I am leading them," Thom replied ostensibly to him, but actually to someone else who was listening.

"Well, then, a fortnight should give us plenty of time to

apprehend the slavers on the plain before meeting Fanchon," Vogelsong said, then turned at a burst of laughter behind him. Placing his napkin on the table, he said, "That looks rather amusing. Surchatain?"

"You are dismissed," Ares told him, and Vogelsong rose to join the dance.

Nicole, pale, also rose. The officers at table sprang to their feet. "I see that you have much to discuss with your men, my lord. Will you excuse me?" she said, eyes downcast.

"Of course, Lady," Ares said. She curtsied and departed the table, but did not join the snaking line. She left the hall.

When Ares came up to his quarters an hour later, he found Nicole in bed, under light cotton sheets beside a low-burning fire. She lay on her side facing away from the door, eyes open.

Seeing that she was not asleep, he tentatively sat on the edge of the bed. "Nicole, you seem . . . unsettled." He stroked her shoulder under the linen bodice.

Without turning to face him, she observed, "You used to invite me to your war councils. Or at least, kept me informed."

"I am not leading the Regiments against the slavers," he said hastily.

"I know that now; Thom informed me tonight," she said.

"Well, then," he murmured, leaning down to kiss her shoulder, but she was cold and unyielding. In exasperation, he said, "Nicole, what would you have me do? I have promised to give up Symon to him. If I do not, Fanchon will use it as an excuse to make war on me. Is that what you want?"

She rolled onto her back to face him. "You used this pathetic man to spy on everyone, then when he fell prey to Renée's schemes and was no more use to you, you decided to turn him over to be tortured to death on false promises from this Fanchon to deliver his friends to you. It appears to me that you are all playing these games of power and intrigue in which I see nothing of the hand of God." She turned back to wipe wet eyes on the feather pillow.

Ares sat biting his lip. "It is no game, Nicole. I am trying to rid my province of these slavers."

"By conspiring with a liar and a cheat? A cruel and evil man?" she flung back at him.

"Symon earned his fate," Ares argued. "He caused the death of a Surchataine. He almost threw Bonnie down the well!"

Nicole sat up abruptly. "Do you really believe that Twomey could have thrown Bonnie down that hole?"

"No," Ares admitted. "But he laid hands on her!"

"For which he should have his eyes ripped out and joints broken backwards?" Nicole cried. "And how quickly you dismiss his part in saving her from Tobias. She was in far greater danger from *him*," she pointed out.

"And as for the Surchataine, I believe that she, being free, made her own choices as to the conduct that led to her downfall and the manner by which she died. I sympathize less with her than with the pawn that is about to be sacrificed," she said.

Nicole seemed to have no recollection of the personal grievance she herself had with the jester, as if it was irrelevant. With tears in her eyes she pleaded, "Ares, this is beneath you. You are too good a man to stoop to the methods of Fanchon."

He dropped his head under the weight of such an

argument. In so doing, he saw her linen bodice slipping off her shoulders and her trembling chest underneath it. Distracted, he picked up her hand to kiss it, and she caressed his head with her free hand. "I love you too much to see you become like him," she whispered.

He opened his mouth in dismay, then blinked once or twice at an inspiration that came unbidden, straight from a pitying God. "I . . . may have a way to satisfy Fanchon and save the jester," he said.

"What?" she asked eagerly.

But, being a man in bed with a beautiful woman whom he loved, he bent to press his lips against her neck and bare shoulder. She unlaced her bodice while placing her fingers prohibitively at his lips. "Tell me first," she whispered in his ear.

While he shrugged out of his clothes, he told her his plan. After considering it, she was satisfied, so she, as implicitly promised, satisfied him.

Early the following morning, Ares watched Commander Thom, his Second Rhode, Captain Crager, and Captain Paramore depart at the head of columns of Blue and Red. Standing on the western parapet to see them off, Ares deeply wished that he was leading them instead. He hated being left in Westford to pace and wait a week or more, until word should come as to how many slavers they caught—if any at all.

It all depended on how reliable Henry's information was, and on the circumstances in which he had come by that information, but Captain Yonge was irritatingly brief in conveying that. So when all the Lystran soldiers had passed out of the gate heading west, Ares returned to his receiving room to reread Yonge's letter.

He said that Henry had killed Dorn weeks ago upon his

arrival (how? where?) and that he had overheard the specifics of this meeting before killing Urias. So, essentially, Ares had sent out the best of the standing army at Westford strictly on the word of a young new Blue.

Ares sat back at his table to think about Henry. How was he faring? Perhaps a letter of encouragement was in order? So Ares pulled out parchment and dipped the quill in the inkwell, then held it dripping while he tried to think what to write. His mind was a blank. He did not know what Henry needed to hear right now. He did not know what he might say to guide or strengthen his adopted son. So Ares reluctantly pushed the parchment aside. Whatever he could do for Henry must have already been done or left undone; the time for teaching had passed.

When Nicole came out to the receiving room dressed for the day, Ares summoned Renée—then waited quite a long time for her. She arrived in flustered irritation, as she liked to do when summoned, to demonstrate that she had more important things to do. "What is it, Ares?" she asked impatiently.

"Forgive the disruption of your day, Chataine. I fear to think of what I might have interrupted," Ares said dryly, and Nicole fought to keep from smiling, although Renée was not looking at her. "I will be brief. Of everyone in the palace, you seem to have developed the most—thorough knowledge of our friend Twomey. So I would like to know . . . what is the best way I can put his mind to rest? To get him to trust me?" Ares asked.

"Trust you?" Renée laughed.

"That is—how can I soften him so that he willingly pursues a course which is—painful, while it is strictly for his good?" Ares asked.

"Oh, well, now that you put it that way, he loves

mincemeat pies," Renée said. "Short of offering him a lady's foot to stroke [she glanced at Nicole] mincemeat pies should do it."

"I see. Thank you, Chataine," Ares acknowledged. After she had flowed out, he looked to Nicole; she smiled and he shook his head.

Over the next few days, Ares became almost unfit to live with. He paced and muttered; he was restless and irritable; he swore a hundred times that he should have gone with Thom and knew it. The only thing he looked forward to—that gave anyone around him any relief—was his daily drilling of the Greens. Then, he became focused, calm, and rational. He attended their ignorant questions seriously, and painstakingly demonstrated the same basic maneuvers over and over. He was approachable and attentive to them.

Nobles who had suffered rebuffs from Ares over what they considered minor infractions (such as calling Renée "Surchataine") were disgruntled over this strange sort of favoritism. In his typical manner, Ares would not bother to explain to them that he was looking for the next Henry or two among the Greens. Also—and this is what caused some speculation that the Surchatain was losing his mind—he began sending one mincemeat pie a day down to Twomey in dungeon.

Finally, four days after the troops had set out from Westford, a messenger arrived from Thom. Ares summoned Vogelsong, Oswald and Nicole to his receiving room to hear the messenger report: "Surchatain, the Commander advises that his advance scouts have discovered about fifty slavers gathered at the meeting place. He determined to hold back the army to see if more would arrive, but will report to you daily."

Ares glanced at his wife and officers, then grudgingly nodded. "Thom is doing exactly the right thing. You may go tell him that." That was all he could say.

During these days of waiting, Ares slept fitfully at night, which meant that Nicole got little rest, either. But for all his impatience and restlessness, he knew that he was on the right path because the dreams of the white knight had stopped.

Since it was now apparent that there was some credibility in Henry's report, it was time for the next step of Ares' plan. So about a week prior to his scheduled meeting with Fanchon, he went down to the dungeon to speak with Twomey.

While a sentry preceded him with a torch, Ares descended the slippery, open-sided stairway into the dark hole. Moss clung to the eternally wet stone, and the sound of dripping water echoed through passages cut into the rock.

The dungeon was now only a third of the size it had been in the past because the underground streams had risen to flood the very lowest passages. Considering that a sign from God, Ares did not attempt to dig more cells—he either fined its occupants and released them, banished them, or, when conscience dictated, simply let them go.

Stooping for the low roof, Ares followed the sentry down a rough tunnel to a cell. Here the sentry sconced the torch and slid back the bolt of the rusty iron door. Ares stood at the door, declining to enter the muddy, excrement-filled pit of a cell. Eyeing the form huddled in the dark corner, he said, "Twomey. I have something for you."

With a quick intake of breath, the jester hurried to the door with many bows, grinning and twisting his fingers in his grubby shirt. "Oh, wonderful Surchatain Ares. What a kind man you are to poor Twomey, Surchatain."

"Sit here and eat it," Ares said, nodding at the relatively clean corridor floor. Twomey sat like a child, and the sentry handed him a fresh mincemeat pie. With a squeal of joy, Twomey brought it up to his chapped lips. Ares looked at his erupted skin, his trembling hands, his watery eyes, and did pity him.

While Twomey relished his treat, Ares knelt in front of him. "Twomey, I have promised to give you up to Fanchon. I have to honor that promise, or he will make war on us." Twomey acted as if he hadn't heard him, and Ares understood why. To think on what was about to happen would drive him insane. All he wanted to do was enjoy this pie.

"Surchataine Nicole felt great pity for you, Twomey, and desired that we do something to deliver you. So I have a plan, if you are willing. It will not be easy, and it may not work. But I believe it is your only hope of escaping Fanchon's torture chamber."

The jester slowly looked up, pieces of pie clinging to his face. "Anything. I will do anything you say."

"So be it." Ares stood to order, "When he is finished with his pie, take him up to Doctor Savary. Guard him 'round the clock."

"Surchatain," the sentry replied, saluting. With a last glance at the sad jester, Ares turned out of the dungeon corridor.

The following day, another message arrived from Thom: seventy-five slavers and/or mercenaries were now accounted for at the meeting place. Thom was holding his army well back to await more.

The next day brought two similar messages: one

hundred, then a hundred fifteen slavers had arrived. But with the last message, Thom reported his fears that he must attack soon or risk discovery. If the slavers got wind of the army hanging several miles south (and how could they miss 3500 men?) and fled at night, they'd be hard to catch.

So Thom was spreading his ranks to begin encircling the camp. At least by now, the Lystrans knew that Henry's information had been wholly correct. In reply to this last message, Ares told Thom to be sure to send messengers west to Odea, as well.

The next three days brought no word at all, which drove Ares to a state of distraction that Nicole had seldom seen. His appointment with Fanchon was in two days; it was already too late to send a message to Corona asking for more time. If Ares received no word from Thom by tomorrow morning, the only way to postpone the exchange would be to ask Fanchon when he arrived at their meeting place north of Eurus. This would rouse his suspicions and his ire, which Ares did not want to do.

While he was enmeshed in this state of preoccupation, all attempted diversions or entertainments seemed to irritate him, and he could hardly sit for more than a few moments without springing up again to pace.

Dinners became awkward, as he sat staring pensively into space the whole time. At this point, Nicole was actually grateful for Renée. Her self-absorbed chatter, while strictly limited to topics of interest to her, did lighten the mood of the table. Usually.

Tonight at table Renée was saying, "So I told her, 'Well, of course, the dress is lovely, but so clingy that it gets all tangled up in your legs dancing, and then what kind of sight are you, with your skirt twisted around you like toffee?'" There was some tittering in response, and more than one woman self-consciously spread their skirts a little on their chairs.

"But, there's no use worrying about the state of one's dress *here*, of course, since there's no dancing to speak of anymore," Renée sighed sadly. "It is quite a shame that such lovely Chataines aren't taught the new dances they're doing in Eurus and Crescent Hollow. Can you imagine going to your first fest and having no clue what they're doing on the floor?" Renée said to Bonnie.

Bonnie turned around to her mother. "Mama, I want to start taking dancing lessons again."

"Of course, dear," Nicole said smoothly. "All we have to do is get someone to practice with you. Let's see. Henry is gone, so I suppose the next best choice is Worster."

"Worster? That big boy who sweats?" Bonnie asked in alarm.

"Yes, he does perspire somewhat, but he dances well enough when he doesn't land directly on your feet, so you just need to wear good, stiff shoes while you're dancing with him," Nicole said. Bonnie's lip curled in disdain. "But if you don't care to dance with him, I believe Torkel is available."

"Torkel? Uncle Giles' errand boy?" Bonnie screeched. "Mama, he *belches*!"

"Is it so awful having a boy belch in your ear while you're learning romantic dances?" Nicole asked, bemused. As Bonnie stared at her, she shrugged and continued, "Well, he's just about the only other young man that can dance. We can find someone *older* to dance with you, of course, like Uncle Giles [who was still in Crescent Hollow]. And to learn properly, you'll have to put in hour after hour on the floor with his arms around you—"

"I don't want to learn any more dancing, Aunt Renée,"

Bonnie said firmly. "Neither does Sophie."

"Let darling Sophie speak for herself. She's always willing to learn new things," Renée said, looking across the table to her last hope. "Sophie?"

Head down, she murmured, "I'll wait for Henry to practice with me." Ares woke up and looked at her.

Nicole said briskly, "That's fine, then. I'm sorry, dear Renée, the girls don't appear to be interested." And Renée sat studying the most underrated player on the field.

A sentry appeared in the hall. Striding to the head of the table, he saluted and said, "Surchatain, the army has returned."

Ares stood abruptly, but so did half a dozen other people, including his officers' wives. So Ares sat back down, and they slowly followed suit. Then Ares told the sentry, "Have Thom and his men wash up and come eat. They will make their report to me here."

18

Shortly, Commander Thom entered the hall with his officers Rhode, Paramore, and Crager. In deference to the guests at table, the soldiers had washed off the worst of the grime and changed into clean uniforms, but they still had the rough air of men who had been sleeping on the ground, fighting in frantic bursts, and marching for days. After taking one look at them, Ares determined never to stay behind again. He would go as flag-bearer, if necessary, but he would not waste away in the palace in safety.

"Have a seat, gentlemen," Ares said, which caused upheaval at the table as the guests moved down to make room for the officers at their usual places. No one took offense at this because Renée still occupied Giles' seat and the rest of those at table were too pragmatic to be thin-skinned about it.

When the men were seated and wine goblets filled in front of them, Ares leaned back. "What news, Commander?"

Thom took a draught from his cup, then held it behind him for a refill. "Surchatain, we attacked the camp at daybreak two days ago. No one escaped. By the time we lined them all up, we counted four hundred and five men."

Gasps of surprise went around the table. "All of them slavers?" Vogelsong demanded.

"Most were mercenaries hired by the slavers, Counselor," Thom replied. "We divided them into groups to search them and question them. All carried arms, and most carried chains and shackles. These, numbering three hundred fifty-one, were set apart to one area. Another forty-four carried keys to the shackles, so they were set off in a second area.

"The last ten carried not only keys, but were in possession of tents with moneyboxes or ledgers. They were put off each one by himself. So we began to question them." Thom paused as a bowl of steaming lamb stew was placed before him, but he did not begin to eat.

"We questioned the lowest mercenaries first, to see if they could point out who hired them, or tell us anything about who was in command of this operation. Most knew nothing, so as soon as we determined what they did or did not know, we killed them. The ones who carried shackles began pointing out a man with four fingers on his right hand—"

"Ticzon!" Vogelsong interrupted excitedly, then apologized, "Er, excuse me. Please continue, Commander."

Thom glanced at the stew, having not eaten since morning, but resumed, "Yes, Counselor. A man with four fingers—and gold rings on all of them—had been occupying one of the larger tents. So we continued our interrogations, and others who had charge of shackles identified a large, fat man as Morguloff. He also had a tent.

"By this time, we were filling a deep pit with bodies in sight of the ten remaining slavers, each of whom was asked his name. Ticzon identified himself with prideful scorn, but none of the others. Morguloff would give no name, but was identified by four of the others. They, in turn, gave varying names for themselves and the eight remaining, none of which we recognized, so they were either lying well or new to the slaving game. We killed them all and confiscated their gear and gold, which amounts to over five thousand royals," Thom concluded.

"Four of the six," Vogelsong said in tense excitement. "That accounts for at least four of the six traders that Fanchon claims to have."

After a moment of silence, Rhode added, "Among the spoils we found maps, Surchatain. They show the new routes that the slavers favor through the Poison Greens and the location of hidden camps."

Ares eyed him, and Thom added, "They were most clever in picking this location to convene, Surchatain—it is relatively desolate, yet within striking distance of heavily populated, lightly defended areas. To my knowledge, the slavers have never attempted a cooperative venture such as this before.

"Had we not known of this gathering, they would have been able to strike south into the vineyards and east into Crescent Hollow, taking a thousand people captive and disappearing overnight—that after setting fire to the vineyards, as we found evidence that this was in the works, as well. They would have crippled us with one blow."

Ares barely nodded, his eyes hazy. Had he been lured into war with Fanchon to the north, then he would have been all the less able to deal with the unification of slavers to the west. He remembered the cemetery he had seen spreading over the land in his dream.

But because of one pawn on lonely patrol in Odea, Fanchon's slave traders had been checkmated. Day after tomorrow, Ares would make his first move against Fanchon himself. "Well done, Thom," he said. "Eat now."

Two days later, before sunrise, Ares collected Twomey and dressed him, then set him on a horse and escorted him out of the palace gates with Thom, Rhode, Oswald, Paramore, Crager, and ten lesser soldiers in attendance, including Ben. The Blue Regiment followed at a distance, under orders to remain unseen south of Eurus unless summoned.

The party of seventeen rode at a steady gallop up the northbound market road, weaving in and out of traffic as it appeared, or leaving the road altogether to prevent oncoming travelers from driving their carts into ditches upon encountering them.

Eurus was less than a day's ride from Westford, but the designated point of exchange was north of the city. And because Ares would not ride through Eurus, going around it would add another hour to their trip. Hence the early departure: Ares wanted plenty of daylight remaining when he met Fanchon face to face for the first time. They also had to allow rest stops for Twomey, who was weakened by his two months' stay in the dungeon.

But the primary reason Twomey kept begging to stop along the way (which he did to the point that Oswald reached over and shook him in the saddle) was that Ares had allotted *two* mincemeat pies for the jester on the road today. He carried them wrapped in a cloth bag that hung on a string from his neck under his clothes.

They encountered light rain for miles north of Willowring Lake, but nothing that impeded travel nor caused great discomfort. The Scyllan farmers were no doubt appreciative of the rain, given that the party also passed many acres of newly sprouted wheat along either side of the road.

Upon their first break to stop and eat, they found a grove of birches off the road to provide a little cover from the rain, as well as from curious eyes. While the men stood to eat bread and cheese out of their packs, Twomey took out the first of his treasured pies and sat under a tree by himself to devour it lovingly.

With Thom and Oswald nearby, Rhode came up to Ares to mutter, "The jester seems to have little fear of the ploy working. I'd admire his courage if I didn't think him such a weasel."

"I don't think he's thinking about it," Thom responded. "I've decided he doesn't think about things in advance. He just does whatever he feels at the moment."

"A losing strategy, in my view," Paramore interjected, handing his Commander a water skin.

Eating a chunk of nut bread himself, Ares watched Twomey lick his fingers. "For Nicole's sake, I hope it works. For *my* sake I hope it works," he amended. For if Nicole was unhappy, there was little chance of her making him happy.

They returned to the road, and a few more hours of steady riding brought Eurus within view. With increased traffic, they detoured from the road to ride through the fields in formation: Ares and Thom leading, Rhode and Oswald forming the rear guard, and the remaining soldiers on either side of Twomey, blocking him in and blocking him from sight.

At about the halfway point around the city, as they were riding through pastureland, Ares raised his hand in a signal to stop and turned around to Twomey. "Do you want to eat your last pie before we go any farther?" Ares asked.

Twomey caressed the treasure dangling against his chest. "No, no," he said. "Twomey keeps the pie for later. Later."

Ares' officers glanced at each other—it was highly speculative that Twomey would live to enjoy "later," but Ares said, "As you wish. Proceed." The group spurred ahead.

By late afternoon, minutes after leaving the city behind, Ares spotted a tent in the field off the road up ahead. "There he is, waiting for us." The riders from Westford were spotted in turn, for a Selecan soldier stepped out into the road, waving to the right, toward the tent.

Ares stopped his men, turning in the saddle to tell them, "Officers, with me. The rest of you keep him hemmed in." While the soldiers remained behind with Twomey in the midst of them, Ares spurred ahead with Thom, Oswald, Rhode, Paramore, and Crager.

They approached the white canvas tent to be met by a score of Selecan soldiers, armed and watchful. Ares and his men carried long swords on their hips, standard with the uniform. None of the Lystrans wore armor—Ares was in his dress blacks—but as he dismounted, he watched Fanchon emerge from the tent in white armor, with the crest of the gryphon on the flaps of the tent.

Ares' officers dismounted behind him, and Thom glanced at the Selecans behind Fanchon in sudden apprehension. He did not like their look, nor the way they edged forward, subtly trying to surround the visiting officers.

Thom glanced at Rhode beside him, who wore a similar wary expression. Crager turned to eye the Selecans advancing toward his back, and the line paused.

But now the Lystrans perceived that they were

essentially trapped. Fanchon had the Surchatain of Lystra, his Commander, and all their top officers contained in a tight pocket of soldiers, while Twomey and his guard sat back on the road. Scouts from the Blue were no doubt watching, but if they were summoned to attack, they would be too late to save the Surchatain.

Thom glanced at the soft black brocade coat Ares always wore, and his jaw tensed. Then he looked at Ares' face, and saw it impassive, as usual. He had to know they were surrounded, so he must play his hand well.

Clearing his throat softly, Thom watched as the two Surchatains drew up face to face. Fanchon, in full armor with a coroneted basinet covering his head, was a large man, taller than Ares, even. There was a moment of silence while the Selecans waited, poised. Then Ares spoke clearly and calmly: "I am Ares of Westford, coming as agreed. Do you require full armor to parler with me?"

The demand for parler dispelled something in the air. Fanchon could still attack and kill them, but it would be—unsporting. A coward's move.

Uttering a laugh, Fanchon removed his helmet. "Ares of Westford, I think to recognize you anywhere. I am Fanchon of Seleca." He was a robust man, with brown hair sweeping to his shoulders and a thick moustache. "You are always reputed to wear black," he added. His underlings broke out in laughter at the joke: that Fanchon would recognize him by his clothes and not his scar.

Ares conceded, "That I do." He did not glance at his officers behind him to make sure that they were studying Fanchon as hard as he was, but that was his motivation for bringing them. He wanted them to be able to recognize Fanchon on the field of battle at some later date.

That was also the reason Ares wished to meet him

himself: so he would recognize him when they met again.

"So, Ares of Westford, is it not time for two great provinces to open our borders and embrace trade with one another?" Fanchon asked. "Wine for the Surchatain," he instructed an underling.

Ares held up his hand to forestall him. "No, thank you, Surchatain; I require no refreshment. And let us see how today's trade satisfies each of us before we progress to— further dalliance." A quiet chuckle rose in the throat of one of the Lystran officers behind him. (Later, all were to deny being the guilty party.) Ares continued, "I believe you have something for me."

Fanchon snapped his fingers. From behind the tent his soldiers produced a string of six men, gagged and chained together by shackles on their wrists. "As requested, I have brought you Morguloff, Dorn, Saracini, Urias, Ticzon, and Ransweiler." So saying, Fanchon pointed to each down the line, then presented Ares with the key to their shackles on a gold chain.

Ares took the key, stepping forward to study the men one at a time. Fanchon had done a good job procuring substitutes: the one reputed to be Morguloff was large and fat; Dorn had a scar on his forehead—not a large scar, but an old one. All of them were approximately the right age and build of the men in question. But as Ares walked down the line looking at them one by one, he saw only fear in their eyes—not the defiance, nor sullenness, nor lack of conscience that made a man a slaver.

When Ares came to the fifth man, the one reputed to be Ticzon, he looked down at the man's hands shackled in front of him. The right hand was missing the fifth digit. However, Ares noted that it was a new injury, still healing.

Turning away from them, Ares said, "I confess that I

am surprised, Surchatain Fanchon. I had not thought it possible for you to apprehend all six. But you have."

"Indeed, Surchatain Ares," Fanchon said, grinning. His officers grinned behind him.

"Take them." Ares gave the key to Oswald, who took the chains of the first to begin leading them away. The line of Selecan soldiers behind them parted reluctantly.

"Now, I believe you have something for me, Surchatain Ares." Fanchon's voice had a coarse, lustful tinge to it. It was a lust for screams, and blood, and the sound of bones cracking. If he went through with this charade of a trade, he'd have something to show for it, by jove.

"I do, Surchatain Fanchon." Ares gestured to the riders standing off for Twomey to be brought forward.

"Alive? Is Symon alive?" Fanchon demanded, straining to see his long-sought quarry.

"Yes, Surchatain, he is alive," Ares answered, "but I must tell you that we just discovered he is sick. I brought him straight from the care of the doctor to you."

"Just so that he lives to Corona," Fanchon grunted. "What's wrong with him?"

But at that moment the guard around Twomey fell away, and he slid down from the horse to advance by himself. The horrified Selecans watched the white shroud flutter around the wretched figure while he staggered toward them, lifting his recently branded hand and crying, "Leper! Unclean! Unclean!"

"That is his affliction, Surchatain. Do with him as you will," Ares said.

Fanchon's soldiers scattered in panic at the approach of the leper. With his white bristly hair and the sores on his arms and legs, he was a convincing picture of the inexorable decay of the disease. "Leper! Unclean!" he continued to cry with grinning lips over blackened teeth.

"Stay!" Fanchon's commander shouted at Twomey. "Surchatain, order him back! He will be the death of us all!"

Torn between bloodlust and survival, Fanchon wavered while Ares watched in mild curiosity. No Selecan drew his sword, for the blood of a leper was held to be teeming with the disease. Fanchon turned a dark eye on Ares, and his desire to have *someone* in his torture chamber was written large across his face.

But then Fanchon raised his eyes and saw a thousand Lystran soldiers standing off at attention. Paramore's lieutenant, Fawler, apparently did not like the behavior of the Selecans, either. He did not advance, as he had not been ordered forward, but—he wished to be seen, and seen he was.

Scowling, Fanchon turned away with a short gesture. "Bah! Go die elsewhere, leper! Die in agony!" At this dismissal, Twomey skittered away into underbrush.

Fanchon gave orders for camp to dismantle. On a hopeful thought, he turned back to address Ares. "I hope he hasn't infected your capital, Surchatain."

"Only time will tell," Ares replied grimly.

"Well. You have yours, at least." Fanchon nodded at the chain of men. "Good evening, Surchatain Ares."

"Surchatain Fanchon." Ares nodded in return.

As Ares mounted with his men and turned south, he heard a hissing from the area of the brush. Riding toward it, Ares saw the jester's face peeking out. "God bless you, Surchatain. You are a good man," he whispered.

"You are on your own, Twomey. But if you cannot find shelter elsewhere, the leprosarium south of Westford will be open soon," Ares said.

"Surchatain," came the hissing whisper in reply, and then Twomey was gone.

Ares looked at Thom, who said, "He'll shed the shroud and start wearing gloves for his next job."

"Perhaps," Ares said wryly.

Rhode leaned forward. "What's to be done with those men, Surchatain?" He jerked his head to the line of men who were being released from their chains and gags by Oswald. "They're not slavers. They're probably farmers or day laborers."

Ares looked them over. "No doubt. We'll stop long enough in Eurus to feed them, find out who they are, and let them go." Gesturing forward, he said, "Gentlemen, let's head home."

Alphonso was a busy man. He had so many friends to visit in Nicole's Harbor and Mcelyea that he rather took his time getting back to Odea. Not a fun place, the outpost, so who could blame him that he wasn't anxious to get back? But arrive he did, finally, on this very day. And when he arrived, he made good his word to his old friend Derrick: he delivered a long-delayed letter.

"Henry!"

At the sound of his name, he paused over his shovel and looked back. He was cleaning manure out of the stables, as he had done every day since bringing Lieutenant Moeck's horse back.

"Sir?" Henry said even before seeing whether it was an officer or not. It wasn't.

"Captain wants to see you, Henry."

Returning the shovel to its rack, Henry muttered, "What now? I haven't had a fight in weeks." Tramping from the stables, he paused by the well to wash away some of the disagreeable odors, then trotted up the steps to Captain Yonge's quarters.

Henry knocked and entered, saluting. "Captain?"

Yonge made a face. "Henry, when you come from the stables, leave your boots at the door!"

"Sorry, Captain." Henry hastened outside to shuck off his boots, then reentered the Captain's quarters in dirty socks. "Yes, Captain?"

Yonge leaned back in his chair, scrutinizing him. While calmly meeting his gaze, Henry began an inventory of his numerous recent infractions in an attempt to isolate which one this session might involve. "So, I heard you came back from your last patrol wearing a leper's shroud," the Captain finally remarked.

"Yes, Captain. You see, the merchants who try to bust the border aren't under a death edict—despite what Giles would like—but if I just chase them away, they circle around and find another way in. But if I ride up to them wearing the shroud, and showing my hand, and making a big fuss, then they think the whole province is infected. They run like the devil!" he laughed. "Sometimes they drop goods. That's where the new kitchen pots came from."

Yonge nodded. "I see. Nonetheless, the shroud is disturbing to the rest of the camp at large, so please remove it before you reenter the compound."

"Yes, sir," Henry said, relieved. "Is that all?"

"Not quite." The Captain held out a soiled bit of parchment to him. "You got a letter, Henry. Tad late, I think."

In wonder, Henry accepted the letter. When he saw the seal and the handwriting, his gut constricted. "Thank you, Captain. Uh—may I—?"

Yonge waved him away. "Yes, finish your duty after you've read your letter. Dismissed."

"Thank you, sir." Forgetting to salute, Henry retrieved his boots from the steps outside and carried them underarm while he walked across the compound looking at the letter.

Periodically stumbling into people or objects in his path, he made it back to his barracks. He dropped his boots outside the door and went in to sit on his pallet in the deserted room. Then he broke the Surchatain's seal and opened the letter.

There were no windows, but large holes in the roof above allowed light to shine down on the faded, smeared lettering. The whole of it was not long—only a paragraph, but Henry stared at the words for a long time, trying to digest them, trying to understand the meaning of one- and two-syllable words. Finally, his grey eyes wandered from the wrinkled parchment to focus on dust particles floating in the narrow shafts of light.

"Henry!" He jumped at the sound of his name, stuffing the letter under his pallet. The speaker stuck his head in the door. "There you are. The lieutenant's looking for you, and he is not in a happy way. You're not done at the stables."

"Blast," Henry muttered, springing up. "Where is he?"

"In the mess, looking for you there."

"Can you waylay him so I can get back to the stables without his seeing me?" Henry asked.

"I'll try," the other grudgingly allowed. "But I don't want to get stuck shoveling manure with you."

Henry patted his shoulder. "Lie convincingly, friend, and you won't." Peering out the door to see that the coast was clear, Henry darted down the steps in the direction of the stables. Then he came to a careening halt, backtracked to grab up his boots, and resumed a dead, furtive run across the compound while his friend sauntered innocently in the direction of the kitchen.

Henry arrived at the stables and threw himself down on dirty hay to jerk his boots back on. Then he seized the shovel to begin filling it from a stall floor and emptying into a cart just outside the stable doors with wondrous energy. This he repeated ten or twenty times without pausing.

When no one appeared at the door right away, however, he slowed to a stop. Standing the shovel upright, he leaned on it, gazing blindly at the hindquarters of the nearest horse while his mind went over and over what he had just read. She had written him. Sophie had finally written him, and—

"Henry!"

(The story continues in *In Extremis*.)

The 18th day of February in the year 8082 from the creation of the world

Dear Henry:

Papa told me about the terrible accident of the branding. I was so sorry to hear of it. It must have hurt very badly. And then to know that you will carry it around when it does not mean anything. That is so sad. But it does not change my mind that you may court me. I have thought about it, and I know that it would not be easy making everyone understand that you are not a leper, but if I have learned anything from Papa, it is that a mark on your skin does not change who you are inside. I say prayers every day for you, and hope you are safe, and that I will see you again soon.

Your friend,
Chataine Sophie

28th April of the year 8082

Dearest Chataine Sophie,

I have only today received your letter, and am writing late at night. (I have had a lot of extra duty lately.) Thank you for your concern. The brand hurt at first, but it doesn't bother me at all now, and I have learned to use it, so it can actually be a good thing.

I do not know how to express my gratitude that you intend to stand by your decision to allow me to court you, but if at some later time you see better how difficult that will be, I will not hold you to your word. I think of you all the time. I miss you and Ares and Nicole, and some days when I do not have anyone to annoy, I miss Bonnie.

Thank you for your prayers. Somehow I know that they have done me good. If you could write me now and then, I would be especially grateful. I may be here for a long time, so you know where to send the letters.

Your servant,
Henry

Glossary

Alphonso (al FONZ oh)—a lieutenant in the Lystran army

amanuensis (a man you EN sis)—a secretary

Ares (AIR eez)—Surchatain of Lystra

Aron, Lord—jeweler of Westford

Artavia (are TAY vee ah)—a courtly friend of Bonnie and Sophie's

basinet—a small, round helmet, often with a visor, worn with armor

Ben—a young soldier; a favorite of Ares' who had been his page

Birondo (beer ON do), **Father**—the priest in the palace at Westford

bocce (botch EE) **ball**—a game similar to croquet except that the balls are tossed or bowled by hand

Bonnie, Chataine—twelve-year-old daughter of Ares and Nicole; twin sister of Sophie

Breckett—the confectioner in Westford

camail—chain mail descending from the helmet to protect the neck

Carmine (CAR men)—Counselor at Westford, ex-husband of Renée

Cedric (SED rik)—son of the usurper Talus; father of Renée and Henry; was murdered as he attempted to execute Ares

Chatain (sha TAN)—son of the ruler of a province; the feminine is **Chataine** (sha TANE)

Conteria (con TER ee ah)—Surchataine of Seleca; Fanchon's wife

Corona—capital of Seleca

Crager (KRAY ger)—a Captain in the Lystran army

Crescent Hollow—capital of Calle Valley before that province was annexed to Lystra

Dansington—small hamlet in desolate northern Lystra

Deirdre (DEE dra)—(1) wife of Roman the Great; (2) Commander Thom's wife

Derrick—a Captain in the Lystran army; in charge of the outpost at Nicole's Harbor

Dorn—a slaver identified by a large scar traversing his forehead

Efrain—a soldier in the Lystran army

Eleanor—Renée's maid

estoc (also called a **tuck**)—a sword specialized for thrusting, with the geometric-shaped blade (viewed in cross-section) sharpened to an acute point

Eugenia (you JEN ee ah)—the province west of Lystra, ruled by Klar

Eurus (YUR is)—capital of Scylla

Evangeline—wife of the Second Oswald

Fanchon (FANCH un)—the Surchatain of Seleca

Fawler (FOLL er)—a lieutenant with the Lystran army

garderobe (GAR de robe)—a water closet, indoor commode

Garren—a member of the Blue Regiment of the Lystran army

Gathing—a tailor of Westford

Genevieve (JEN e veeve)—Steward Giles' wife

Georges (JEOR jes)—dinner master at Westford

Giles (hard *g*, long *i*)—the Steward at the palace of
Westford

Glinda—talkative laundry maid at Westford

Gowin (GOW in)—the top-tier flower vendor of Westford

Green Lady—the mountain range on the southern coast,
which resembles a woman lying on her side

gryphon (GRIFF en)—a mythical beast with the body and
hind legs of a lion and the wings and head of an eagle

Hauffe—Carmine's personal attendant who now serves
Renée

Henry—former Chatain of Lystra, Renée's 20-year-old
half-brother

hippocras—a spiced, sweetened wine, often served hot

Hoose—a soldier, a friend of Henry

Hornbound—capital of Qarqar

Jared—a Lystran soldier

kumyss (KOO miss)—fermented milk; see the Appendix

Lieterstad (LEE ter stad), **Lord**—a rich nobleman,
originally of Calle Valley

Lystra (LIS tra)—province once ruled by Roman the
Great, now ruled by his descendant Ares

Magnus (MAG nus)—Surchatain of Scylla; his early
marriage to Renée ended with his rejection and
humiliation of her

Mayra—the nursery mistress at Westford

Mcelyea (mac EHL yah)—a port town west of Prie Mer

Melva—former Chataine of Qarqar

Menchal (MEN shel)—Chataine Sophie's maid

mincement—a mix of chopped apples, spices, suet and
raisins

Moeck (moke)—a lieutenant in the Lystran army

Morguloff—a very tall, very fat slaver

motley—a comical garment of various colors

nesselrode—an ice pudding based on chestnuts which are poached in syrup and then rubbed through a hair sieve

Nicklos—nephew of Lord Lieterstad and previous husband of Renée

Nicole (ne COLE)—Ares' wife, Surchataine of Lystra, and mother of Bonnie and Sophie

Ninian (NIN ee an)—Chataine Bonnie's maid

Notham (NOTH am), **Lord**—a nobleman of Westford, father of Lady Rhea

Odea (oh DAY ah)—the outpost in desolate far western Lystra on the border with Eugenia

Oswald—Second in Command of the Lystran army under Commander Thom

Paramore (PAIR ah mor)—Captain of the Blue Regiment of the Lystran army

parler (PAR lay)—French, "talk"; *à parler*, "to talk"

Pearcey—a soldier in the Red Regiment of the Lystran army

pence, copper—the smallest monetary unit traded in the southern Continent; 20 pences equal a silver piece

Pervalley Highway—the east-west road through Lystra, running south of the Poison Greens

Poison Greens—the mountain range dividing Lystra and serving as a boundary between western Lystra and Qarqar

Polontis (po LAWN tis)—mountainous province far northeast of Lystra, home of the hardy, courageous, but unsophisticated **Polonti** (po LAWN tee)

Preus (proose), **Lord**—the once-premier dressmaker in Westford

Prie Mer (pree MARE)—small coastal town, Nicole's birthplace

Purdy—childhood friend of Nicole's, now overseer of livestock at Westford

Qarqar (KAR kar)—mining-rich province to the northwest of Lystra

quenelles—meat forced through a purée-sieve, seasoned, and then forced through a tube into boiling water

Ransweiler (RANS wy ler)—a notorious slave trader

Renée (ren AY)—ex-wife of Counselor Carmine; Henry's 32-year-old half-sister

Reynard (ray NARD)—Talus' brother who saved the life of young Ares

Rhea (ray), **Lady**—Lord Notham's daughter, who had been stringing Ares along before he met Nicole

Rhode (road)—Second in Command of the Lystran army under Commander Thom

Riley—Chataine Bonnie's newest guardian

Roerich (ROE rick)—the administrator of the palace at Crescent Hollow

Roman—the first great Surchatain of Lystra; author of Roman's Law; great-great-grandfather of Ares

Roux (rue)—a courtly friend of Bonnie and Sophie's; Giles' niece

Rupe—a gambler at Nicole's Harbor

Ryal—Thom and Deirdre's oldest son, now eight

sabatons—plate armor for the feet

Saracini (sair ah SEE nee)—a notorious slave trader

savarin—pastry with rum sauce

Savary (SAV a rie)—the physician at Westford

Scroggs—a soldier, a friend of Henry

Scylla (SILL ah)—the province east of Lystra, ruled by Magnus

Seane (shawn)—Chataine Sophie's guardian

Seleca (SEL e kah)—once-great province to the northeast of Lystra, now riddled with slave markets

shatranj—the medieval precursor to chess

Sophie, Chataine—twelve-year-old daughter of Ares and Nicole; twin sister of Bonnie

Soucie (SOO see)—wife of the Second Rhode

Stengi (STEN ghee)—Giles' assistant

Sulander (SOO lan der)—a losing challenger to the throne of Lystra

Surchatain (SUR cha tan)—the ruler of a province; the feminine is **Surchataine** (SUR cha tane)

Symon (SI mon)—a monk at the court of Corona

tabor—a light, tambourine-like drum played by hand

Talus (TAL us)—the Commander who murdered Surchatain Bobadil (Ares' grandfather) and seized the throne of Lystra; Renée and Henry's grandfather

Thom—Commander of the army of Lystra

Ticzon—a slaver with only four fingers on his right hand

Tobias (toe BI as)—Chataine Bonnie's guardian

Tockhorn—the province immediately north of Seleca

Tor—Thom and Deirdre's youngest son

Torkel—Giles' errand boy

trebuchet (TREB you shet)—a war machine which flings heavy projectiles over great distances at fortress walls

Twomey (TOO mee)—the new jester at the palace of Westford

Urias (yur EYE as)—a notorious slave trader

Van Laeke (lake)—a member of the Gold Regiment of the Lystran army

Veola (vee OH la)—the kitchen mistress at the palace of Westford

vielle—a stringed instrument, precursor to the violin

vigneron (VEEN yer ohn)—the person responsible for planting and tending grapevines

Vivian, Lady—Renée's mother

Vogelsong (VO gel song)—Counselor at Westford

Wasserleben (vass er LAY ben)—a complex couples' dance

Westford—capital of the province of Lystra

Wigzell (WIG zul)—the long-time palace physician at Westford who died years ago

Wordie—a member of the Red Regiment of the Lystran army

Worster—a boy at the court of Westford

Yonge (yung)—a Captain of the Lystran army; the officer in charge of the outpost at Odea

Appendix

Kumyss

(from a 1915 Fleischmann's Recipes booklet as reproduced on http://theoldentimes.com/kumyss_recipe.html)

Heat two quarts milk to blood-heat (100 degrees). Add half a cake Fleischmann's Yeast and two tablespoons sugar dissolved in a little warm water. Let stand for two hours, then bottle and stand for six hours in a moderately warm room; then place on ice. Kumyss will keep four or five days if kept cold, but it is better if made fresh every day or two.

Books by Robin Hardy

The Streiker Saga
>*Streiker's Bride*
>*Streiker: The Killdeer*
>*Streiker's Morning Sun*

The Annals of Lystra
>*Chataine's Guardian*
>*Stone of Help*
>*Liberation of Lystra*
>(first published as *High Lord of Lystra*)

The Latter Annals of Lystra
>*Nicole of Prie Mer*
>*Ares of Westford*
>*Prisoners of Hope*
>*Road of Vanishing*
>*Dead Man's Token*
>*Games of God and Men*
>*In Extremis*
>*All Mirrors and All Suns*
>*The Laughing Side of the World*

The Sammy Series
>*Sammy: Dallas Detective*
>*Sammy: Women Troubles*
>*Sammy: Working for a Living*
>*Sammy: On Vacation*
>*Sammy: Little Misunderstandings*
>*Sammy: Ghosts*
>*Sammy: Arenamania*
>*Sammy: In Principle*
>>(continued on next page)

Sammy: Grave Agreement
Sammy: Love Shouldn't Hurt
Sammy: The Consolation of Bucephalus

The Idecis
*Unknown Name, Unknown Number: A Wimsey
Reade Mystery*
Padre and its sequel *His Strange Ways*

Edited by Robin Hardy

Sifted But Saved: Classic Devotions by W.W. Melton